'Will you be silent?' His hands gripped her shoulders. The heat of him burnt through her clothes. 'Or do I have to stop your mouth?'

'Someone has to say these things.' She stared at him. His mouth was inches from hers. He swooped down and claimed her, branded her. Phoebe stilled as warmth pulsated through her, searing her with its fierceness. His lips called to something deep within her, turned the warmth into a raging inferno.

The kiss lengthened, deepened. Her lips parted and he feasted, devoured her like a starving man. This was no gentle persuasion or chaste kiss, but the sort of kiss a pirate captain might bestow. Plundering and taking. His arms went around her and held her body against his. Her breasts were crushed against his chest. Her melting softness met his body. His lips trailed down her throat as he entangled his fingers in her glorious hair. Held her there.

The mantel clock chimed the hour, bringing them back to reality. He stepped away from her, a stunned look on his face.

'Miss Benedict… I…'

Phoebe looked at him, turned on her heel and fled.

Author Note

You may have met Simon Clare in A QUES-TION OF IMPROPRIETY. In fact, he and his son Robert very nearly took over his sister's book. The events in this story happen several months after the events in A QUESTION OF IMPROPRIETY. The book is a stand-alone story, but does revisit the world I created. Hopefully you will enjoy this story as much as I enjoyed writing it.

If you are interested in the early development of railways, *Steam and Speed: Railways of Tyne and Wear from the Earliest Days* by Andy Guy is a thoroughly useful book. And, if possible, I would recommend a visit to the Beamish Open Air Museum and a ride on the Pockerley Waggonway. Another great joy of writing these books was rediscovering the Literary and Philosophic Society in Newcastle. Its largely unchanged reading rooms date from 1825, and they have the original prototype of George Stephenson's safety lamp in a case.

As ever, I love getting reader feedback—via post to Mills & Boon, through my website, www.michellestyles.co.uk, or my blog, http://www.michellestyles.blogspot.com/

IMPOVERISHED MISS, CONVENIENT WIFE

Michelle Styles

First published in Great Britain 2009
Large Print edition 2009
Harlequin Mills & Boon Limited,
Eton House, 18-24 Paradise Road, Richmond, Surrey TW9 1SR

© Michelle Styles 2009

ISBN: 978 0 263 20673 9

Set in Times Roman 16 on 18½ pt.
42-0809-76983

Harlequin Mills & Boon policy is to use papers that are natural, renewable and recyclable products and made from wood grown in sustainable forests. The logging and manufacturing process conform to the legal environmental regulations of the country of origin.

Printed and bound in Great Britain
by CPI Antony Rowe, Chippenham, Wiltshire

Born and raised near San Francisco, California, **Michelle Styles** currently lives a few miles south of Hadrian's Wall, with her husband, three children, two dogs, cats, assorted ducks, hens and beehives. An avid reader, she became hooked on historical romance when she discovered Georgette Heyer, Anya Seton and Victoria Holt one rainy lunchtime at school. And, for her, a historical romance still represents the perfect way to escape. Although Michelle loves reading about history, she also enjoys a more hands-on approach to her research. She has experimented with a variety of old recipes and cookery methods (some more successfully than others), climbed down Roman sewers, and fallen off horses in Iceland—all in the name of discovering more about how people went about their daily lives. When she is not writing, reading or doing research, Michelle tends her rather overgrown garden or does needlework, in particular counted cross-stitch.

Michelle maintains a website, www.michellestyles.co.uk, and a blog, www.michellestyles.blogspot.com, and would be delighted to hear from you.

Recent novels by the same author:

THE GLADIATOR'S HONOUR
A NOBLE CAPTIVE
SOLD AND SEDUCED
THE ROMAN'S VIRGIN MISTRESS
TAKEN BY THE VIKING
A CHRISTMAS WEDDING WAGER
  (part of *Christmas By Candlelight*)
VIKING WARRIOR, UNWILLING WIFE
AN IMPULSIVE DEBUTANTE
A QUESTION OF IMPROPRIETY

For Pam Brooks. Because, as E. B. White said in Charlotte's Web, *it is not often that someone comes along who is a true friend and a good writer. Pam is both.*

Chapter One

End of January 1814—
Ladywell, Northumberlandf

'We have arrived, miss.'

Snow swirled around the Honourable Phoebe Benedict as she alighted from the carriage. Not the soft downy flakes of her Cotswold childhood, or the coal-flecked ones of London, but hard biting snow with a wind to match, the sort of snow that crept into the bones and lingered. Phoebe peered through the veil of white. The house rose up in front of her—grey, stern, without a hint of candle-light to welcome her.

For the first time since she'd started this journey, her optimism vanished and the nerves coiled around the pit of her stomach, waiting to strike. She was truly alone here, without friends or family. Phoebe gave her head a decisive shake, banishing all thoughts of failure back to that dark and lonely place. She would demonstrate to all her family and acquaintances that she was capable of more than visiting and pouring endless cups of tea.

'Are you going to take this…this creature with you, miss?' the coachman asked, reaching into the carriage and withdrawing a wicker basket. He looked at it with distaste as the 'creature' in the basket gave an angry cry.

'Yes, of course.' Phoebe took the basket and peeped under the cloth at the scrawny kitten. A pair of green eyes blinked up at her before the cat let out another ear-piercing yowl. She hated to think about what could have happened if she had not spotted it lying beside its dead mother, friendless and alone. 'I refused to leave the creature to die in the cold of the inn, and I am hardly likely to leave it now.'

'I have no idea what Mr Clare will say about a cat.' The coachman grimaced slightly. 'The big house doesn't have any, like. No pets whatsoever now that Miss Diana…I mean Lady Coltonby… has left with her terrier. I should have said at the time, but I just wanted to get on with the journey. Mr Clare is not going to like it.'

'Cats are a useful addition to any home.' Phoebe tucked the basket under her arm. She would find a way. How could anyone turn a helpless kitten away? Simon Clare's sister, Diana, Lady Coltonby, was the epitome of grace and charm combined with practicality. Her brother was bound to be the same. He would see the necessity of keeping a cat, if he did not already possess one. 'They help to keep the mice down and only ask for a saucer of milk and a warm place by the fire in return.'

'You are braver than I. The master doesn't take kindly to his will being crossed. I can tell you that for nothing.'

'Once Mr Clare understands the situation, I feel certain that he will be amenable.'

'I say nothing.' The coachman shook his head gloomily. 'Mr Clare gave me orders to return with Miss Diana or not to come back at all. Mayhap we should have stayed in London.'

'Lady Coltonby specifically sent word.' Phoebe juggled the basket with her large portmanteau and withdrew a letter. 'She assured me that this would suffice. Lord Coltonby agreed. Mr Clare wants help with his son. I am here to provide it. It is a sensible, practical solution to the problem.'

'I just wouldn't want to cross him, not on

account of a kitten that was likely to die anyway.' The coachman tapped the side of his nose. 'You ain't seen him in a temper, miss.'

'One must do one's duty as one sees it. One's destiny is not written until it is lived. Something had to be done.' Phoebe looked towards the house again and knew she had to believe the words. This was about more than saving a kitten. She had to face Simon Clare and break the news that his sister would not be returning to Northumberland as he demanded. Mr Clare had to accept the inevitable.

A blast of freezing air drove the snow into Phoebe, hitting her like a thousand pinpricks, making her stagger back. With one hand she clasped her bonnet, and, with the other, the basket and portmanteau. Slowly she struggled towards the house. The door crashed open. A tall dark figure stood silhouetted as he held a lantern aloft. Great arcs of yellow illuminated the white of the driving snow. 'Is that you, Diana? You took your time. Come into the warmth at once, you will catch your death in this perishing cold.'

'Miss Phoebe Benedict. The Countess of Coltonby sent me in her stead.' Phoebe started forwards, but the snow brushed against her skirt, weighing her down, making her footsteps heavy, as if even the weather had decided that this was a bad idea. 'I have a letter.'

'John, Diana is there, isn't she?' The man's voice held a note of impatience. 'I sent you to bring back my sister, not some stranger off the wayside.'

'No, Mr Clare, I brought this one on your sister's expressed instruction. Miss Diana sent her with her best wishes. It ain't my fault.'

'Throw her back at once.' Mr Clare lowered the lantern. Phoebe put her hand to her mouth, unable to stifle a gasp. The light suddenly highlighted a black eye patch and a scarlet burn that covered half the man's face. His hair was far longer than fashionable, flowing ragged about his shoulders. She had thought to meet a model of urbanity, but Mr Clare bore a closer resemblance to a wild savage. 'I sent for Diana. She is the only one who can help! I do not have time to waste on strangers.'

He began to swing away. In another moment, the door would be closed, and her chance gone, all down to her weakness and indecision. She would have to go back cap in hand to her sister-in-law and admit that she had failed and had been utterly wrong to try. Phoebe tightened her grip on the basket. Impossible after the scorn the Dreaded Sophia had poured on Phoebe's head when she had explained her determination to save James from his fate. And how could she condemn her stepbrother to life in a debtors' prison because a man's appearance shocked her into inaction?

Phoebe squared her shoulders and looked directly at Mr Clare, willing him to keep the door open. 'Lady Coltonby sent me. I have a letter from her in my portmanteau explaining.'

'The devil she did. Who precisely are you?'

'Phoebe Benedict.' She made sure her words were clear and precise. Said it slowly so that he could understand. 'I am Lord Coltonby's second cousin.'

'And why in the name of all that is holy should Diana send you? Why should she wish to foist you on me? My sister should know her duty. When you have finished gawping at me, you may go.'

Phoebe winced, hating that he had seen her bad manners.

Whatever had happened to the man, it was not his fault. Nor was it any of her concern. Her concern was with James and the aid that Lord Coltonby would give him because she had agreed to this task. The Benedicts might be poor now, but they would never stoop low as taking charity. There had to be a payment for the favour. 'I have had experience with scarlet fever. My younger stepbrothers had it several years ago. Lady Coltonby felt I was ideally placed to look after your son.'

She refused to flinch under his gaze and ignored the stubborn downturn of his mouth. She could be immovable as well. She returned his dark brooding gaze, measure for measure. Suddenly something flared in his eyes and she knew she had won a small victory.

'Miss…Miss Benedict, it is all very well and good, but I sent for my sister. I specifically requested her. Why isn't she here? Why has her husband sent you? Jenkins! Jenkins! Where is that butler when I need him?'

'Is there a problem, master?' A tall man appeared behind Mr Clare. 'Where is Miss Diana? I heard the coach.'

'Lord Coltonby has kept her from me and has sent this person in her stead.' Mr Clare gestured imperiously with his cane. 'Once again Coltonby has turned my world upside down.'

'Lord Coltonby told me that I was specifically to inform you that he opposed my coming here.' Phoebe drew a calming breath. She had worried her cousin was being sarcastic, but now she saw he had known the sort of welcome she might encounter. 'It was my cousin's considered opinion you would not allow me past the front door and would waste everyone's time, pigheaded idiot that you are—his words, not mine. He was most insistent that I say those words to you. I apologise for them.'

'I know what my brother-in-law is like. I am well acquainted with his way of speaking.' The scar on his temple throbbed. 'Continue with the story.'

Phoebe kept her head up and concentrated on the warm enticing pool of light behind Mr Clare, rather than on his thunderous scowl. She did not have the luxury of walking away. There was more than her pride at stake. 'Lady Coltonby disagreed. She felt you would understand her reason. It was only through her pleading that Lord Coltonby relented.'

'Ah ha, why didn't she send her maid Rose? Rose understands the situation. She knows Robert and his escapades.'

'Lady Coltonby's reason for remaining in London is not something I would like to discuss during a blizzard. May I come into the warmth?' Phoebe took several steps forward. Another blast of arctic air drove the stinging snow against her body. Her toes and the tips of her fingers no longer appeared to possess any feeling. He couldn't be such a monster as to slam the door in her face, not after she had journeyed all this way. 'Your coachman and I have been travelling almost straight from London, with only brief stops to change horses, and I am near perished. If you will not allow me entrance, Lord Coltonby indicated that I could rest at his house before returning to London.'

'You had best come in, then. I refuse to give my brother-in-law the satisfaction.' Simon Clare gestured with his cane. 'Say your piece. In the morning, you may return to London and inform Coltonby that I require my sister. But I will not have put it about that Simon Clare fails to provide hospitality to Coltonby's messengers or relations on a night like this!'

Phoebe closed her eyes and willed herself to hang on to her temper. Mr Clare was upset that his sister was not there. She had seen his letter with its bold spiked handwriting and terse demand for his sister to return, but she had also glimpsed the blotch under his name as if he had hurried the words and had been far too worried to let the ink dry properly.

'I would not like to be in your shoes, miss. The master appears to be in a right royal temper,' the coachman said in an undertone. 'I ain't seen him like this for years.'

'He has had his expectations dashed.' Phoebe

eyed the man in the doorway whose fury appeared to grow with each breath. 'He will understand once I give him Lady Coltonby's letter. He will see the sense in what his sister and I have done.'

'I will be ready in the morning, miss, early, like. I'd go now but them horses will only be fit for the knacker's yard if they don't get some rest.'

'I refuse to depart without performing my task. I have given Lady Coltonby my word.' Phoebe fought to keep her voice steady. 'All Mr Clare has done is to make me more determined.'

'Like I said, miss, the morning will suit me fine.' The coachman touched his hand to his hat and began to lead the horses away.

Phoebe straightened her spine and marched towards the house without a backwards glance. But suddenly the bone-rattling coach seemed far more hospitable than the large, grey house.

Crossing the threshold, she closed her eyes for a second, savouring the warmth. Hearing an impatient cough, Phoebe opened them and discovered she was staring into Simon Clare's furious face. He had been handsome once, but one side of his face bore fierce red marks, and he had a blaze of white running through his hair. He leant heavily on a cane as if his side pained him. Antagonism bristled from every pore as he moved slowly to let her in. Phoebe revised her opinion—not a savage, but a pirate captain, someone who wanted to bend the world to his will.

'I believe you said my sister sent a letter, explaining her reasons.' He held out a stern hand. 'I will have it now.'

The ticking of a large clock filled the silence as she waited for Mr Clare to finish reading. With each ponderous tick, a little more of her easy optimism faded, vanishing until it became the merest wisp. This scheme was not going to work any better than the half-a-dozen plans she had rejected. She should never have attempted it. Mentally she tried to rehearse the words she would use when she returned to Atherstone Court and begged Sophia's pardon. Her brief moment of triumph and independence was over before it had truly begun.

Phoebe struggled to keep herself upright. She refused to give this pirate captain the pleasure of seeing her burst into tears. She would simply have to pretend; if she pretended long enough, everything might work out. 'As you can see, Mr Clare, everything is straightforward.'

'So you say.' Simon Clare stared at the woman

standing in front of him in the entrance hall and attempted to control his temper. Her cloak was fine, but worn, and her bonnet not of the best quality, but her voice held an educated tone. The woman was no demure and downcast servant. Instead she stood there, shoulders back and eyes blazing.

Exactly where had his sister found this woman and why had she sent her when his instructions had been precise? Robert needed someone who would understand. The simple words resounded in his brain. *I am unable to come. She is immensely capable.* The truth hit him. Diana had refused his simple request. Simon ignored the pulling of his shoulder. The pain behind his eye rose to a blinding crescendo. He had had such hopes. Diana would have instinctively understood what to do with the boy. Once she'd arrived, everything would have gone back to normal. Only now he was faced with some harpy of a cousin. 'Why did she send you?'

'Lady Coltonby assured me she had put the details in her letter.'

Simon glanced up at the ceiling, trying to regain control of his emotions. He hated being infirm, hated the indignity of asking for help, but most of all he hated that Diana had abandoned him.

Abandoned him for her new husband and the bright lights of London. Even her letter was a single uncrossed sheet. He folded it and put it in his pocket. 'I must wonder what part of my letter my sister failed to understand.'

'Your sister indicated that you might be taken back, but you would see the sense of the thing in the end.' The harpy calmly undid her cloak and her bonnet before handing them to Jenkins as if she were here on a visit rather than on sufferance.

He revised his opinion. Not a harpy at all, but a woman who, despite being past the first blush of youth, radiated beauty. Although her gown hung like a sack, he could see that she possessed a magnificent figure—generous bosom, narrow waist and long legs. His jaw tightened. It was far worse than he had thought. Not a harpy, but some sort of faded débutante from the south. What ever had possessed Diana to send such an unsuitable creature? Had London turned her wits?

'The sense of the thing eludes me,' he said as they went in to the drawing room. 'I will wish to understand precisely the terms on which you agreed to come up here.'

The embers were dying, but the room remained pleasantly warm. The débutante went over to the fire and warmed her hands. The fire tinged her cheeks pink, and caused the golden highlights to stand out in her hair. Definitely a woman who belonged in the ballroom, rather than the sick room.

'You make no answer, Miss Benedict. What have you agreed with my sister? Why precisely did she send you of all people?'

She tilted her chin and her steel-grey eyes met his. 'I agreed the terms with Lord and Lady Coltonby. You do not need to worry about being inconvenienced. Or out of pocket!'

'It is not the money I am worried about. It is the boy's reaction. He wants his aunt.' Simon tried not to think about Robert's increasing bouts of temper and the exhortations of his current nurse. Or the uproar that would ensue when Robert learnt about his aunt. Simon shook his head. Not an hour before he had been counting the minutes until Diana saved him once again, just as she had done when Jayne had died. How wrong he had been. 'Robert has a forceful personality.'

'It will be my pleasure to meet him. Your sister spoke fondly of him.'

'What sort of condition prevents my sister from travelling? Is she ill? At death's door?' Simon glared at the woman, ignoring her polite smile.

First Jayne and now Diana. How many more people would he lose? Could Coltonby be trusted to look after Diana properly?

'You may ease your mind. Your sister is well. She is blooming. London agrees with her and she is in safe hands there.'

'That is not what I am asking and you know it.' Everything was conspiring against him today— the snow-blown weather, the sputtering fire in the grate of his study, and now his injuries from the accident last autumn were playing up. He wanted to sink down in his armchair, but he refused to show how weak he felt. 'Tell me the truth. What are you hiding from me? What is wrong with Diana?'

'The Countess is in a delicate condition.' She said the words slowly as if speaking to a particularly dim-witted child. 'The Earl refuses to risk her or her unborn child.'

Diana pregnant? Simon's head throbbed with fresh pain. He should have anticipated it. Another worry. He tried to put it from his mind. Diana had always been strong. Never ill. She would survive. And yet he found it impossible to fault Coltonby for being cautious. 'Where is her maid? Robert appears fond enough of her. Surely Diana could have spared Rose.'

'Lady Coltonby's maid is about to be wed to Lord Coltonby's valet and is therefore unavailable. Her brother has just returned to this country. He only has a short leave from the Navy. This scheme was discussed.'

Simon regarded the gilt of the ceiling and regained some measure of control over his temper. Everywhere he turned, there was another excuse, another reason why he must yield and give way. Why he must accept this thoroughly unsuitable woman. 'I suppose we must all bow in the face of love and romance.'

'My cousin concurred with me about the solution, considering the Countess's condition and her maid's situation. Everyone was agreed that you would see the logic.'

'*Everyone* neglected to consult me.'

'Your letter stressed the urgency. I barely had time to scrawl three lines to my stepmother once the scheme was agreed.'

Simon resisted the temptation to swear long and loud. As if forgoing letter writing to one's stepmother was somehow akin to his situation. 'You will be rewarded in heaven.'

'There is no need to blaspheme, Mr Clare.'

Simon pressed his lips together and held back a

few more choice words. 'And how precisely are you related to the Earl?'

'As I've already mentioned, I am the Earl's second cousin. Our maternal grandmothers were sisters. The connection sealed the matter. Your sister had no wish for some stranger to look after her nephew. I am not a stranger, but a relation.' Her lips curved in a placating smile.

Simon tightened his grip on this cane. Same obstinate arrogance as his brother-in-law. Same assumption that they ruled the planet and all must give way. He did not need arrogance; he needed help with Robert. 'Let me see your bare hands.'

She held out a delicate hand, long fingered and smooth without a callous or blemish. 'I have no fear of work.'

Simon resisted the urge to ask if she had ever lifted anything heavier than a china tea pot.

'What sort of qualifications do you possess? My son has had scarlet fever. The worst has passed, but he remains weak. He will require proper nursing, not someone to wipe his brow with eau de cologne.' Simon refused to think about the nights he had spent by his son's bed. Silently he cursed the school for not noticing, and then sending him home in a cold carriage. Whatever happened, Robert would be educated elsewhere. And he refused to think about the other problem, the tendency Robert had begun to exhibit. It had to be temporary—the boy would return to his old self in time. Diana would have brought him back.

'Your letter did indicate the nature of the illness. It was what made Lord Coltonby adamant. I know how to run a sick room, quite probably better than your sister.'

'An unusual accomplishment. I would have considered dancing lessons or water colours to be more your forte.'

'My father was a viscount, and my mother the daughter of a baronet, but that does not preclude me being able to nurse.' Her chin angled higher and her tone became more clipped. 'One does what one must and I need to support my family, regardless of my parentage.' Her mouth became thin, but her gaze did not waver. Simon felt a glimmer of respect rise within him. Angrily he dampened it down. 'My stepbrother James requires a commission in the army. I happened to be at Coltonby House, seeking advice, shortly after your letter arrived. It seemed the best way. Lord Coltonby will help my brother and I will assist you. One cannot accept charity, Mr Clare.'

'And why does your family not assist your stepbrother? Surely you have male relations capable of the task. Why does he seek to hide behind petticoats?'

Simon was gratified to see Miss Benedict glance down at the floor. Two bright spots appeared on her cheeks and for the first time in their encounter her poise appeared shaken. She rapidly recovered.

'My eldest brother died a year ago. His carriage turned over on the way to visit me. There is no one else, no one else who cares.' She plucked at the lace on her collar. 'He left a wife and a son who will never know his father. It is my sister-in-law Sophia who is head of the family now, and she…she has other concerns.'

Simon pursed his lips. The undercurrent to her words was obvious. The sister-in-law had quite rightly decided to stop the allowance of some feckless aristocrat. It was admirable in a way that Miss Benedict wanted to help her brother. But he doubted that she was the right person for Robert. Even Robert's current nurse had problems and she had arrived with a string of recommendations and references. All he had to do was find the right words to refuse Miss Benedict's assistance.

Just then an earsplitting yowl emanated from the

basket as it rocked on the woman's arm. She immediately started to make cooing noises to whatever creature lay under the cloth and the din subsided.

'What in the name of all that is holy is that?'

'A cat.' Her cheeks had the grace to develop a slight pink tinge. 'Little more than a kitten, actually. I discovered him at our stop near Catterick. The poor thing was mewling its head off beside its mother. The innkeeper wanted to drown him.'

'And you decided to save its life. How saintly.' Simon stared at the basket. 'What are you planning on doing with this cat?'

'All the kitten wants is a bit of milk and a warm corner in which to sleep.' Her voice was low and she appeared to be talking to his boots. 'A chance to live.'

'Are you prone to picking up stray animals that happen across your path, Miss Benedict?' Simon raised one eyebrow, intrigued. She knew he was about to dismiss her and she was trying to distract him.

'I will let you know when I discover the next animal in dire need.' She tilted her head to one side. 'Surely your heart has been touched by this animal's plight, and you will not refuse him shelter.'

'It has been claimed that I have no heart.'

'Having met your sister, I find that impossible.'

Simon gritted his teeth. He would allow Miss Benedict to stay the night, but in the morning, she would have to go. Back to Coltonby with a warning—he had managed thus far on his own and did not need to depend on the kindness of strangers. There would be no need to trouble Robert.

'Master, Master!' The upstairs maid's frightened voice echoed from the hallway, interrupting him. 'It has started again! Worse than ever. Mrs Smith says to come quickly.'

'Stop that unholy racket!' Simon thundered, ignoring Miss Benedict's questioning glance, and the maid's wails ceased. Simon tilted his head as a better solution occurred to him. If Miss Benedict saw Robert in this state he had little doubt that she would flee on the first coach, cat and all.

'I am sorry, truly I am, but young Master Robert is being impossible. He has heard the carriage and swears that it will be her ladyship.' The maid had burst into the room without knocking. 'And now Jenkins has told Mrs Smith that Miss Diana is not here after all. And the nurse refuses to go back in. Not after what he did to her the last time. He is the very devil incarnate. Mrs Smith says that I must come and fetch you. I am not to take no for an answer. You must see your son.'

Simon raised his eyes to the ceiling. The day had descended from awful to disastrous. There was no telling what measures would be required to restrain the boy.

'Mr Clare, are you going to introduce me to your son?' Miss Benedict stood there, her face composed and her shoulders relaxed. 'I believe he is awake. He will want to know that his aunt is well.'

Simon felt an overwhelming urge to join Robert in screaming. Miss Benedict was standing there, so calm, so smug, so certain that she could control Robert. Last time it had taken two footmen and the nurse to get the laudanum down his throat, and even then one of the footmen had ended up with a black eye.

Miss Benedict wished to meet Robert? Very well. Let her. Let Coltonby's saviour fall at the first hurdle. He doubted that she would last five minutes before she began bleating for the coach. He would delight in writing to Coltonby and explaining the spinelessness of his cousin.

'Miss Benedict, you may accompany me to the sickroom. Robert has set his heart on his aunt returning.'

'But what is it that you want me to do?' She crossed her arms. 'I have never met the boy.'

'You are my sister's emissary. It falls to you to explain why she has declined to return.' Simon bit out each word.

'To me?' Miss Benedict had the grace to look wary. 'But surely the explanation should come from you, as his parent. I will wait here.'

'No, from you.' Simon glared at the woman—in his mind, he consigned her to a dark place. '*You* can explain to the boy why the one person in the whole world that he wants to see is not coming. We will deal with your cat later. I do hope you have a strong constitution, Miss Benedict.'

Chapter Two

The heart-rending wails hit Phoebe as she mounted the stairs—pitiful wails to make any adult wince with pity, pleas for his aunt to come upstairs. But with each new piercing sound, Simon Clare's face became more stonily resolute and the maid only appeared concerned that her evening had been interrupted.

'Who is Mrs Smith?' Phoebe asked.

'Robert's nurse.' Mr Clare stopped and a wry smile crossed his face. 'Surely you do not expect me to leave Robert under the care of a scullery maid, or perhaps lying on his own, unattended? Mrs Smith came highly recommended from Lady Bolt. She has excellent references. But Robert wants his aunt.'

Excellent references. Phoebe's heart sank. Had

she entirely misjudged the situation? She had been positive that his letter had asked for a nurse. 'It would appear that I have made a mistake.'

'It would appear to be the case, Miss Benedict. And you may explain the situation to Robert.'

Another loud, long echoing plea issued from the room. Phoebe's heart squeezed. How would he react when she explained about his aunt? Would he understand any better than his father? And then what?

She glanced at Mr Clare's stern back. His coat twitched as if he knew she would get her words wrong. Suddenly she wanted to rush down the stairs and demand to be returned to London. But that would be admitting failure.

Phoebe allowed herself three steps of panic and then regained control. She knew why she was here. James deserved his chance in the army. A friendship with the Earl of Coltonby was not to be underestimated. Who knew where it might lead not only for James but for Edmund as well? She owed it to her stepbrothers. After all, she bore some responsibility for their predicament.

She took another step and knew there was more to it. She had seen the tears in Lady Coltonby's eyes and knew how torn she was between her love for her nephew and her need to protect her unborn child.

'Miss Benedict, I am waiting. Unless of course you want to give up before you have begun.'

Phoebe gathered her skirts in her free hand and marched up the final few stairs. 'Quit before I have begun? Never!'

'Well said, Miss Benedict. I hope you will not have cause to regret those words.'

He flung open the door. Phoebe stifled a gasp. The single guttering oil lamp threw shifting shadows on to piles of broken toys and dirty linen, and an overturned bowl of congealed brown liquid oozed on the floor. A freezing wind blew through an open window as a young boy with only a few shreds of hair on his head stood screaming on the bed, his hands clenched around the rails of the iron bedstead. Phoebe shivered slightly and fought to keep her stomach from churning as all around her the echoes of his cries rose. How could anyone with an ounce of compassion in their body permit this to happen? Where was this misbegotten nurse who had been hired?

She glanced up at Mr Clare, but his face had become even more set, harder and more forbidding.

'Robert, be quiet this instant! You will do yourself injury!'

'Aunt Diana. I want Aunt Diana.' A tear trickled

down the boy's face as he rocked back and forth. A terrible squeaking from the bed combined with the wailing to create an unholy din. 'She is here! I heard the coach! You promised!'

'Stop this racket!' Mr Clare thundered. 'Immediately, Robert Clare! You are ten, not four! Behave yourself, boy!'

The boy stopped his screaming so abruptly that the silence seemed unnatural. Everything appeared suspended in time as if she had inadvertently stepped into one of the panoramas at the Exeter Change. The scar on Simon Clare's face stood out bright red against the paleness of his cheek. His hands curled tightly as if he was making a supreme effort not to hit the wall. His son's pleading face was turned towards him.

Her stomach knotted. She felt helpless standing there watching the scene, but her voice refused to work.

A gust of wind rattled through the room bringing with it a flurry of hard stinging snow, breaking the spell.

'Who opened the window? The room is freezing.' Simon struggled to contain his temper. The window had been opened to the elements. Against his expressed orders. Windows were to be kept tightly latched at all times. He had been very clear on that. Every one of the staff knew the order. It could only have been one person. The blackness of his nightmare was complete. 'Robert, did you open this window?'

Robert slowly shook his head as he hugged his arms about him. 'I am cold. I want a fire!'

Simon slammed the window shut and threw a bucket of coal on the fire, before he turned towards the boy. 'Somebody must have! Windows do not magically fly open!'

'I…I have no idea.' Robert's teeth chattered as Simon eased him back under the covers. 'It just opened! When I woke, I was cold.'

'My orders are quite strict on the matter! No window is to be opened!' Simon struggled to hang on to his temper. Memories of the last time he had discovered a window open like this assaulted him. 'Are you sure it wasn't you, Robert?'

'It wasn't me!' Robert looked up at him with injured eyes.

'If not you, then who?'

'Mrs Smith did,' Robert mumbled, ducking his head. 'She did it, because I was naughty.'

'Mrs Smith? You will have to do better than that, Robert. Mrs Smith is a trained nurse. I cannot abide a liar. Who threw the beef jelly on the floor?'

'Hate beef jelly. Particularly when it is cold.'

Behind him, Simon Clare could hear Miss Benedict make a little tutting noise in the back of her throat, judging him and finding him wanting. His humiliation was complete. And Robert had been exposed as the liar the nurse had said he was. Why had his life come down to this?

He glared at Mrs Smith, who had come into the room with a superior expression on her face. She was the fifth nurse he had hired for Robert. 'Did you open that window against my expressed orders?'

The woman looked uncomfortable, but did not speak. The back of Simon's neck prickled.

'I did, sir,' Mrs Smith said finally. 'I thought the cold air would calm him. In such cases—'

'Balderdash. I have no wish to hear about other cases and theories. You disobeyed me!' Simon fought to retain a leash on his temper. For once Robert had not been lying. Did the foolish woman not realise what damage she could have done? The nurse cowered slightly as if she expected to be beaten. He heard Miss Benedict's sharp intake of breath. Simon sighed. When had he ever had a servant beaten? He might shout, but it was beneath him to discipline his servants in that fashion. He was no boorish aristocrat who gave way to his passions.

'But…but…please, sir, it was the only way. He was yelling something fierce. I thought it would shock him back to his senses. He threw beef jelly at me.'

'Never, ever disobey me again!' Simon banged his cane down on the floor. 'In fact, get out of my sight and pack your bags!'

'You need not ask me twice. No amount of money would make me stay and look after that…that monster of a child!' The nurse turned on her heel.

He shook his head in disgust. Yet another staffing problem to deal with.

The pain in his head grew, throbbing and blotting out everything. He gave his head a shake and with an effort forced the pain to recede.

He thought that once Diana arrived, everything would get easier, and he could dispense with the nurse. But instead he had been landed with a former débutante and Robert was becoming more unmanageable by the day.

He refused to even think about what the doctor had said about how Robert's mind could be affected by the illness. He wouldn't let it happen. Robert would get well. He wanted his boy back.

'I want Aunt Diana. I heard the carriage.' Robert's green eyes blazed defiantly as he banged his hand against the iron bedstead. 'Aunt Diana! Aunt Diana!'

'And this is the way you behave? Creating a mess like this? To get attention? You would make your aunt cry.'

'Mr Clare,' Miss Benedict said in a soft voice, as if he had done something wrong.

'I want my aunt!'

'You have shamed me, Robert. Truly shamed me.' Simon shook his head. 'When this is cleaned up, then we will discuss your aunt.'

Robert closed his mouth, attempted to draw a breath and failed. As Simon watched in horror, the boy's limbs and face began to jerk uncontrollably.

A small noise came from Miss Benedict behind him in the doorway. Simon wanted to tell her that this was not the Robert he knew.

'Stop that, Robert! You can control yourself if you want to. Concentrate, boy!' A surge of fear swept through him as Robert gave no indication that he had heard. He wanted to do something for the boy. He wanted to prevent what was coming next. 'Cease that noise this instant!' He put a hand to his head and whispered, 'Please!'

'Shall I get the footmen and the rope, sir?' The maid peeped out from behind the door. 'It is the way I had to do it last night when Mrs Smith refused to help. The boy will not take his medicine. It is more than a body should have to deal with. Like Mrs Smith said—he should be sent away to one of them hospitals.'

'Are ropes really necessary? The boy seems frightened enough,' Miss Benedict asked in a clear voice, breaking through Simon's desperation. 'Does he have to be tied down?'

'I am trying, Papa. I can't seem to stop.' The boy's limbs began to move of their own accord, jerking and dancing. A ghastly parody of the boy he knew and loved.

'You must stop, Robert. Or else you will leave me with no choice…'

'I am trying, Papa.' Robert struggled to contain his movement but the jerking and rocking only increased. 'Truly I am.'

Prior to Robert's illness Simon had considered the accident when his travelling engine had exploded to be the most frightening experience of his life, but now he knew it was far more dreadful to watch Robert suffer this torment. Robert raised two trembling hands. The night shirt fell away from his wrists and the red welts from last night were clearly visible.

Simon winced, hating the necessity of restraining the boy. He had no other choice. Robert had to take his medicine. It was a fight for Robert's soul, but it did not mean that he had to like the method.

The boy's breath rattled again, an awful sound. Simon cursed his own useless arm. Once he would have been able to administer the medicine himself, but no longer. 'Bring two footmen. Quickly!'

He heard the maid's footsteps hurrying down the hall. He forced his hand to pick up the beef-jelly bowl, heart sick at his own failure. Behind him Robert's wailing rose and fell.

'I wish to speak with you, Mr Clare. In the corridor.'

'Is there some new problem, Miss Benedict? Has the noise disturbed your kitten per chance?' A bitter laugh escaped his throat. 'If you will excuse me, other matters are more urgent.'

'We need to speak.' Her eyes became rapiers. 'Now, Mr Clare, before you make a big mistake.'

He looked down at her, tempted to brush her aside. The avenging angel with the flawless skin and disapproving beestung mouth, so righteous in her indignation, so sure in her clipped tone of voice—what did she know about his fears? Or how the laudanum appeared to return Robert to his former self for a few hours? He knew what Mrs Smith thought and what the four nurses before her had thought.

All he wanted was for Robert to get well. A great weariness descended over him. Every particle of his body ached. He hated this. He would loathe himself afterwards, but it was the only way to get Robert to take his medicine.

'As you wish.' Simon ran his hand through his hair and waited. He had had such hopes when the carriage had arrived back, but now all he had was an interfering, meddlesome woman. He did not need to be told that tying down his son with ropes was wrong. With her disapproving look and crossed arms, Miss Benedict failed to understand that he was doing the only thing he could to save his son. Robert had to take the medicine whether he liked it or not.

'I highly doubt that Robert has done this on purpose.'

'He tries to avoid the laudanum. The nurse was right. The boy has become ungovernable.' He forced a ghost of a smile. 'And it is entirely my fault.'

'You are taking the nurse's word. The woman

who opened an invalid's window during a blizzard! She could have given him lung fever! How could you have allowed such a creature in this house?'

Simon clenched his hands. What other new great insight could Miss Benedict give him?

Miss Benedict clamped her mouth shut, but her eyes burned with an even greater intensity. 'You should have checked…'

'I note you do not offer any references of your own. You ask me to take you on trust.'

'I can certainly do a better job than that…that slattern!'

'The footmen have already been called.'

'Listen to my plan.' Phoebe forced her voice to be calm. She had to get through to this man. The boy was in trouble. She could see his blue lips and uncontrollable shuddering. This was no act of defiance or a wish to get attention. This was something else entirely. 'He may not be to blame.'

Mr Clare's face blazed with a barely controlled fury, but she stood her ground and refused to flinch.

'Do you not think every way has been tried? Tried and failed? I have had experienced nurses. This is no tea party, Miss Benedict. This is real life. The boy must take his medicine or risk dying.'

'But not that way! It is cruel and is making matters worse! We need to speak if I am to help the boy.'

A faint sardonic smile touched his lips. 'I am rather busy at present. If you disagree with my methods, you know where the door is.'

'You will listen to me.' Phoebe ground the words out. 'Will you tie me down as well or will you listen to what I have to say!'

Mr Clare glanced at the boy and his face appeared to soften momentarily. Phoebe silently pleaded that somehow her words had penetrated, that he would finally agree to listen.

'You have five minutes, Miss Benedict, to explain yourself.' His quiet words filled the room. 'After that, my coach will return you to your home.'

Phoebe blinked. He had agreed! Tension flowed from her shoulders, leaving her weak and giddy.

Mr Clare led the way into the hallway as she heard Robert's sobbing increase, but the squeaking of the bed slowed. The fit was ending. She gave one hurried glance, but saw that the boy appeared to be coping. She carefully closed the door.

She looked Mr Clare in the face and sought to find the concerned, loving parent, rather than the stern savage who had greeted her at the door.

'That boy is far from being mad.' Phoebe

crossed her arms and met his intense gaze. 'He is frightened beyond measure. The threat of ropes and being forced to take the medicine is making matters worse. He had already begun to calm down when the medicine was mentioned. Yes, he is excited, but—'

'What do you suggest should be done with him?' Mr Clare raised an eyebrow. 'He bit Mrs Smith two nights ago. I saw the teeth marks on her arm. Others have tried to tell me that it is my duty to send him to the madhouse. But not Robert! Not while I have a breath in my body!'

Tiredness made Phoebe's mind clumsy, but she fought against it. All she knew was that tying the boy down was wrong. He was a frightened little boy in need of understanding. He had had scarlet fever, not brain fever. 'Did she say why he had bitten her? Did anyone see it happen? She went against your wishes about the window.'

Mr Clare's face took on an even more ruthless demeanour, became even more piratical. She suspected that he longed for a plank so that she could be ordered to walk it. 'She attempted to give him his laudanum. And I saw the bite.'

'Perhaps the nurse tried to force it down his

throat—against his will. He reacted in the only way he had left.'

'He must do as he is told, Miss Benedict.' Mr Clare regarded her with disdain. 'All of us must do things in this life that we dislike, but we do them. It has been explained to Robert, several times.'

'Have you ever had medicine forced down your throat, Mr Clare?'

'Does it matter?'

'It matters a great deal.'

The air crackled between them, replete with some raw elemental emotion. His hard look intensified. Phoebe resolutely refused to turn her gaze away as the heat between them threatened to sear her. Suddenly he turned his face. The breath exited her lungs with a whoosh.

'My stepbrothers never had to be tied down when they had scarlet fever, not even the youngest, and he contracted rheumatic fever,' she said quietly. 'I think the nurse has frightened Robert badly.'

'Your stepbrothers were not Robert. If he will not take his medicine, measures must be taken.' Mr Clare's mouth became a thin white line. 'Is that all you wished to speak me about? Your time is nearly up.'

'Have these fits been happening long? Did he ever

have episodes like this before she started to care for him?' Phoebe asked quickly, seeking to regain the upper hand. 'Your sister never said that he suffered from any affliction. Did the fever cause this?'

'They started within the last few weeks. Just before Mrs Smith started or just after.' Mr Clare ran his hand through his hair. 'Then this started happening—these fits of madness. I knew Diana was my last chance. Robert's cries were unbearable.'

Phoebe pressed her lips together. Thank goodness Lord Coltonby had seen the sense of it and had prevented his wife from travelling. This sickroom was the last place where Lady Coltonby should be.

'Have you had the doctor in? What does he say?' Tiredness made her head fuzzy, blocking her thoughts.

'Doctor MacFarlane says that only time will cure him. It is out of our hands.' Simon Clare crossed his arms and gave her a dark brooding look. 'Robert must be nursed here.'

Robert was not mad. It was his illness. He had contracted rheumatic fever. It had to be. It bore all the hallmarks of what Edmund had had. St Vitus's dance. Phoebe paused, unclear how best to proceed. Then she decided that she would simply have to say it, tell Mr Clare the worst. But hopefully, once he knew, then he would stop using the ropes. It had to work.

'My youngest stepbrother, Edmund, contracted rheumatic fever after his bout of scarlet fever. His limbs and face would shake and move. Our doctor called the condition St Vitus's Dance. It affected his heart, not his mind.'

'And how does he fare now?' Simon Clare's hoarse whisper echoed down the corridor.

'He can run as well as any man, better than most. He has finished his last term at Oxford.' Phoebe could not resist a note of pride creeping into her voice. Of all of her stepbrothers, Edmund was the one she felt closest to. He made her feel as if she was not an outsider, as if he truly cared about what happened to her. 'He hopes to join one of the Inns of Court soon and train to be a lawyer. Hardly the actions of an imbecile.'

She forced her gaze to meet Mr Clare's green one, felt it bore down into her soul as if he were searching for something. Every inclination in her body told her that he would yell and storm, but she kept regarding him, refusing to flinch. He looked away.

'Is it not an affliction?' Mr Clare's voice was a husky rasp. 'Will Robert recover? Will he return to his old self? Do you promise me?'

'I have every reason to hope Robert will recover as well. He looks so much like Edmund,' she whispered. 'It may take a long time, but there is hope. You do not need to use ropes. He must be kept calm. Please let me try. Your sister believed I could help.'

'You have seen him at his worst and have not run. It is more than several of the maids were able to stand. Perhaps Diana's judgment was not misplaced.' The colour drained from Simon Clare's face, but his shoulders straightened. 'What do you propose?'

'Keep him quiet. Speak to him gently. Reasonably. He looks to be an intelligent boy.' Phoebe forced her voice to be calm and matter of fact. Excitement surged through her. She had this one chance to prove her worth. 'He is not to be put under any undue stress.'

'But he needs to take his medicine. I refuse to allow him to become a little savage. I refuse…' His voice tailed off in exhaustion.

'Allow me to handle this. I will get him to take the laudanum.' Phoebe said the words with far more confidence than she felt. 'Allow me to prove that I can nurse Robert. If I can't, I will leave in the morning and you can hire another nurse with references.'

'You have ten minutes.' He held out his hand. 'And, Miss Benedict, he must take his medicine.'

Phoebe swallowed hard and touched her fingers to his. They curled around hers for an instant, warm and strong. A pulse went up her arm and she rapidly withdrew her hand. 'It will be enough time.'

Silently she prayed that her words were true.

Chapter Three

Ten minutes to get Robert to trust her enough to take his medicine quietly. She had made a bargain with the devil. But it did give her a slim chance. Phoebe pushed open the bedroom door as the wails started again. Her legs threatened to give way and her stomach knotted. Her easy words to Mr Clare echoed in her head. She could get this frightened child to take his medicine. She gave a half-smile and wondered why it was so easy to say things, but so difficult to actually achieve them.

She placed the wicker basket down at the entrance and willed the kitten to stay there. She would not need the ropes. All she had to do was to believe. A calm firm voice and slow movements—the same way she had captured the kitten earlier in the day. The same way she had nursed her stepbrothers.

At her approach, Robert stopped crying and regarded her with eyes that were too large for his face. His entire body went still. Behind her, she was aware of Mr Clare's looming presence, watching her every move, doubting her ability. It irritated her that she was intensely aware of every little movement he made—the fierceness in his eyes, the way his fingers curled into a fist, the warning hunch of his shoulders. She stopped, turned back and shut the door with a decisive click.

'Who are you?' Robert shouted. 'Go away! I want my aunt!'

'Robert, your Aunt Diana sent me in her place. I have a message for you.'

'A message?' Robert tilted his head to one side. 'What sort of message?'

A breath escaped Phoebe's lips. She had his attention. Everything would turn out fine. She made her voice sound sing-song, unhurried, easy and light as if it did not matter that time was sliding through her fingers. 'Your aunt is very sorry. She wanted to be at your side, but she can't come.'

'Who are you?' His face was a reflection of his father's except his eyes seemed to dominate his shrunken face.

'Phoebe Benedict. I am to look after you until

you get well. I have come all the way from London at your aunt's request.'

'I want my aunt! I miss her.' A small hand scrubbed at his eyes. He looked all of about six, instead of the ten that Lady Coltonby had said he was.

'She is…going to have a baby. Soon you will have a little cousin to love and cherish.' Phoebe looked directly at the boy. Her entire being tensed. Would he go into another fit? And then what would happen? Why had she made such a rash promise? 'They would not let her come. She wanted to, very much. You must believe that, Robert. She told me to tell you that she loves you and wants you to get well.'

'I miss her.'

'And she misses you too. It is why you must be a good boy and get well.'

Phoebe pressed her hands together and willed him to stay quiet and to trust her. She resisted the temptation to brush the sweat from the back of her neck and simply stood there, hands outstretched.

'Are you going to tie me up?'

'No ropes.' She held out her hands and showed him they were empty. She bent down so her face was level with his. 'I don't believe in tying boys up.'

'Me either.' Robert gave a decided nod as his

limbs began to convulse again. 'But I don't like this either.'

'You need to relax and the spasms will ease.'

'What is happening to me?'

'You are ill. You need to rest. Your body wants to get well.' Phoebe kept her voice soothing. 'Take a deep breath, Robert. In. Out.'

'I can't catch my breath. It frightens me. Really frightens me.' His eyes swam with tears. 'I want to live and not go to hell like Mrs Smith said I would.'

'Your body will find it easier if you are quiet.' Phoebe cast her eyes upwards and wished she could throttle the nurse. What was Mr Clare thinking when he hired her?

Robert closed his eyes. The trembling and jerking in his limbs subsided slightly. Phoebe risked another step towards the bed, willed him to keep calm. She touched his forehead and breathed a sigh of relief. Cool and without fever. The worst had passed, but Robert would need a long time before he recovered his strength. Phoebe lifted her hand from his forehead and stared at the wallpaper. A mixture of anticipation and misgiving filled her.

She had written to her stepmother that it would be for a few weeks at most. She had never considered that the time might run into months. Months.

Maybe her presence would be missed. Maybe they would realise they missed her and how much she tried. She wanted them to be proud of her, to feel that she was part of their family, instead of part of the furniture. She had given her promise and she would see that this boy became well. She paused. As long as she could get him to take his medicine.

'Why did you do that?' Robert asked, bringing her back to the present.

'Because I wanted to see if you had a fever.'

'And do I?' Robert screwed up his face. 'I have had such strange dreams. I want them to go away. They frighten me.'

'The doctor has left something to keep the fever and the dreams away.' Phoebe reached for the medicine bottle.

'What are you going to do?' Robert rubbed his shaking hand across his eyes.

'I am going to give you something to drink. It will make you feel better. A little sleepy, but better.'

'I don't want any medicine. Nasty.' Robert pulled a face. 'I won't take it. I won't!'

'Robert!' Mr Clare's voice echoed throughout the room as the door came open. His footsteps resounded on the floor and Robert's eyes grew wide again.

Inwardly, Phoebe cursed and willed Mr Clare to the devil. She had gone too quickly, she knew that, but little time remained. She could get Robert to take his medicine if only Mr Clare would be quiet. 'It will help. I promise you that. It helped my youngest brother when he was ill like you.' Her tongue flicked over her lips. 'Shall I tell you about Edmund? I started looking after him when he was a boy about your age.'

'I want my aunt. She won't make me drink anything!' The boy's voice started to rise again. 'Aunt Diana! Aunt Diana!'

'Miss Benedict!' She heard Mr Clare's warning sound behind her.

'My time is not up! You promised!'

She spun around and nearly collided with his hard chest. Behind him, two footmen stood with ropes dangling from their fingers.

'No!' Phoebe put out her hands and placed her body between Robert and the men. 'I won't let them pass. He will take it! Give him a chance! Give me this one chance!'

'Stand aside, Miss Benedict! He must take his medicine. You had your chance and failed. My only consolation is that I was correct in my assessment.'

'Ten minutes. I want ten minutes.'

'You can see what Robert is like.' Mr Clare nodded towards the bed. 'Why are you intent on making him suffer?'

'You are frightening him. Please let me try again. You didn't give me ten minutes.' Phoebe glanced at Robert. His mouth was set mutinously as his eyes flickered between them. 'What harm will a few moments do?'

'Miss Benedict! No one defies my orders in this house!'

'Mr Clare! Someone should!'

She stood toe to toe with the man, aware that with one sweep of his arm she could be brushed aside. But she refused to allow her gaze to waver. Each breath she took seemed like an eternity.

Finally he bowed his head and took a half-step backwards. 'Very well, a few moments. One more chance.'

'I rescued a kitten earlier today,' Phoebe said, speaking rapidly and praying that her words would provide a distraction. She kept her eyes trained on Robert, but every particle of her body was alert to Mr Clare's movements. 'Would you like to see it? Shall we see if your cries have made him wake?'

Robert's mouth closed and he lifted a thin

shoulder. Phoebe ran to where she had placed the basket and opened the cover. Despite the uproar, the kitten had gone to sleep.

Carefully she carried the basket over to the bed. The kitten gave a loud purr, but did not open its eyes. Robert put his fingers to his lips. 'It's asleep. I don't want to wake him.'

Phoebe replaced the cover and placed the basket beside the bed.

'He's sleeping now. It would be a shame to disturb him. Shall I let him sleep here? We must be very quiet, the kitten has had an exhausting day.'

'I will try, truly I will try, miss, but it is hard. Sometimes…' He closed his eyes and his face became stiff with concentration. Phoebe forgot to breathe. 'Will the medicine help me to be quiet?'

'It helped my brother. Truly it did.'

'Then I will take it…for the kitten's sake. He looks tired. And sweet. I have always wanted a kitten.'

'Good boy.' Phoebe glanced back over her shoulder at where Mr Clare stood. He lifted one eyebrow. With a trembling hand she poured the liquid on to a spoon and held it out to Robert. He made a face, but swallowed it with one gulp.

'Is the kitten for me? As a gift?' Robert asked, wiping his hand across his mouth. 'I have never had a cat before. We used to have a dog, but…he went with my aunt.'

Phoebe gave a slight laugh. 'Cats can never be given. They choose their owner.'

Robert pursed his lips and nodded. His brow knitted together, but he remained quiet. 'That makes sense.'

'He is a wee thing and his mother has just died. I wanted to protect him. He is quite a lively thing when he is awake.' Phoebe kept her voice light as she knelt beside Robert. The storm appeared to have passed. Somewhere her prayers had been answered.

'My mother died as well. We can be friends, the kitten and I.' He paused and his bottom lip trembled. 'Will you protect me? I am not ready to go to heaven or to the other place. Mrs Smith says that I will burn for ever in the torment.'

'Who says that you will die?' Phoebe looked at him, shocked. How much had he heard of her whispered conversation with Mr Clare? How much about his condition did he know? 'Did your papa tell you that? Or the doctor?'

'They thought I was asleep—Mrs Smith and Gladys, the maid. I will go to hell because I am wicked through and through.'

Phoebe heard a growl behind her, but she held

up her hand, stopping Mr Clare from speaking. She had to do this.

'Sometimes you only think you hear things and really you are dreaming. It is best not to think on such things.' Phoebe grasped Robert's hand and his fingers folded around hers. 'Shall I look after you for a little while? Your aunt would like that.'

'You do not smell of barley water or peppermints.' Robert's lips turned up and he gave a tiny laugh. 'And you have a kitten. I have often longed for a kitten. Do you think it might choose me?'

'There is no accounting for kittens, but when you are stronger, I will introduce you.' Phoebe did not dare to glance at Mr Clare. She could feel the heat of his gaze from where she knelt. Maybe he had learnt his lesson. He wouldn't dismiss her as some silly woman who did not know how to run a sick room. 'And you will only get stronger if you keep taking your medicine.'

'Did…did my uncle say anything before you left? Did he send any message?' His shoulders tensed. 'He is not disappointed that I have had to come home from school, is he? I had promised him that I would stay at school, but they sent me home.'

'Your uncle did indeed give me a message.' Phoebe strove to keep her voice light. 'He said that if you were to get well and strong, then he'd see about teaching you to drive a carriage, regardless of what your dear papa says.'

She ignored the outraged growl behind her.

Robert collapsed back against his pillows and all the tension eased out of him. 'I want to get strong again. All my puff seems to have gone. The littlest thing appears to bother me.'

'My cousin strikes me as a man who keeps his word.'

'Uncle Brett does.'

'And I will work with you to get you strong again.' Phoebe gritted her teeth. Mr Clare would have to eat his words. She believed that she had proved him wrong. She would do all in her power to get Robert strong enough to drive carriages, with or without Mr Clare's consent.

'I will.' Robert's lashes fluttered closed. 'I like you, Miss Benedict, you and your kitten.'

She watched him for another moment as his lips turned up into the sweetest smile and sleep claimed him. She pulled the blanket up to his chin and tiptoed out. A small glow of triumph filled her. She had succeeded. She could do this. This really would be a new beginning. All her debts would be paid and her stepbrothers would get the start in life that her father would have wanted them to have.

'Very neatly done,' Mr Clare said softly from where he stood watching her. 'You seem to have a knack, Miss Benedict. It took Gladys and two strong footmen three hours to calm him last night. And the maid before her only lasted until Robert tossed a bowl of porridge at her. My words to you were hasty and ill thought out.'

Phoebe tucked a stray lock of hair behind her ear. She longed to say that she had told him so, but she would be magnanimous in her victory. He would never know how deeply his remarks had wounded her. 'One learns a lot about boys and their ways when one has three stepbrothers. The so-called nurse did far more harm than good.'

'She will be gone by morning light. I shudder to think what she nearly did…what she nearly had me believe. Her references were excellent.'

'No doubt sent by people who were pleased to be rid of her!' Phoebe wiped her hands on her gown. 'I will need to freshen up and then there is the question of the boy's care. We should discuss this downstairs, away from Robert.'

Mr Clare caught her elbow, stopping her progress. 'It would appear my sister was correct to send you. You will work admirably if you wish to stay.'

'There is no need to apologise.' Phoebe attempted to ignore the sudden flood of warmth on her cheeks. 'It must have come as a huge shock.'

'I never apologise, Miss Benedict, for stating the truth. In this instance I was mistaken. I judged you too harshly.'

'The important thing is that Robert is now sleeping.' Phoebe clung on to the remnants of her temper.

'Shall we quarrel about that as well?' A smile touched Mr Clare's face, transforming it. 'I fear my sister will have misled you. My temper has become far shorter since the accident. I do assure you, Miss Benedict, that my bark is worse than my bite. Above all else, I want Robert to get well.'

'Hopefully, there is a room near Robert's where I can store my things.' All the exhaustion from her long journey returned, crashing over her in one great wave. All she wanted was a warm bath and the welcoming embrace of clean sheets, but these would have to wait until Robert was better. She knew her duty. Phoebe stifled a yawn. Even the armchair in Robert's room would be welcome after the hard springs of the coach.

'I refuse to allow you to start tonight. You have just arrived. Someone will watch over him.'

Someone? Gladys, the upstairs maid? Did she dare risk another confrontation? Phoebe forced her body to relax. She had to be content with her small victory. He might decry arrogant aristocrats, but Mr Clare was without a doubt one of the most pigheaded people that she had ever met.

She willed a smile to cross her lips. Her time in the *ton* had taught her how to be polite to the rudest people. 'Robert's health is more important, Mr Clare. I want to hear if he cries out in his sleep.'

'Very well, if you wish.' He made a dismissive gesture with his hand. 'Jenkins, put Miss Benedict's things into the little room next to Robert's rather than in Miss Diana's old room. She appears determined to look after him. You will be able to hear Robert if he cries out.'

'Your sister entrusted me with his care. I gave her my promise.'

'How much did my sister tell you about this house?'

'Very little. There was not time. Speed was of the essence according your letter.' Phoebe kept her voice steady. 'I expect I will learn the house rules as I go on.'

'There is one request I must make of you, Miss Benedict.' His face became stern. 'On no account speak to Robert about his mother.'

'Why ever not?' Phoebe's eyes widened and she wished that she had questioned Lady Coltonby more closely about the precise nature of the situation. What had this boy's mother done before she died?

'I have no wish to encourage morbid fantasies. His mother is dead and that is the end of the matter.'

'But—' Phoebe stared at the man. Surely he had seen the hunger in Robert's eyes when he mentioned that his mother had died. She knew what it was like to be alone and motherless. She knew what it was like to be without a family. Did Mr Clare?

'That is the one charge I make on you.' Mr Clare inclined his head. 'I have agreed reluctantly to my sister's scheme, but I will have the rules obeyed in my house.'

'I will take it under advisement.'

'You will obey my orders.'

'If I had obeyed your orders, Robert would now be tied to his bed. Or, worse, in a madhouse. Robert is seriously ill and has been treated badly.'

Mr Clare opened and closed his mouth and his scar became a livid red. A small thrill of satisfaction ran through Phoebe. She enjoyed seeing the barb hit home. It might make her wicked, but she felt Mr Clare deserved it.

'You speak very boldly.'

'I fight for those who need it. And I will fight for Robert.'

'Then I must be grateful that you intend to do that.' Mr Clare gave an imperious nod and turned away down the hall.

A soft noise woke Phoebe from where she slumbered on a narrow cot. It took a few moments to work out where she was. She forced her muscles to relax as she realised that it was not Atherstone Court and she would not have to see her sister-in-law today.

She listened again, hoping against hope that Robert was not about to experience another fit. The noise appeared to have stopped. She nodded and forced her breathing to come easy.

She was safe here. No men would come knocking at the door, demanding money for unpaid bills, no stepmother would look at her with injured eyes when she suggested economies. No sister-in-law to roll her eyes when Phoebe suggested starting a dressmaking or millinery shop, rather than sinking slowly into the mire of impoverished gentry.

Here, she was giving James a chance. He had not asked for Father to go walking on the frozen Thames. He had not been the one to refuse to join him on that stroll, preferring to stay at home and trim a bonnet. She knew who bore that guilt. And he had not caused Charles to take the corner too fast, overturning his carriage on his way to mediate a dispute between her and Alice. She trusted that Lord Coltonby would do as he had promised. Then there would only be Edmund to worry about. She hoped all of them understood the sacrifices she was making and why. Far too often they seemed to take her feelings for granted. Phoebe pushed away the thought. They were the only family she had and belonging to a family was important. She would keep her mind only on the good things, the way forward.

She'd concentrate on the little boy and his heartless parent. Imagine having your only child looked after by a creature like that and in such conditions. It was not as if they lacked money. The whole house screamed money, but it lacked love and tenderness. It lacked a heart.

The noise sounded again. It appeared to be halfway between a sob and a wail. Phoebe's heart sank. She did not want to think about confronting Mr Clare at this hour.

She wondered if Mr Clare had been true to his word. Robert could be alone in there or with someone as unfeeling as that miserable maid. She refused to let that happen. The boy needed help.

In the moonlight, Phoebe fumbled for her shawl and wrapped it around her body. She lit a candle and held it aloft as she tiptoed over to the door that separated her from Robert. She opened the door slightly, but kept to the shadows.

Robert appeared to be asleep, but a figure knelt at the side of the bed, head bowed, one arm stretched out on the coverlet.

She raised the candle higher, trying to discern who was there. The too-long hair and finely moulded shoulders could only belong to one man. Simon Clare. For confirmation, she spied the cane lying by the side of the bed. She started to tiptoe out when she heard a hoarse whisper.

'Let me take his place. Please…I will do anything. Punish me, not him.'

Phoebe put her hand to her mouth. She had inadvertently intruded on this man's grief. How she could have thought him heartless? A sudden fear gripped her. 'Is everything all right, Mr Clare? Is Robert…?'

At the sound of her voice, the quiet groans ceased. He lifted his head. His white shirt was open at the throat, revealing his golden skin. In the darkness, his face had become all shadows and planes, but she could clearly see how handsome he was. He was no monster, but the personification of masculinity.

'Robert is asleep. All is well, Miss Benedict.' His voice held a singular raw note.

'That is good to hear. I…I heard a noise.'

'I regret having disturbed you.'

'You…that is…I am a light sleeper. Years of practice with my stepbrothers, I am afraid.' She gave a small shrug and felt the shawl starting to slip off her shoulder. Her hand clutched it tighter about her.

'You looked after them.'

Phoebe wet her lips. 'Someone had to. My stepmother was not maternal and the maids were unreliable, even before my father died.'

'How good it is that someone cared.'

He stood up, seeming to fill the room. His gaze slowly travelled down her body, then back up to her face. She clung on to the thin shawl, aware suddenly that she was dressed only in her nightgown; her hair flowed over her shoulders and her bare toes peeped out. Hurriedly she smoothed her gown, and covered her feet. She wished that she had thought to wear a cap. Her hand shook slightly, causing the wax to drip on her wrist. She stifled a cry.

'You should be more careful, Miss Benedict. Wax burns.'

'I will be fine.' Phoebe attempted to ignore the searing pain.

He took a step towards her. 'Let me inspect it. There is little that I do not know about candles and burns. My father was a tallow merchant to begin with.'

She stayed still.

'Surely you are not afraid? Not the brave Miss Benedict.' His voice mocked her.

Phoebe held out her arm. 'It is but a small burn.'

'Let me be the judge.' His fingers encircled her wrist, lightly touching the spot. They were cool against her skin, but sent a strange trembling ache through her. Then abruptly he let go. 'You will live.'

'Hardly anything in the grand scheme of things, you see.' Phoebe tried to keep her gaze away from his face and the way the candlelight turned his skin golden.

'I know you think me unfeeling, Miss Benedict, but I do want what is best for the boy. I want him to get well.' His voice rippled over her like smooth thick velvet.

'There are other ways.' She breathed and took a step backwards. 'Ways that are kinder. Ways that treat the patient like a human and not an animal.'

'I realise that now. I wanted my boy back. I want him well and whole again. You do not know how much it pains me, Miss Benedict, to see him like that.'

'He will get better, but you need to look after yourself as well.' Phoebe made a small gesture. She hated to think about how he had sacrificed his own bed to sit there. And how she had condemned him before without understanding. 'Your injuries must pain you. Night air will not be good for them. I will sit here if you like. I have had my sleep and feel refreshed.'

'Goodnight, Miss Benedict,' Mr Clare said, turning back to the bed, settling down once again. 'Your watch will begin in the morning.'

She had been wrong. Wrong about so many things. Mr Clare was complicated. He did care about his son, but why did he wish to pretend otherwise?

Phoebe lowered the candle and closed the door, trembling. The bed creaked slightly as she pulled the covers up to her chin. She willed her body to relax, but thoughts kept racing through her brain. The image of him standing there holding her wrist, shirt open at the neck, appeared to be scorched on her eyelids. She screwed up her eyes tight and bid the vision to be banished but her wrist continued to tingle from his touch for a long time.

Chapter Four

'Can I name the kitten now?' Robert asked before Phoebe had even fully entered the room the next morning.

'The kitten belongs to me…for the moment,' Phoebe replied carefully, easing her way around the piles of discarded clothing. The sick room in bright sunshine was even more dismal than the night before. It was a wonder that Robert had survived at all amidst this squalor. It was a crime that the nurse had been allowed to behave in this fashion.

'He likes it here.' The kitten chased a dust ball across the room.

'Yes, but he will like it better once the room is tidied up. And it is for your father to decide if the kitten stays.'

'Papa doesn't care.' Robert's lip trembled. 'He

told Mrs Smith that if I couldn't be kept quiet, I was better off dead.'

'Mrs Smith had a singularly overactive imagination.' Phoebe disentangled the kitten from the curtain. 'I would hardly be here if your father wanted you to die.'

Robert pursed his lips, thinking. 'He never notices anything that I do right. He only notices when I am naughty.'

'And you want him to notice you.'

'Well, he is my papa. It is proper. I know that I must have done something wrong. A long time ago, he used to spend time with me. He used to draw me things like carriages…then he stopped. He even sent me away to school when I did not want to go.'

Phoebe closed her eyes and counted to ten.

'Robert, your father does care…' Phoebe paused. She refused to lie, but the boy seemed desperate for his father's love. Why was it that people who did so little, commanded so much? It hurt that James and Edmund always took her stepmother's part, that they did not see all that she had done for them. 'He wrote to your aunt and asked for help. She sent me and I will ensure you get better.'

'If I get better, will Papa like me?' Robert asked in a small voice. 'Will he let me keep the kitten?'

Phoebe swallowed hard. It would be easy to become attached to this motherless boy. She could well remember her own childhood and how everything had gone wrong once her mother had died. How she had wanted her father to smile again, and how he had only done so once he had married Alice. She gave her head a small shake. Her time was limited here and she could not afford to become attached to the boy. 'The important thing is to get better, and you will get better faster if all this mess is cleared up.'

Robert wrinkled his nose and flopped down amongst the pillows. 'Don't like clearing up. I am too weak.'

'Then you are too weak to name the kitten.' Phoebe crossed her arms. 'This room will be cleaned up and kept that way. I run a tidy sickroom. And you, young man, need fresh bed linen and a clean nightshirt.'

Robert shrugged a thin shoulder. 'After that, can I name the kitten?'

'We will see, but I think it can arranged.'

Robert's face broke into a sunny smile. 'I hope the kitten can stay for ever…and you as well, Miss…Benedict. Can I call you something different? One of the masters at school was called Mr

Benedict and he used a cane. He was particularly cross when he found my frog in his inkstand.'

Repressing a smile, she said, 'you may call me Miss Phoebe if you like.'

'Yes, that would be good, Miss Phoebe.'

Phoebe turned her face away and busied herself with tidying the toys and the discarded papers. Robert would be very easy to love indeed.

Simon jammed his arm through the black superfine coat, and heard the material tear. He swore. Ponsby, his valet, said nothing, but handed him another coat. Simon gritted his teeth. 'This time, man, hold the coat properly.'

'As you wish, sir. I will see that the coat is mended.'

'Ponsby, the shaving water was cold this morning.'

Ponsby made no reply, but merely gave a correct bow. 'I will endeavour to have it warmer next time. Yesterday it was too hot.'

Simon ran his good hand through his hair and grimaced. He refused to stoop to the indignity of quarrelling with his valet. But this morning, every little thing pricked at his temper.

He hated the accusation in Miss Benedict's eyes that he had been somehow at fault for the state of

Robert's room. His only mistake had been to trust that misbegotten nurse. Next time, he would know better than to ask Lady Bolt for her recommendation. And now he was stuck with a débutante as a nurse. A débutante with all her high-handed ways and a kitten. Exactly what he didn't need.

What had Diana been thinking when she'd dispatched Miss Benedict? Matchmaking? Simon rejected the idea instantly. Diana knew his feelings on the subject of remarriage. She would never dream of sending such a person.

He pursed his lips. It was quite possible the suggestion had come from Miss Benedict. He would not put it past her. She would learn that he was not the marrying sort. Jayne had cured him of that for ever.

Unbidden, the image of Miss Benedict rose in his mind with her nightgown swirling softly about her ankles and the faint scent of stephanotis and lavender rising like a cloud around her, her face lifted towards his with her lips softly parted. He frowned and made a sweeping gesture with his good arm, banishing the image. He would never stoop so low as to make a guest in his house, a gently bred lady, his mistress. He was better than that. Even the thought appalled him, and yet the image lurked in the back of his mind. He made another effort to clear it.

His hand knocked the shaving bowl, sending a stream of dirty water onto his dressing table. With impatient fingers, he righted the thing and dabbed ineffectually at the spreading foam and mess. He bellowed for Ponsby, but the valet did not appear. Simon gritted his teeth and redoubled his efforts.

The sooner Miss Benedict departed, the better.

'What are you doing, miss?' the butler asked Phoebe, standing so that her progress down the passageway was blocked.

She tried to balance the assortment of toys and linen in her arms. All morning she had laboured to clean up Robert's room and not once had Mr Clare appeared or sent word. She had thought surely he would want to know how his son was doing. It was only when she accosted the little under-housemaid that she had been able to find clean linen for Robert.

'These will all have to be burnt. Bedclothes, curtains and these wooden toys. They will be a mass of infection and germs.'

'Have you asked the master about this?' The butler looked down his nose. 'It was my understanding that he did not wish the young master to be unduly disturbed. Those are some of his favourite playthings. I would hate to think of the fuss the young master will make. You saw what he can be like. And when the young master makes a fuss, the master gets cross. It pains his head.'

'Do you wish to tell Mr Clare that you have condemned his son to an early grave for a bit of peace and quiet or shall I?'

She stared long and hard at the officious butler. The man lowered his gaze.

'One of the stable lads can do it,' he said in an impassive voice. 'The blizzard appears to have passed and the sun is out. Yes, it can be done as long as you will vouch for it, mind. I won't have anyone saying it was one of the staff that did it. Mr Clare is not a man to cross and we all value our wage packets.'

'Thank you, Jenkins. I will take full responsibility for this.' Phoebe held out her bundle and willed him to accept it.

'I sincerely hope you do, miss.' Jenkins lowered his voice. 'The young master before his illness was lively, but he meant well. We all want him well again. We were ashamed about the mess, but we are all frightened, like.'

'And, Jenkins, I wish to speak with Mr Clare.' Phoebe kept her gaze level and prayed that her cheeks would not flame. It was necessary—but would the butler think she was making up excuses? The memory of Mr Clare's fingers against her wrist rose in her mind's eye. She banished it and regained control.

'Is the young master worse?' Jenkins's face turned grave and he shook his head. 'Gladys was predicting such things, muttering darkly as she left. She says the house is cursed, what with the master's accident and now this. She cannot wait to leave, having done her best for no reward.'

'No, he is not worse,' Phoebe replied slowly. She wished she could strangle Gladys and her folk wisdom. 'I simply wish to send for the doctor, to have him confirm my diagnosis and give me some idea of the latest treatments. Mr Clare's mind will be more at ease if he hears the truth from a medical man.'

'The master is like a bear with a sore head today. Try another day.' Jenkins shook his head. 'His breakfast came back untouched. It is always a bad sign. Even his valet has gone to ground. I heard Mr Clare bellowing for more hot water only a little while ago.'

'Mr Clare's problems with his valet are none of my concern.'

Jenkins tapped the side of his nose. 'Perhaps it

is best to wait, miss, until the air is calmer. I have no wish to lose any more members of staff. You have no idea how difficult it is to find someone suitable. You will learn. The master is not to be provoked. It saves trouble in the long run.'

'Is Mr Clare generally of bad temper, then?' Phoebe asked carefully. 'Both you and John the coachman have mentioned his ire.'

'He has become more difficult since the accident and Miss Diana's marriage and her departure to London have only made matters worse. She used to smooth over his upsets. She was in charge of the household, you see. She did all the menus, hired the staff, and generally ran the place. Now all we have is Mr Clare.' The butler paused. 'It is best to wait and ask him later. For the sake of all of the staff, if not your own health. The one thing Mr Clare desires above all else is quiet and his orders are to be obeyed.'

Phoebe gritted her teeth. Was it any wonder that this house appeared to be inadequately cared for if the staff were walking around on tiptoes? Mr Clare was the worst sort of tyrant. She wished again that she had quizzed Lady Coltonby more closely on her brother and his household. It had seemed enough that Lord Coltonby was able to help her brother and she was able to do something in return. She had never thought to ask about how difficult this man might be.

She drew a breath and thought of the alternative. He could not be any worse than her sister-in-law—the Dreaded Sophia. Her complaints and tantrums over the slightest flaw or fault had driven Phoebe to despair.

'Do you think he will see me?'

The butler was silent for a long while. Phoebe's insides tensed.

'He is in his study, miss,' the butler said finally. 'Where he always is these days.'

'Did he used to go somewhere else?' Phoebe tilted her head to one side. 'I had understood that Mr Clare was a gentleman.'

'He used to be down at the colliery or on the staiths, but these days he prefers to stay here, seeing as few people as possible. Then he shouts when things go wrong or things are out of place. The house has not been properly cleaned for weeks. It makes for an unsettled life.'

'You should give your notice.'

'Mr Clare pays me extremely well, miss, and I gave Miss Diana my word.'

Phoebe lifted her eyes to the ceiling. Her responsibility was to Robert and not to his father. She had to do what was best for him, and not what was easiest for her.

'I feel certain that once he understands the reason for my intrusion, he will pardon it. He will agree that it is best to act swiftly. Robert must get well.'

The butler inclined his head. 'Ground floor, second door on the left. You won't be able to miss it.'

'Thank you, Jenkins.' Phoebe straightened her spine and wished it did not feel like she was about to go into battle. 'Would you mind asking the cook for a saucer of milk? My kitten is a bit hungry. Robert appeared to enjoy watching it chase a piece of string this morning.'

'That I will, miss. And it is good you stood up for Master Robert.'

Phoebe went down the stairs, heartened at the thought that the staff supported her actions. She started to open the second door when there was no reply to her knock. It was a bit stiff, but gave way when she applied her shoulder to it. 'Mr Clare, I would like to speak with you.'

A faint light shone through the shutters, but the room was shrouded in dust cloths. A faint dusty dank smell pervaded it; in the corner, a single dried rose lay abandoned.

Phoebe took a half-step inside. A ballroom, rather than a study. She had made a mistake with the butler's instructions.

She would simply grab the rose and tidy up, the work of a moment. It seemed so sad and lonely there with cobwebs festooning the chandelier. A lonely reminder of some happier time. She half-closed her eyes, imagining what this room must look like when filled with light and people. It must be truly magnificent with an orchestra in the background and the excited chatter. A cloth covered most of the floor, but where it was pulled back, she could tell it was highly polished. Out of the corner of her eye she spied a spinet, its dust cover half off. Phoebe hesitated, looking at the black keys. Some servant had undoubtedly been careless and had left it open.

Quickly she walked over, intending to cover it, but her fingers brushed the keys. A low sound came out and her heart turned over. How long had it been since she had played? Of all the things they had lost, her spinet had hurt the most. But economies had had to be made, even if Alice had at first refused to see it.

Softly she picked out a simple tune, listening to the bell-like quality of the instrument. She closed her eyes, letting the music flow over her, holding her in its embrace.

A door behind her opened, and she froze, hands poised over the keyboard.

'Ah, Miss Benedict, I fear you have lost your way. This room is never used. What precisely are you searching for? And why did you think you might find it here?'

Her cheeks burned as if she had spent hours in front of a roaring fire. Such a foolish thing to do. To play an instrument without permission.

Mr Clare watched her from the door across the hall with a sardonic expression on his face. He looked so very different from the man she had glimpsed in his shirt sleeves last night. Once again he was the pirate captain, prowling the deck of his ship, looking for people to feed to the sharks.

'I appear to have mistaken the butler's directions.' Her hands smoothed her skirt. Absurdly she wished that she was wearing a colour better suited to her complexion than jonquil. 'I was searching for your study.'

She left the ballroom without a backwards glance.

'Indeed.' He reached out and closed the door with a bang and then turned the key in the lock.

'Endeavour to remember precisely what your business is. And where you conduct it.'

'I doubt I will have any need to go in there again.' Phoebe pressed her hands together, knowing that her cheeks flamed. It had been wrong of her to play, but at the same time it had felt so wonderful to have music flowing from her fingertips again. She doubted that Mr Clare would understand the lure of music. 'I am here to look after your son, not to attend dances or to play the spinet.'

'For future reference, my study is across the hall. I trust you will not be lost again.' His face turned cold.

Phoebe forced her lips into a smile as inside she fumed. She of all people should have known better than to be swept away by such things. Wool-gathering, her stepmother called it. Sophia would sniff and call it something worse. 'With you to lead the way, how could I be?'

'Is your tongue often tart, Miss Benedict? You certainly seem to have no fear or hesitation of speaking your mind.'

'Only when necessary, Mr Clare.'

'That makes a change.' A faint smile crossed his face. 'Here I was thinking you spoke it all the time, and the devil take the hindmost.'

'It is one of the disadvantages of mixing with my stepbrothers. My tongue has become far too free.'

'And how many do you have?'

'Three.' Phoebe drew a deep breath. 'I took an interest in my stepbrothers and their well-being. They have had their scrapes, but they have all turned out well. My eldest brother's carriage accident had nothing to do with his upbringing and everything to do with taking a corner too tightly.'

'And where was your stepmother? Did she take no interest in her children?'

Phoebe bit her lip. How did one begin to describe Alice, the Dowager Viscountess? Her nerves and her sudden enthusiasms, none of which included her children. Phoebe banished the thought as unworthy. Her stepmother was a good woman in her own way, and it was not her stepmother's fault that her husband had perished in the way that he had. Phoebe knew where the fault lay with that. And after her father's death, her stepmother had been incapable of anything but wallowing in self-pity. Someone had to comfort the boys and make sure they were brought up properly. 'My stepmother is not one of nature's nurses.'

'And you are?' His voice was liquid honey, flowing over her. Seductive and smooth.

Phoebe kept her eyes firmly on the Turkey-patterned carpet in the hallway. Was he mocking her? 'I have reason to believe so.'

'How pleasant it must be to have this passion to look after other people. To know what is right for them. Pure arrogance, Miss Benedict.'

'To make them well, to make them whole again.' She glanced up into his ravaged face. Her breath stopped. Did he need healing as well? Her cheeks heated at the wayward thought.

'Nothing will make me well again, Miss Benedict.' He inclined his head. 'I charge you to remember that. I have no need of a nursemaid or a helping hand.'

'I never…' Phoebe clutched the folds of her skirt, twisting them about her fingers. Rapidly she schooled her features. 'I am here as Robert's nurse, not yours. And the only person I will pity is anyone foolish enough to attempt to look after you.'

'And do the rest of your family also have this passion for sticking their noses into other people's business? Going into closed rooms?'

'It…it has been a long time since I have seen as fine an instrument as that spinet, let alone played one. I have begged your pardon. That should be the end of it.'

'I sincerely hope it is, Miss Benedict. Temptation can be a dangerous thing. As you wish to examine my study, you might as well satisfy your curiosity—I see I will get no peace until you do.'

Phoebe brushed past him and into the study with as much dignity as she could muster. In stark contrast to the shrouded and mummified ballroom, the study burst with light and warmth. A fire crackled merrily in the hearth and the curtains had been drawn back to allow the winter sunshine in. Every surface had paper piled high on it. In one corner a model of a travelling engine stood. Phoebe stared at it, puzzled, but at the sound of rattling papers she turned her attention back to Simon Clare, who had sat down in an armchair.

'Now that you have seen the study, is that all? Or was there something more than the urge to gawp?'

'I…I…'

'You appear at a loss for words.' Mr Clare stretched out his legs. 'Surely you are not coming to say that you wish to leave.'

'No, not that.'

'Very well. Your visit here saves me the trouble of climbing up the stairs. Precisely why did my sister choose to send you?' He indicated a sofa.

'Please sit. Should you remain standing, I would be forced to stand up again.'

Phoebe opened her mouth to protest, but then she saw the deep circles under his eyes. The man had spent the night by his son's bed. Exactly how bad were his injuries?

She sank down on the sofa and kept her hands tight on her lap. Here was her chance to begin anew and to explain why his sister had felt it necessary to send her, why she had to stay and why the doctor should be sent for.

'Lady Coltonby assured me that she had given a full explanation,' Phoebe replied, keeping her head up. She was not going to think about the fate that awaited James if she left. Sophia had made it very clear that she was unprepared to help either James or Edmund. In her view, the boys had become men and should be responsible for their own livelihood, but Phoebe knew they would drift without help. Their potential had been cut cruelly short, first by their own father's death and then by their older brother's. She had a duty towards them, even if both Alice and Sophia denied it. Families should help each other out.

'She wrote very little. What are you hoping to gain from this exercise? I do not believe that you came here out of purely altruistic motives. People seldom behave in that fashion. What are you escaping? Or have you been compromised and are seeking a refuge?'

'How dare you, sir! My reputation is spotless.'

Their gazes warred until he suddenly developed an interest in the carpet. 'I want to know the sort of woman I have under my roof. False protestations of modesty do neither of us any good, Miss Benedict.'

'It is not for my sake that I travelled up here, but for my stepbrother James.' Phoebe leant forwards. He had to understand that she was not doing this for her own gain. James had to have this one chance to make something of his life. Her father would have seen to it that he had a commission, if he had lived. 'Lord Coltonby has agreed to help James get a commission. Not one of the most fashionable, but a solid regiment with a chance for advancement. I believe it will be the making of him. It was the perfect solution—each of us helping the other's brother.'

Mr Clare lifted an eyebrow. 'And why did your stepbrother not make use of the connection before now? Surely he can speak.'

'My stepbrother is unconnected to Lord Coltonby. I felt obliged to ask. His enthusiasm for the army has happened quite recently.' Phoebe shifted uncomfortably. She had no wish to go into the details about James's debts or the need to prise him away from his troublesome companions. He was not feckless, as Sophia claimed, simply young and in need of a purpose in life. The army would give him that purpose. She had counted on Charles to look after James and Edmund, but with his death, there was no one to provide a steadying hand but her.

'I am certain that had you but asked…Lord Coltonby would have been delighted to help. My brother-in-law is like that.' The faintest hint of irony laced his voice. 'He has a great love of organising people and situations.'

'I…I…'

'You know I speak the truth. Has Coltonby refused your request?'

Phoebe summoned all her dignity. Mr Clare was being deliberately awkward. One could not ask for favours, one had to give something in return. It was understood. She would never have gone to Lord Coltonby if she had thought otherwise. In any case, she had only gone for advice. That Lady Coltonby had received the letter only hours before her visit was fortuitous in the extreme, a sign that it was meant to be. She had acted decisively because she had to seize every opportunity. She knew how quickly doors could be slammed when you no longer had anything to give.

'My family does not accept charity. Lord and Lady Coltonby have promised to do all they can for my brother and I will try to help your son. It is a fair exchange.' Silently she prayed her words would be enough.

'And who exactly is your family? You say that you are Coltonby's second cousin, but your stepbrothers are unrelated.' His voice was cold. 'Your accent is far too fine for you to have been some poor relation. It oozes London quality.'

'My eldest stepbrother was the fifth Viscount Atherstone. His baby son is now the sixth.' Phoebe forced her tongue not to stumble over the name.

'Your father was the fourth Viscount Atherstone?' Mr Clare's eyes narrowed and his body stilled, but there was an alert look to it.

'Yes.' Phoebe kept her head up and met his gaze full on. 'Were you acquainted with him?'

'We had business dealings many years ago. We were fellow shareholders in a canal. I lost touch with him recently, though. When did he die?' The words were deceptively casual, but his entire body had become alert, poised.

'He died eight years ago.' Phoebe forced her voice to sound calm and prayed that Mr Clare would not enquire into the exact circumstances. There again, he might already know. Was he one of her father's creditors who had hounded him until he had gone for a long walk on the frozen Thames? The river had given up his body when the ice had melted that spring. Because her stepmother was prostrate with grief, Phoebe had claimed the body. She shivered slightly. No one could ever say if he had intended to fall or had merely slipped.

How could she explain her part? How her father had asked her to go for a walk with him, and she had refused, being more concerned with the trim of a new bonnet? How she had not realised how deep was the state of melancholy that he was in? She bore her responsibility with fortitude. She did not explain her troubles or her duty. She still had her pride.

'My condolences.' His eyes were remote. He picked up a pen and toyed with it. 'A bad business. What I had seen of your father I liked. He treated all men alike.'

'It was a long time ago. I am surprised you remember him. I do not recall ever meeting you at any of the dinner parties my stepmother gave.'

She knew she would have remembered him, and the prowling way that he moved.

'He and I did business shortly after I married. One does not have to move in the same social circles to do business.' Icicles dripped from his voice. 'It had to do with docks in London, but I remember his courteous behaviour. I had not realised that he was in financial difficulty…until it was far too late.'

'I am grateful for that.' Phoebe discovered a sudden lump in her throat. 'You would think, after all these years, I would be able to speak of it with an even voice.'

'But I begin to understand why you might have difficulty with accepting charity. I take it your circumstances altered after your father's death. Was the settlement not all you had hoped for? I had understood Lord Atherstone to be a very wealthy man.'

'He made a mistake. The entail saved the estates for my eldest stepbrother, but there was little left over. Of course, once Charles died, everything went to his infant son. My sister-in-law's brother administers the estate.' Phoebe gave a small shrug, but her fingers twisted a fold of morning gown. 'My father invested unwisely in Peruvian silver mines—both my late mother's portion and his other wealth. And then he died.'

'Ah, he was caught in that scheme. I feared as much. I did try to warn him about it when he wrote asking about mining engines. When I invest, I like to see what I am getting. To know a mine, you must walk every inch of it. You must understand its inner workings.'

Phoebe forced her fingers to relax. 'If you are satisfied with my antecedents, perhaps we can speak about your son.'

'And what will happen to you after Robert recovers?'

'That will be many weeks away… Rheumatic fever takes a long time.'

'But it will happen and I presume you are planning to stay until then.'

'I will not abandon the boy.'

'Good.'

'I am hoping a great-aunt will take me. She lives near Tunbridge Wells and is not without family feeling, or so I am told.' Phoebe kept her eyes on the clock behind Mr Clare. She had no wish to see pity in his eyes. She should have thought that he might have known her father. Her father had been fascinated with mines and machinery. 'I wish to call the doctor. I wish to speak to him.'

'You wish to change the subject.' A sardonic

smile played on his lips. 'You dislike speaking of yourself, Miss Benedict. It is not so easy to be put under the microscope?'

'Robert understands the necessity of the doctor. I see I must explain it to you as well.' Phoebe started to explain what she was doing and why. She noticed that Mr Clare's expression became more thoughtful as she went on. Phoebe gave an inward smile—the treatment of invalids was something she did know about.

'Please, Miss Benedict, spare me the lecture. I have the general idea. You know what you are doing and you will do it that way whatever I say, or you will argue with me until my head aches more than it already does.' He held up his hand and stopped her as she was about to explain why it was necessary to be firm but kind with invalids. Phoebe shut her mouth firmly. 'I would like to institute a regime so I can discover how my son is doing. I have no wish for a repeat of last evening. It is my understanding that a good nurse wishes to have free rein in most matters and I accept that.'

Phoebe gazed at Simon Clare in astonishment. Did he think that she intended to bar him for the sickroom? 'You are more than welcome to come into the sickroom whenever you wish. I am sure

Robert will want to see you. He was asking about you this morning.'

'He needs to get well. These episodes disrupt the entire household.' Simon Clare leant forwards. 'Trust me when I say that I know this. My presence appears to agitate him and brings on the fits.'

'What do you wish me to do?'

'I would appreciate being kept informed as to his progress. You may come down each evening and tell me.'

'I want to speak to the doctor about Robert and hear for myself what he wants done. It is best to follow the doctor's advice in these matters. Medical science is improving so quickly that there may be some new procedure that I know nothing about.'

'If you must… Doctor MacFarlane will be more than agreeable about coming out. I pay in hard coin.' Mr Clare waved a dismissive hand. 'You appeared to know what you were doing last night.'

'Sometimes I have a way with stubborn boys.' Phoebe forced her lips up. 'My stepmother always used to say that, but I have no wish to second-guess medical science.'

'And was she right?'

'She had little patience…particularly after…'

Phoebe allowed her voice to trail off. 'I will tell Jenkins to send for the doctor, then.'

'And you might ask him his advice for yourself.'

'For myself?'

'You appear a bit pale, Miss Benedict.' He tilted his head to one side. 'I would hate to think you were sickening. I am counting on you to nurse Robert back to health.'

'Possibly just a little tired. The journey was quite an arduous one.' Phoebe attempted to ignore the lump in her throat. How long had it been since someone had asked about her health? Always it seemed that she was the one to ask or to notice, and no one cared enough to ask about her well-being. Just when she really wanted to dislike Mr Clare, he asked something like that, treated her like a person.

She took a step backwards and stumbled. His firm fingers caught her elbow and remained there. All she could do was to look up into his face for what felt like an eternity. His breath touched her forehead, warm, sensuous. Her fingers itched to brush away the lock of hair that tumbled into his eye patch.

Then it was over and he had put her away from him, his face contorted with something that looked like anger. At her? Phoebe's insides trembled and she summoned the remnants of her dignity. 'I will go to see Robert now.'

'Do send him my regards.' Simon Clare gave a nod, dismissing her. 'Tell him that…I am thinking of him and wish him well.'

'Yes, I will do that.'

She backed out of the room and then buried her face in her hands. How utterly vexing. She had behaved with no more dignity than a stammering school girl at the end. What must he think of her! Alice's argument about why she should never become a governess echoed in her mind. How governesses were too easily seduced and ruined, bringing shame on the whole family. For an instant, she had forgotten her duty to her family.

Phoebe put her hands on either side of her face, feeling the burning heat. It was nothing, merely a reaction brought about by tiredness. She knew where her duty lay and thoughts about Mr Clare had nothing to do with it.

Chapter Five

Phoebe watched the doctor's carriage depart the next morning. He had confirmed her diagnosis but had declined to speak with Mr Clare. In fact, he had taken great pains to avoid Mr Clare, and had reminded Phoebe before he left that he had made no mention of bleeding the boy, and to be sure to apprise Mr Clare of this fact.

'Begging your pardon, Miss…Miss Benedict, may I have a word? I wouldn't ask, but Jenny… Jenny Satterwaite, like, said that you were kind.'

Phoebe started as a roughly dressed man approached her. 'Can I help you?'

The man twisted his cap. 'It's like this, you see. Jenny told her ma about you and the master. Her ma told me wife. How you stood up to him and how you sent that nurse packing.'

'Mr Clare was worried about his son. I really had nothing to do with it.'

'Now you got Dr MacFarlane to call. Never in a month of Sundays did Jenny think that would happen, but I saw his carriage going off as I came up the drive.'

'Jenny should not be bringing tales home.' Phoebe pressed her lips together. It bothered her that the maids were spreading stories. 'I will have a word with her. Thank you for bringing this to my attention.'

'Don't get angry, miss. It is just that she knows how worried I am about things at the colliery,' the man said quickly, putting an arm up to bar her way. 'And I thought it might be right to have a word. Mr Clare doesn't know what is going on there. He used to know every inch of the place, above and below ground, could walk it blindfold and still know where he was, like. Or leastways, it was what the men thought. But now he relies on Mr Dodds to tell him. And it ain't the same. Things could happen… I fear for me mates, see.'

'I have no control over Mr Clare. I am sure he does what is best.' Phoebe couldn't get involved in this. 'You should go and see him. I feel certain that he will listen to your concerns.'

'But men's lives might be at stake. The third tunnel's timbers are weak in spots. I have been on to Mr Dodds, and he says that there isn't the money and them timbers are sound. But I know Mr Clare. He would replace them in an instant if he knew. He is like that, refuses to take the risk with the men.' He gave his cap a final twist. 'Anyway, I have said my piece. You can throw me out if you like, but don't go blaming little Jenny.'

Phoebe regarded the miner's troubled face. She wished that she could do something. 'I am sorry. It is not my place.'

'I know that, miss. I thought maybe if you asked him to go to the colliery that he'd take the notion into his head.'

'Mr Clare does not go anywhere from what I understand.'

'He used to. He was right canny. Always willing to speak about machines and the like. Patient. I have seen him spend hours on getting an engine to run smoothly.'

'Patient?' Phoebe nearly choked on the word. She had never thought to hear it used in connection with Mr Clare.

'Ladywell Main is becoming just like the other mines now. It's a pity. And I really thought his travelling engine was going to work.' He gave a crooked smile. 'It used to be great working there. Now it is the same as any other colliery. I just wanted to avoid an accident.'

Phoebe regarded the deep blue sky. This miner was not asking much of her. 'If there is an opportunity, I will say something.'

'Aye, I'd appreciate it. Jenny said that you were a right canny lass.'

'I shall take that as a compliment.'

'Aye, do.' The man touched his fingers to his cap and was gone.

Phoebe stared after him. She had to remember that she would only be here for a short while. She refused to get involved with other people's problems, but would it do Mr Clare any harm to stop being such a recluse?

Simon regarded the book on mechanical engineering in the flickering candlelight. The decanter of port stood on the side table. He reached over and topped his glass up before returning to the book and the intricacies of high-pressure steam. However, every time he attempted to think about the engine,

Miss Benedict's face rose in front of him, looking up at him, with long eyelashes and red parted lips. Tempting him. Enticing him to lower his mouth. To behave like something less than a gentleman. To become one of the men he despised.

Angrily, Simon downed the port in one gulp. The fiery liquid did nothing to banish the image. Or the desire. Her flesh had trembled under his fingers. He was certain of it. But then he had seen her eyes, unguarded. There was something indefinable between them. Or was it simply his fancy? He had had enough of these foolish thoughts. He had correspondence to answer.

He walked slowly over to the bureau, pulled out the drawer where he kept his spare blotting paper and clumsily spilt the contents on the ground. He swore, giving vent to his anger. It cost him to bend down to pick the items up and when he tried to force the drawer back in, it refused to go. He pulled it out again, and felt for any obstruction. His hand brought out a crumpled piece of parchment. Simon brought it out into the light and cursed again. He had considered the miniature to have gone missing long ago, lost in some cleaning frenzy.

The colours remained as brilliant as ever. The soft blonde curls and rosebud mouth. A tiny pointed chin. The sort of face that was the toast of six regiments in its time. Once he had believed himself the luckiest man in the word to have won her. To have been honoured with the favour of her hand.

Simon's lips twisted into an ironic smile. That young man's fancy had gone long ago. Jayne had crushed it with her dainty spoilt fingers. A good reason not to think on Miss Benedict's figure or on how her hair had looked unbound, falling about her shoulders late at night.

He fingered his scar. His own looks had not improved over the past few years. What was it that the Honourable Miranda Bolt had called him last autumn—a fiend? She had not known that he was standing there, but he had heard the words as they had departed.

And even if his face was not that of a hell-born imp's, he knew his insides were. Twisted and bitter from his experience with Jayne. Miss Benedict deserved better. The very purity of her goodness shone from her. He had no wish to infect her with the burdens he carried. No, his outside was merely the reflection of his soul. Miss Benedict's destiny was for a better man than he could ever be.

A discreet knock sounded, bringing him back to reality.

'Enter.' Simon contemplated tossing the miniature on the fire, but instead he placed it carefully back in the drawer.

Miss Benedict stood in the doorway. Her hair curled softly at the nape of her neck and her dark blue gown contrasted with the cream of her skin. It was hard to believe that he had thought of her as a harpy. Simon gave a half-smile. But one should never underestimate the steel in her backbone. He had found that he'd spent the entire day looking forward to crossing swords with her, and the way her eyes sparkled when she passionately defended her position.

'Doctor MacFarlane has called. He was most helpful in explaining his view of Robert's condition. He sends his regrets at not staying to speak with you as he does have other patients to attend to and does not have the time to spare.'

Her lips turned down at the corners as if she did not approve of the doctor's attitude. No doubt she considered that the doctor should have berated him for allowing Robert to get into that state. Personally, he offered up a small prayer of thanksgiving. The doctor had taken the threat Simon had made on his last visit as the truth.

How much had MacFarlane told her of his reasons?

Simon made a mental note to send a few extra coins with the bill. MacFarlane had shown sense by not coming to see him and offer his usual litany of queries about his eye and his arm. The pain had not gone away like the doctor had promised. No specialist would be able to do anything either. It was a judgment, a reflection of his insides. He would live with it, but he refused to explain it to anyone.

'The doctor has already come and gone.' Simon gave a short laugh and poured another glass of port. 'No surprise there.'

'He said that there was no need for him to see you as you remained as stubborn as you always were.' A ghost of a smile touched her lips as she lowered her lashes. 'I did agree that you were stubborn.'

'I am the most mild mannered of men, Miss Benedict, except when provoked.'

'And have you been provoked?'

'Continually!'

'I gather you objected to Dr MacFarlane bleeding Robert the last time he called. He was at pains to stress that he had no intentions of doing anything like that without your permission.'

'Robert was not in a fit state. He remains in an unfit state.'

She raised an eyebrow. 'Surely the doctor should have been the judge of that. Bleeding is an accepted practice.'

Simon clung on to his temper. The insufferable doctor no doubt had made great play of his seemingly irrational behaviour, but suddenly it mattered to him that Miss Benedict understood his reasoning, that she saw the truth in his words.

'Bleeding never did a weak person any good, Miss Benedict, in my experience.'

'But it happens all the time.' She tilted her head to one side. 'Threatening to throw a doctor down the stairs does not endear you to them.'

'My father died after he had been bled. I am certain that it hastened his death. I saw my wife grow weak after being bled continually, until she begged me to have it stopped. Doctor MacFarlane knew my views before he came to administer to Robert. We have argued over them at the Reading Room before.' Simon slammed his fist against the table, making the glass clang into the decanter. 'My views may be unfashionable but I am still the master in this house and no one is bled here. I trust you did not allow it to happen.'

He waited for the shocked intake of breath. She merely raised one perfectly arched eyebrow as if he were some naughty school boy. A grudging respect grew within him. Normally, the servants made a quick departure when he was in these moods. Even Diana had found excuses.

'Doctor MacFarlane did not bleed Robert.' The aristocratic tilt was back in her chin. 'While he was here, he kept looking over his shoulder. You should perhaps give more consideration to his expertise.'

'As long as he obeyed my orders, I am content. As I said, Miss Benedict, I am not an unreasonable man.'

'It is a wonder that Dr MacFarlane returned at all…'

'Dr MacFarlane understands that I pay in coin and promptly. That is more than most do in this neighbourhood.' Simon began to pace the room. He hated it when people kept things from him. Perhaps he should have seen the quack. He picked up the glass and regarded the ruby-red liquid. No, that would have invited unwanted comment. 'Now out with it, how does the boy fare? What does the good doctor recommend aside from bleeding? He has obviously talked to you.'

'As I did not threaten him, he was most congenial. Doctor MacFarlane spent a great deal of time examining Robert. Robert enjoyed his jokes. He even managed to laugh once without losing his breath.'

The image of Robert gasping for breath entered his mind and refused to leave. Simon's eye throbbed and he was forced to sit. He breathed deeply, trying to control the pain. He should have been there. He glanced up and saw Miss Benedict looking at him with a concerned expression on her face.

'Continue, if you please, Miss Benedict,' he said when he could finally trust his voice. 'My infirmity returns to plague me at the oddest times.'

Phoebe stared at him and choked back any retort. He was in pain. She had been so concerned with Robert that she had forgotten about Mr Clare's injuries. His face contorted several times and then appeared to relax as the spasm eased. She waited with hands clasped for a few moments before finally continuing. She concentrated on the half-empty decanter of port, rather than on him. 'Robert is improving. He recommends more beef tea and toast because Robert needs to regain his strength if his heart is not to stay weak.'

'His heart is weak. What else has the good doctor chosen to conceal from me? Did he speak of removing Robert to a place of safety? Robert will be nursed in my home, Miss Benedict.'

Phoebe winced. Mr Clare's scar shone red against his skin. Her natural inclination was to flee, but she forced her feet to stay rooted to the spot.

'The St Vitus's Dance—the fits stem from the rheumatic fever. Both the doctor and I have every hope…' Phoebe spoke quickly, hoping to calm him, to make him understand that Dr MacFarlane agreed with her assessment. 'Time is a great healer. Sometimes, it is the only thing we can do.'

'Spare me your platitudes, Miss Benedict.' He leant his head back against the chair and waved a hand of dismissal.

Phoebe straightened her spine and held her head high. She wanted to shake him. He had wilfully misunderstood. 'Not platitudes, the truth.'

Silence filled the room. Phoebe looked hard at Mr Clare, willing him to say something, willing him to call her a liar. She wanted him to yell and rail against the world. His hair had fallen forwards, hiding his face. And his knuckles were white against the stem of the glass. 'Is Robert going to recover?' His hoarse whisper echoed in the room. 'Or will he remain bedridden forever?'

'Both Dr MacFarlane and I feel certain he will recover. Quite probably before summer.'

'And his mind?' The words were a harsh whisper, but echoed in the book-lined study.

'His temper tantrums are the result of over-indulgence and that benighted nurse scaring him.' Phoebe kept her voice matter of fact. There was no use criticising the former nurse. She could not change the past. 'The doctor is cautiously optimistic. Robert is taking his medicine and seems far quieter, less agitated. He looks like an angel when he sleeps.'

Phoebe stopped as the blood drained from his face.

'Mr Clare?' Phoebe whispered. 'Is everything all right?'

'I once wanted him to be good and to stop his naughtiness, but not like this,' he whispered in a low voice. 'I want Robert back. To think how angry I was when he made a stink bomb. Or when the school wrote home about his many transgressions of the rules.'

'Robert is going to live. You must believe that your son will live. Soon you will forget that he was so ill.'

'I will never forget. I had feared so much. My boy...' Myriad emotions crossed Mr Simon Clare's face, but then he appeared to regain control of himself. He swirled the ruby-red liquid in his glass. 'How is he now?'

Phoebe moved away and busied herself with straightening the items on the mantelpiece. Anything to get away from the overpowering urge to gather him in her arms and hold him until the pain in his gaze ceased.

'He is asleep. Jenny, the under-housemaid, is sitting outside the door. If he makes the slightest peep, she is to run and tell me. Jenny appears to be a sensible child, even if her mouth bubbles like a brook.'

'Jenny Satterwaite?' His forehead puckered, then cleared. His face became remote once again. 'Yes, yes, I know the girl. Diana told me that I had to hire her. Her brother has gone with Lord Coltonby to London. Now I must attend to my business.'

Phoebe breathed again. The moment had passed. She was going to have to control herself. Becoming attracted to a man like Simon Clare was simply not done. She was here to nurse Robert and to repay Lord and Lady Coltonby for their kindness. No one had ever said anything about Mr Clare and his troubles.

'And your business is that important that you cannot spare five minutes for your son? I had hoped to persuade you to visit Robert and see the improvement for yourself. You practically live in this study, according to Jenkins.'

'Does it matter to you, Miss Benedict, what my habits are? Do you listen to servant tittle-tattle? I go about my business when I need to. It is not neglected. I can run my empire from the study as well as being there.'

Phoebe took a deep breath. Here was her opening. She might never get a better chance. Mr Jameson was correct. He did need to know. 'I thought that a mine could not be run properly from an armchair.'

'I run my mine from a desk. I employ honest men that I trust.'

'I thought you had to be able to walk every inch of a mine blindfolded to truly know it. Or was that a sop to explain my father's mistake?'

His lips became a thin white line. 'Is there anything else? Anything else to berate me with?'

'Your sister asked me to report on how you looked. She worried that you might be hiding from the outside world. I had hesitated. What should I say?'

'I do not hide.' Simon Clare toyed with his glass. 'My sister oversteps the mark. I am being cautious. I was nearly blown up last autumn, and then after she had left on her wedding trip, I tried to return to the mine and was injured again.' His fingers touched the white blaze in his hair. 'For once I am following the doctor's orders.'

'The doctor you refuse to see.'

A muscle in Mr Clare's cheek twitched. 'Yes.'

Phoebe shifted uneasily, and wondered whether she dared. She decided that someone had to. He might throw her out, but at least she would have said something. 'It might better for everyone if you did.'

She waited with bated breath, wondering if she had gone too far.

'I will keep it under advisement, Miss Benedict. And I do expect a report every evening. My injuries prevent me from climbing the stairs as nimbly as I might wish.'

'You may visit the sickroom whenever you choose.' Phoebe laced her hands together. 'We are willing to overlook any injuries or pained expressions, simply for the pleasure of your company.'

'Be careful about the pleasure that you are seeking.'

'I am speaking of Robert's pleasure.'

'I am not.'

Phoebe stumbled out of the room and shut the door behind her. She tried to regain her composure. This was all about Robert and not about the way Mr Clare invaded her dreams. She hated him for implying otherwise, for reminding her that she had thoughts that no gently reared lady had any business having.

Just who did Miss Benedict think she was, coming in here and making pronouncements? Simon paced his study. He was not a recluse. He could go out any time he chose. He never sat around and moped. He just chose not to see people.

The walls appeared to close down around him. He half-started towards the stairs. Stopped. No, Miss Benedict was not going to have it her way. She wanted him to go up there and see Robert.

He danced to no woman's tune.

'Jenkins! Jenkins! Where is that butler when you need him?'

'Here, master. Was there something you require? The cook made boiled beef again as per Miss Diana's orders.'

Simon gritted his teeth. He knew today was always boiled beef. It was why he dined out. Diana had liked boiled beef. He could not stand it, but it seemed wrong somehow to upset the house's routine. It was far too much bother to have to think up new dishes, write out new menus and instruct the cook. At least with the same old food, he knew exactly what he was going to have and exactly how much should be spent on the household budget.

'I want my carriage brought around. I wish to go to the Reading Rooms.' Simon pushed the fringe away from his eyes. 'And send Ponsby to me. I want my hair trimmed before I go out. It has grown rather long. Lord knows what he was thinking about.'

'Yes, sir.' Jenkins's face did not move a muscle.

'You may get on with it!'

Jenkins left and Simon smiled. 'Think you will manipulate me into doing what you want, Miss Benedict? You may think again.'

Chapter Six

'Enter.' Mr Clare's terse command resounded in Phoebe's ears the next evening.

She pushed the door open and peeped in. Mr Clare sat before a chessboard, seemingly intent on the piece. His hair was far shorter and neater with the white blaze nearly hidden. Instead of his usual day clothes, he wore evening clothes, a form-fitting tail coat and cream-coloured breeches. Gone was the pirate captain, and in his place a rather more urbane, but remote, businessman. Phoebe touched her hair and wished she had thought to change or at least tidy herself.

Tonight she would prove that she could act with dignity, instead of like a blushing schoolgirl. She knew that she had avoided him last night, and had sent a short note instead. He had sent a message back that he expected her in person.

The prospect of the meeting felt worse than her first ball at Almack's, when she had nearly spilt punch down Beau Brummell's front and had to wait several heartbeats to hear if she was damned for ever in society's eyes. Mr Brummell had raised his quizzing glass before remarking that given the state of the punch that evening, perhaps it would be best worn on the outside. And the evening had swung from disaster to triumph in a few words.

Suddenly she wished that she had given in to her impulse and had sent a written note again. She straightened her back. No, Mr Clare deserved to hear about his son from her lips. He could ask questions. And perhaps she could impress on him how much Robert wanted to see him. 'You re-quested information about how Robert fares.'

For several heartbeats, Phoebe wondered if he had heard her as he appeared totally absorbed in his chess match. Just when Phoebe was con-vinced that she would have to repeat her message, Mr Clare lifted his head. His good eye appeared to take in everything about her appear-ance, from the blotch of dirt on her shoulder to the slight fraying of her cuffs and the way her hair escaped in tendrils down the back of her neck. 'I have heard no screams today. I presume the boy is doing better. Is that what you wanted to say to me?'

He bent his head and appeared to contemplate the chessboard again. Phoebe shifted where she stood. She should go, but she refused to be dismissed so easily. The man was going to hear about his son. The man who sat by Robert's side at night obviously cared about his son. She wanted to get through to that man, not the one who regarded her with cold impatient eyes.

'He is taking his medicine without protest, you will be relieved to hear he has settled now and is fast asleep. Hannibal is asleep in a basket beside the fire.'

'Who is Hannibal?'

'The kitten. Robert was most determined on the name. The story about Hannibal and the elephants fascinates him. We finally settled on it today.'

'Robert is a barbarian at heart.' Mr Clare had a sardonic look on his face.

'I have not seen these tendencies.'

'You wait, Miss Benedict. Robert has an ability to cause trouble that is unequalled, if his most recent school report is to be believed.' Mr Clare leant back in his chair and pressed his long fingers together. 'The barbarian hordes had nothing on the boy's ability to disrupt an ordered classroom. I have firsthand experience of the havoc he can wreak on an At Home. It took Lady Bolt's nerves many weeks to recover from the beetles in the sugar bowl incident. And we will not go into what happened at Mrs Elton's *musicale*.'

'You appear to have a very poor opinion of your son. Boys can be like that. The tales I could tell about my stepbrothers, and the spiders they put in my hair.'

A half-smile quirked on his lips. 'When you get to know Robert better, you will understand. Robert's natural inclination is to rebel against rules, but he must learn to obey them. Other people's lives will one day depend on him.'

'Nevertheless, Robert has been admirably behaved today. He is sleeping peacefully.'

'I am relieved to hear it. Kitten and boy asleep. You have set my mind at rest on that score. You do appear to have taken some time in achieving this.'

He glanced up at her and their eyes met and held. Phoebe wiped her hands against her skirt, resisting the impulse to smooth her hair back. What was the matter with her? She knew how to handle the most awkward of social situations. Once she had done it with ease. But now faced with this man, she seemed worse than the most naïve débutante. 'It took longer than I expected. He wanted to talk about what might be happening with the war. Robert has a lively mind. He thirsts for knowledge.'

'You have been all this time in settling him?'

'Is this a problem?' Phoebe watched his long fingers.

'Your report was expected earlier. Yesterday, you sent your note before supper.' He moved a chess piece, held it there with his finger poised on the top of it and then returned it to its former position. 'I should like to have your report before my food…in case of indigestion. It was boiled mutton with parsnips, one of the cook's many delights.'

'I had no wish to disturb your supper.'

'I dine alone, Miss Benedict.' A faint smile touched his lips. 'You would have added to the meal rather than detracted from it.'

Phoebe lowered her head and attempted to ignore the little spark of pleasure growing inside her. 'Robert kept me busy. I wanted to make sure that he finished all of his beef tea and did not put the rice pudding under his bed.'

Simon gave a laugh. 'That sounds more like Robert. You have far more to worry about when he is behaving beautifully, according to Diana.'

'But you would prefer him to obey the rules.'

'Rules save lives, Miss Benedict. I may appreciate Robert's spirit, but it must be contained. Being a father is not an easy task.'

Phoebe gritted her teeth. It was not right. Her father might not have been perfect, but she had known his love. And in her own way, she knew her stepmother loved her as well. They certainly would never have relied on anyone else to tell them about their children. They would have checked.

'It does seem that boys are like that,' she said carefully. 'James used to put his green beans down his socks at meal times when he was about Robert's age. And I had a chore to get him to eat. I think he did it for the sheer devilment because now he loves green beans.'

'I will take that under consideration, and will have Robert checked the next time he dines with me. However, coming downstairs to supper is out of the question. Robert needs to eat early and rest.' He tilted his head to one side and the fire light made his eye patch appear more piratical than ever. Phoebe breathed easier. She knew she could deal with the pirate captain. She found the businessman far more of a cipher.

'If he is not to eat with you, then it might be helpful if his food arrived hot, instead of cold. Congealed rice pudding is a test for anyone.'

'Congealed rice pudding sounds dreadful.' A shudder went through Mr Clare as he seemed to realise the full horror of cold rice pudding. 'Has this happened often?'

'Every night so far.'

'And you have spoken to Cook?'

'Yes.' Phoebe kept her voice even. She had not wished to report the words that had passed between them. Or the Cook's refrain of needing Mr Clare's direct orders to change his practice.

'I will have a word. This should not be happening.' Mr Clare frowned. 'Are any of the other servants not obeying your orders?'

'This is the only problem I have encountered so far.'

'I will see to it and please let me know if you discover anything else. I am no monster, Miss Benedict. I want Robert to recover.'

'To become a barbarian again, but a barbarian who obeys rules.'

'Just so.' A smile tugged at his lips. 'You understand my intention.'

A happy glow coursed through Phoebe. She had mistaken his dry sense of humour for indifference. She knew the problems she pointed out would be solved. If she could just get Mr Clare to visit Robert, she felt certain Robert would recover much more quickly. She had to get through to him, to make him want to visit his son. But how?

'How are you finding Northumberland?' Mr Clare asked. 'I fear you arrived in bad weather.'

'Colder than London. Bleaker. The wind whips around the house.' Phoebe went over to the fire and warmed her hands. The subject had very definitely been changed. The tiny opening had been slammed shut. But she would prevail. And if by the time she left, he had a better relationship with his son and the house was running that bit smoother, she would feel as if she had accomplished something. 'But Northumberland has its own beauty as well. I was able to go for a short walk earlier and discovered a clump of snowdrops struggling to push through the snow.'

She forced a smile. She had thought the brisk walk around the house would make her thoughts of him vanish, but they hadn't. It had only increased her appetite to see him.

'Ah, then you are not a pale thing given to remaining indoors all winter. Sometimes London women…'

'I am quite robust, Mr Clare. I do not break easily.'

His eyes travelled down her form and absurdly she wished that she had taken the time to change into a gown that better suited her complexion.

'I can see that.'

Phoebe drummed her fingers against her thigh. She wished that she was in one of her ball gowns, one of the ones she had worn when she had been called an Incomparable, all frothy Belgian lace and net. 'Robust' would not have been one of the words used to describe her then. Words such as *exquisite* and *ethereal* had tripped off lips instead. 'Are you insulting me, Mr Clare?'

'I am merely agreeing with your assessment.' A dimple flashed in his cheek and he adopted an innocent expression. 'If I considered you a shrinking violet, you would have been on a coach back to London the morning after you arrived. This house has no room for fools.'

'I will take that as a compliment, then.' She crossed her arms, and met his gaze measure for measure.

'My words have never run towards hearts and flowers.' His brows knitted together and he appeared to be remembering something. 'Not for a long while at any rate. My sister never minded my tongue, but I dare say others find it difficult.'

Phoebe wondered what he must have been like as a young man, before his wife had died. Had he been charming? Or caustic? He must have loved his wife very much. She had searched amongst the family portraits, but had failed to discover any of her. She had found one of Mr Clare when he was young. The jet-black hair and forthright look had caused her to suck in her breath. And she kept finding excuses to return to the portrait, to see him again.

The silence seemed to stretch between them. Phoebe knew she should make her excuses and go. She had promised herself that was what she would do, but now that she was here, the words seemed to stick in her throat. She wanted to prolong their encounter somehow.

'Who are you playing at chess?' She tilted her head to one side, studying the game. 'Surely you are not playing against yourself.'

'A correspondent. A friend from Cambridge.'

'Ah, I know that sort of game. It can be frustrating. Games take months to finish. And one has to be careful that servants do not move pieces.'

'I have never found that a problem.'

Phoebe pasted a smile on her face. 'I suspect they would only do it once.'

'My sister preferred drawing to such things. The few times we played, she showed a singular disregard for the rules. I developed this method out of necessity.'

'I used to play nearly every night when my father was alive. My stepbrothers and I play occasionally, but they dislike being beaten.'

'And did you do so?' The dimple flashed in his cheek.

'Regularly.' Phoebe gave a little laugh, relieved that the air suddenly seemed easier. 'Edmund behaved quite badly when I beat him six times straight in one evening. In the end he took to his bed with a headache and I had to fetch some willow bark tea.'

'Perhaps your stepbrother is not overly fond of the game. It requires a certain amount of skill and patience. As well as forward thinking.'

'My stepbrother played chess at Oxford where he gained a reputation for being quite skilled.'

'If he had gone to Cambridge…' He clicked his

fingers as if the difference in mental capacity should be apparent. 'Watch and observe as I set a trap for my opponent.'

Phoebe narrowed her eyes and studied the board as he moved his bishop.

'Your queen will be in jeopardy within three moves if you are not careful. And you will be checkmated in four.'

'How so? Pray take a seat, Miss Benedict, and demonstrate.' He gestured to a stool opposite. 'I warn you, I am quite skilled. But I am always willing to learn from someone whose stepbrother went to Oxford.'

'It is the game with your correspondent. I have no wish to ruin it.' Her mouth became dry. Would she be able to do this? She had last played Edmund about a year ago. But the board appeared straight-forward enough. And Mr Clare's intended trap was one that she had encountered before.

'My correspondent can wait. I am well aware of where we are in that particular game.' He gestured to the sofa opposite him. 'Prove your worth. Your idle boast intrigues me.'

'It is far from an idle boast. I speak the truth.'

'Prove it.'

'I shall.' Phoebe's fingers curled around a black

pawn and held it trembling over the board. She glanced up and saw a quizzical look in Mr Clare's face. Quickly she moved it. Waited. As she had suspected, Simon made the easily predicted countermove, blocking her rook and seeming to create an easy chance for putting his king in check, but if she did so, she would put her king into jeopardy.

'I am waiting, Miss Benedict.'

'I am thinking.'

'Not as easy as you claimed, then.'

She moved her knight. Simon's face became serious. He studied the board for a long time. Then played his piece. Phoebe tried very hard not to laugh as she captured his queen with her bishop. 'I do believe it is check, Mr Clare.'

'I am impressed, Miss Benedict, but the game is not over yet.' He drummed his fingers against the chair.

'It is now, Mr Clare. Checkmate.' Phoebe made no attempt to disguise the triumph in her voice as she closed the trap.

'I fear I have done you a disservice, Miss Benedict. I had thought you merely a pleasant face, but you also possess an admirable brain.'

'Another backhanded compliment—you must be slipping, Mr Clare. Two in one night.'

'I speak the truth, Miss Benedict, as always. It tends to save confusion.' He dipped his head and she could see where his trimmed hair kissed the back of his neck.

'I will return the pieces to your former game.' Phoebe started to rearrange them on the chessboard. Her fingers refused to move properly and her heart resounded in her ears. With each breath she took, she became more aware of his masculine strength, sitting there concealed beneath a veneer of civilisation. He was definitely a ruthless pirate who took without asking.

His hand stopped her, closed over her fingers, held them in his warm embrace. Their breath mingled for an instant. Her lips ached with a dull throbbing. 'We could have a proper game.'

Phoebe looked from the entwined fingers back up to his face. The offer was tempting. In the back of her mind she heard Alice's voice from years ago, warning her about men and the need to keep on her guard. Rapidly she withdrew her hand. 'I need to check on Robert. I have left him for as long as I dare.'

'Is that the truth or merely an excuse? You have made no comment about my appearance.'

'You look less like a pirate…more like the successful businessman.'

'A pirate? Someone who takes without asking, who behaves without rules or standards. Without his principles, a man is lost.'

Phoebe knew her cheeks flamed and she wished she had never said the unguarded words. 'Then it is as well you changed your appearance.'

'Until tomorrow, then.' He inclined his head. 'And in person, Miss Benedict. A note simply will not suffice.'

'I will take your request under consideration.'

'And, Miss Benedict, thank you. You have made the time pass most enjoyably.' He paused and a crooked smile played on his lips. 'And that is a true compliment, Miss Benedict. Do not seek to deny it.'

'I never did.'

She fled upstairs, hearing Mr Clare's amused laugh ringing in her ears. It was easy to like Mr Clare, but her purpose was to find a way to bring him and Robert together.

'Miss Benedict, I want to thank you.'

'Thank me for what, Jenny?' Phoebe placed her pen down and turned to face the under-house-maid, Jenny Satterwaite. Her letter to Alice describing how much she enjoyed being in Northumberland would have to wait. It was far too soon to hope for a letter from someone in her family. But as she wanted someone to write to her, she knew from past experience that she would have to write first.

'Tommy Jameson said that I ought to. I hope you don't mind me saying things to me mam. Tommy has been really kind now that our Jimmy is in London with Lord Coltonby.' Jenny took a large breath. 'Anyways, Mr Clare went to the colliery yesterday and found the problem straightaways. All Tommy had to do was mention it, like.'

Phoebe tucked a tendril of hair behind her ear. Mr Clare had found his way to the colliery, but he had not found his way up to the sickroom. She had seen how Robert stilled every time he heard footsteps. Somehow, she would make Mr Clare understand how important it was to Robert that his father pay him attention. She could not order him, but she had to do something to make him want to be there. 'Mr Clare is very good about getting things seen to, if he knows there is a problem.'

'Yes, Mr Clare ordered a full survey of the tunnel. Any weak timbers will be replaced. Tommy is ever so grateful.'

'I did not do anything.'

'If that is what you want to believe.' Jenny's

brow wrinkled. 'But if you don't mind, I will think differently.'

'And, Jenny, no more tales home, please. What goes on in this house stays in this house.'

'Yes, miss.' Jenny bobbed her head. 'I will try to remember that.'

Phoebe watched the little maid hurry off. It would be so easy to get involved here, but she had to remember that her time was limited. She would be leaving as soon as Robert was well.

Simon glanced at the mantel clock, irritated. He had been looking forward to his match with Miss Benedict. The board was set, everything was in readiness, but she was late.

He grimaced and touched his scar. He should have expected this. She wouldn't come. She had spoken to the cook and the cold boiled mutton had vanished, but she had not reappeared herself.

To go up to Robert's room would look like he was desperate for company. And he wasn't. He was perfectly content down here. Alone. Solitary. The way he liked things. He had had quite enough of stares and comments out at the colliery. It was right to go there. The Reading Room at Ladywell had failed to exert its usual charm.

He had lifted his hand to ring for Jenkins when the door opened, and Miss Benedict stood there, mouth turned ever so slightly down, hair twisted up into a knot with a few tendrils playing about her neck. Her blue gown hinted at her curves, rather than revealed them. He felt the tension ease out of his shoulder. All was right with world. She had appeared. He had not had to go in search of her.

'Is there some problem, Miss Benedict?' Simon asked smoothly, forcing his gaze to her face and seeing that the frown had only increased.

'Doctor MacFarlane called again.'

'You have an admirer.'

'Hardly. He brought a book for Robert on elephants as they had a discussion about them before. As he was leaving, he asked whether or not you still wore your eyepatch.'

'What does my eyepatch have to do with my son?' Simon waved a dismissive hand as his stomach knotted. How could he explain why he suffered this affliction? How could he stand to see the disgust in Miss Benedict's eyes? He knew what was inside him, what he had done. 'And what right do you have to mention such things to the doctor?'

She raised a delicate eyebrow and her expression

became cool. 'I did not mention it. The doctor enquired. There is a difference.'

'Was there any particular reason why he asked?'

'Apparently, he has discovered an eye specialist in Edinburgh. He wished me to mention this to you. He makes no promises, but wonders if you have explored the possibility.'

'MacFarlane should have come to see me himself.' Simon gestured about the room. 'I would have made the time. I would have welcomed the intelligent conversation.'

'Perhaps he is afraid to. Everyone who enters gets their head snapped off. You rarely have a good word for anyone.'

'And you are not afraid?' He leant forwards, waiting. The clock ticked loudly and somewhere a door was slammed shut.

'I would hardly be here if I were. I am no coward, Mr Clare.'

'There is little anyone can do with my eye. I have seen the quack in Newcastle. If MacFarlane had concerns, he should come and speak to me directly.'

'I believe he feared that you would not listen. He asked me to write your sister, but I felt it best to tackle you first. Your sister would only worry.'

'Write to my sister!' Simon gripped the arms of

his chair and half-rose up. The impertinence of the man. He could well imagine Diana's blistering letter if she thought he was not attending to his health. 'MacFarlane oversteps.'

'I am certain that he does it out of concern for your well-being. It is a wonder that he mentioned it at all given how rude you were to him.' She crossed her arms.

'Macfarlane knows where his hard coin comes from.'

'If he knows that, why did he jeopardise it? He asked out of concern for you. Apparently he used to see you quite often at the Reading Room. He was sorry to miss you the other day and hopes to see you there soon.'

'People know where I live.'

'Perhaps they did not want to intrude. Your son has been ill.'

Simon drew a deep breath. The worst thing was that she was correct. He was at fault. It did not make things any easier to bear. Robert's illness was an excuse. Excepting the other day when he had been so annoyed with Miss Benedict, he had not been to the Reading Room since before the explosion. It used to be one of his highlights—a chance to speak to his friends and fellow business associates, to find out what was going on in Ladywell. 'Did he leave the name of the specialist?'

'A Dr Cording in Charlotte Square.' Phoebe waited. She hated being the go-between, but Dr MacFarlane had been insistent that she might be able to help. And someone had to risk his ire. 'If you were one of my stepbrothers, I would insist.'

'And is that how you see me, Miss Benedict, as one of your stepbrothers?'

Phoebe examined the carpet, noting how the pattern seemed to shift and change. A brother? Her dreams last night had been full of him—a pirate captain who plundered and took without hesitation. She had woken full of a nameless longing. Her insides twisted. She knew what she should feel and it was very different from what she did feel. 'I see you as Robert's father.'

'That is not an answer.'

'But it is the truth.'

He nodded and did not pursue the matter further. Phoebe risked a breath and forced her shoulders to relax. As soon as she could, she would make her excuses and leave, before she accidentally confessed her true feelings.

'Robert has gone straight off to sleep. Now that he knows the medicine is to help him get better, he takes it with scarcely a murmur. He is hoping for a horse, apparently.'

'I am gratified to learn your theory, but I have made my views quite clear on the subject—no horses. My wife became paralysed due to a fall from a horse.'

'Your son is not your wife. Sometimes, one must take calculated risks.'

'It is a moot point because he must become well, before he can even begin to think about learning to ride.' He gestured toward the chessboard. 'And now to the matter at hand. I wish to discover if you truly do play, or if you had simply seen that strategy used before. You pique my curiosity, Miss Benedict.'

'I look forward to the challenge.' Phoebe settled herself down opposite Mr Clare.

'Then shall we play for a friendly wager?'

'A wager?' Phoebe gave a nervous laugh. 'My stepmother told me never to wager with a gentleman.'

'Your stepmother is not here. My price will be within the bounds of honour.'

Phoebe bit her lip. She knew that she could win, and the offer was tempting. She would force him to go and see Robert. It would mean so much to the boy. She would do it. 'I agree.'

The game began and she rapidly discovered that Mr Clare was a far harder opponent than her stepbrothers. She kept being distracted with the length of his fingers, and the shape of his hands. After he captured her queen, she redoubled her efforts at concentrating, captured several pieces and the game appeared to flow in her favour. She moved her knight. 'I believe it is check, Mr Clare.'

'Would you care to increase the wager?'

'You will lose, Mr Clare. It would hardly be fair.'

'When my back is to the wall, I play my best.' He moved a pawn, taking his king out of jeopardy.

Phoebe glanced at the board. It was very simple. Almost child's play. She moved. 'Again check.'

'But not mate, Miss Benedict.' He moved his bishop and far too late she saw the trap. 'But it is now. I believe I have won.'

Phoebe looked at the board, dismayed. How had she fallen into such a simple trap? She had lost and now she owed the unspecified forfeit. She only had to hope his word was true and that it would be honourable. She turned her king on its side. 'I do believe you are correct…unfortunately.'

'You underestimated me, Miss Benedict. A very dangerous thing to do.' He put his hands behind his head and smiled a very self-satisfied smile. 'I am not often an easy proposition. And a game is never won until the last piece is played.'

'I will have to remember that.' Phoebe stood up and prepared to leave. He had administered his lesson and now she would go.

'You may stay a while, Miss Benedict. We need to discuss your forfeit.'

'My forfeit?' Her voice rose several octaves. 'You have seen me humbled—is there something else you require?'

'You lost. We wagered. Surely you are not trying to run out on the terms of the wager.'

She licked her suddenly dry lips. She should have thought to enquire, but she had been so sure. This was the first time that she had lost since before her father had died. 'And what will you have me do?'

'You need not worry, Miss Benedict.'

'How can you tell that I am worried?' She hated the way her voice stumbled over the words. All her stepmother's warnings echoed in her head. She had already broken a dozen rules.

'Your forehead creases up. You are a guest in my household, I would not do anything untoward. Your reputation is safe.'

Phoebe released a breath. A vague sense of disappointment crept over her. She gazed up at the carved wooden ceiling. 'I never meant to imply…'

He lifted an eyebrow. 'The other day, you played a simple melody on the spinet.'

'It was wrong of me. I should never have gone into the room.'

'It was well that you did. I heard you play. The melody has been echoing in my head.'

'A few notes only.' Phoebe's cheeks burnt. 'It has been a long time. 'Wild Geese' was one of my father's songs.'

'I wish you to play me a tune on the spinet.'

'My skill is very rusty.' Phoebe regarded her hands.

'But you consider it one of your accomplishments, or you would never have touched the spinet.' He lifted an eyebrow. 'Unless you wish to have a different forfeit.'

His eye was firmly fixed on her mouth, making it ache. What would it be like to be kissed by him? She smoothed and re-smoothed a crease in her gown.

'The spinet and I parted company after my father's death.' She made a little gesture. 'It was sold to pay the debts and…'

He nodded.

'After hearing the noise the other day, I discovered that I want to hear music. My sister had a tin ear, but my wife used to sing beautifully. It has been a long time since music filled this house, Miss Benedict.'

'I fear I will cause you a headache.'

'Nothing could be worse than Diana's playing.' Mr Clare gave a slight shudder. 'She can dance, but her forte is painting. You must have a walk out to the summer house when the weather improves. She spent hours adorning it with garlands and flowers. It is more than pleasant to have a cup of tea out there in the summer.'

'I shall look forward to seeing it at the earliest opportunity.' Phoebe kept her mind resolutely away from the changing seasons. With the rate at which Robert was improving, she would not be here to see the spring, let alone the summer. She would be lodged with her great-aunt or some other relation. Sophia's latest letter had shown her that she could not bear to go back there. James's future might be settled, but there was Edmund to be considered. She had to think what her father would want for him. Somebody had to care about them.

'Northumberland is exquisite in the early summer. There is no place like it on earth.'

'I shall take your word for it.'

'And now, I think, the forfeit.' He led the way

into the drawing room, leaning heavily on his cane as if his whole body ached. Phoebe longed to offer her arm, but knew he would reject it as she opened the door.

Alabaster lamps bathed the drawing room in a soft glow. The sofas and armchairs had been rearranged and the spinet had been brought in to sit in an alcove.

'It looks as if it belongs there. As if this room was designed for it. Even the moulding on the surround matches the detail of the spinet.'

'The spinet was moved to the ballroom after my wife's death. Somehow, I never got around to returning it to its rightful place.'

Phoebe touched a black key and listened to the deep melodic sound. Bittersweet ghosts hung in the air as the note faded. 'It was your wife's?'

'A tune, if you please, Miss Benedict.' Mr Clare sat down in the chair, placing his cane by his side. 'After all the hard work that has gone into moving the furniture, it is the least you can do.'

Phoebe kept her gaze firmly on the black keys. The subject had been irrevocably changed. Everything about that time remained shrouded in mystery. She knew how painful her father had found it at first to speak of her mother, and yet there were times when he needed to speak and to remember. She knew it had pained her step-mother that he had only felt able to speak to Phoebe about it.

'There is no music. How can you test my skill, if you give me no music?'

'Play what you played the other day. I wish to hear it all the way through.'

'It was a simple folk melody.'

'It will suffice.'

She sat down on the stool; her fingers trembled over the keys. Then she struck the first note, a false one. She hesitated and tried again, this time going slower, savouring the tune.

The music washed over her and she became lost. She finished the tune and stopped. She glanced over her shoulder and saw that his head lay back against the armchair. A look of perfect contentment.

'You do not have a tin ear, Miss Benedict.'

'I fear my fingers are rusty. I am certain I played the last phrase a bit more quickly than I should have.'

'You may continue, Miss Benedict. Let me be the judge if your playing is worthy or not.'

Phoebe rapidly played another tune, one she re-membered her mother playing to her father. Her fingers had fun with the simple piece. When she had finished, she glanced over and saw his slight nod.

She began softly to sing the words. A low baritone filled the room, combining with hers, a rich voice that flowed over her, singing about how the narrator waited for his love.

Her hands faltered on the keys and played the wrong note. A discordant sound. The next verse was impossible to play. It had been such a bad choice, this song. She would have to hope that he simply assumed she had forgotten the notes.

'I fear I have strained your ears long enough.' Phoebe gave a hiccupping laugh and tried not to notice that he had come to stand behind her. His breath fanned the back of her neck, sent warm pulses coursing throughout her body. All she had to do was to reach out a hand and she would touch him.

'You have done no such thing.' His voice rippled, called to something within her.

She forced her hands to stay on the spinet and hoped that he wouldn't notice the tide of red washing up her face. 'I should never have started it. It gets very tricky at that point and I fear I have forgotten the rest.'

'It was very pleasant. The words were correct, weren't they?'

'I had no idea you sang, Mr Clare.'

'As a young man, I was told I had a very

pleasing voice. The music faded from my life for a long while.'

'Music can provide healing, my father used to say.'

'To those who want to be healed. It has been a pleasant interlude, Miss Benedict.' His voice flowed over her, held her in its embrace. 'I had forgotten how much I enjoy the simple melodies.'

'Then it has been worthwhile.' She closed her eyes and tried to control her pulse. Her lips tingled as if they had been kissed. She ran her tongue over them, surprised at how they ached. All she had to do was turn and she'd be in his arms. Where she wanted to be. The thought shocked her.

'Why did you choose that tune?'

'It was one of my father's favourites.' Her voice sounded high and unnatural to her ears as the compulsion to touch him grew.

Phoebe rose and moved away from the spinet, away from him and temptation. She refused to behave like some wanton woman, a foolish spinster who panted after a man. He had only wanted some music. She dug her nails into her palm, and concentrated on the pain. 'I have paid my forfeit and I will retire.'

'If you wish…'

Phoebe closed her eyes and vowed that she would never play that melody again. It was temptation personified. It made her forget the intervening years and why she was here. She was here for one purpose only—to see that her brother got his commission. She was not here to make sure Mr Clare was healed. When Robert had recovered in a few weeks, she'd leave without a second glance. 'I do wish. Robert wakes with the lark, and there is much to be done.'

The words sounded weak and feeble, but he seemed to accept them. Phoebe offered up a prayer for small blessings. To lust after Mr Clare was not part of her bargain. Lady Coltonby had sent her up to nurse her nephew, not to seduce her brother. It was a measure of how far she had fallen that she could even contemplate such a thing. What would it be like to be thoroughly kissed?

'You have provided a good evening's entertainment, Miss Benedict. I shall have to think up another forfeit for the next time we play chess.'

'As you say, the winner is never clear until the last piece is played.' Silently she vowed that she would not touch the chessboard again. It was foolish to hope that he might have some regard for her. Such things only happened in fairy tales and her fairy-tale days had ended one winter's night eight years ago.

Simon listened to her footsteps on the stairs. Rapid and precise. Running away. Away from him and this room and back to the safety of Robert's sickroom.

He shook his head. He had come so close. Another breath and he would have taken her into his arms and tasted her lips and her creamy skin. It would have been so easy. She had felt it as well. He was certain of that. She was ripe for seduction.

He slammed his palm down on the keyboard. The jarring, jangled sound echoed through the drawing room, bringing him back to his senses. He had come so close to betraying his principles. Miss Benedict was a guest in his house. She was there at the request of his sister. She was not there for him to use for his pleasure. She was there for him to protect. She was a lady, and related to his brother-in-law.

Some aristocrats might argue that she was fair game, a woman alone, looking after a stranger's child, but he rejected that notion. He prided himself on his restraint. He had never behaved in that fashion, had never taken a mistress, even after Jayne refused his bed. He desired Miss Benedict.

She invaded his dreams. But he refused to seduce her. He refused to ruin her.

The only alternative was marriage. A bitter laugh escaped his lips. He had parted company with that institution a long time ago. And he had no wish to return to it. Even for Miss Benedict.

He would have to keep this dark passion under control. He could master it. His eye caught the miniatures of his sister and her new husband on the mantelpiece.

'My God, Coltonby, how you would chortle. You might have been willing to make my sister your mistress, but I am a better man than you. I will not seduce your cousin. And neither will I marry her. I play within the rules.'

Chapter Seven

Sunlight flooded into the sickroom as Phoebe concentrated on mending her stockings several days later, trying not to think about the way Simon Clare's hand had felt beneath hers or the way when his lips turned up in a smile it changed his usual scarred grimace. Nor how good it had felt to play the spinet once again.

Twice last evening she had started down the stairs with the written report in her hand. Each time, she stopped and headed back upstairs. On the third try, she had encountered Jenkins, who informed her in ponderous tones that the master had gone out to a lecture and was not expected to return until late. A vague sense of disappointment filled her. He had not even given her a chance. And that hurt.

Instead she had left the report defiantly in the

centre of his desk, hoping that it would spur him to appear, but thus far, nothing. Not even a summons to his study. Since then she had sent notes and had tried to forget that moment at the spinet.

Phoebe gave a small shake of her head and stabbed her needle into the cloth. Her days of music and dancing were long past. It would take more than a few airs on a spinet to change the march of time. She supposed that she should begin to think about creating a spinster's cap.

Phoebe jabbed the needle in again, banishing the thought, and drew blood. She quickly put her finger into her mouth to prevent the blood from falling. It was easier not to be in the Season at all. No doubt remarks would have been made about her figure being inclined to plumpness in the bosom and how her hair had become unremarkable. She would be better off concentrating on why Alice and Sophia had not yet responded to her letters.

'You are from London, Miss Phoebe,' Robert said, looking up from his drawing. 'Did you ever go to the Season? And see the fine ladies and gentlemen?'

'I was born in the Cotswolds in a little village just outside Broadway, but I have spent time in London, yes.' Phoebe gave a little laugh and wondered where Robert's mind was headed. He had such a quick mind and his thoughts always appeared to be zooming off in different directions. He never seemed to settle on one thing. It made for interesting conversations, but she did not find him difficult, rather eager to learn. His was a mind hungry for knowledge. 'We used to spend the Season there when my father was alive, so I have seen the ladies and gentlemen in their fine silks and satins.'

'And is it exciting during the Season? Did it make your head whirl? Aunt Diana wrote that she had been to so many parties lately that her head is spinning and her feet ache from all the dancing.'

Phoebe paused and placed her sewing in her lap. How did one begin to explain about a London Season and not give the wrong impression? Some parts of the Season were wonderful, but others were dreadful, and some even downright dull. What would a boy of his age understand about the horror of being cut and the necessity of appearing at the correct balls when the correct people were there—not before and certainly not after? Or the tedium of standing for hours in a receiving line? Or how could he understand the thrill of a new ball gown? Or the horror at discovering that that Season's proposed colours did not match her complexion. Or seeing her stepmother's despair when the cards and invitations stopped coming? Or how she suddenly became a wallflower because she no longer had a dowry and all the eligible men found other dance partners?

'I was once presented to Queen Charlotte,' she said carefully. The Court of St James was a suitable topic—full of possibilities for learning and without the necessity of touching on anything particularly personal.

'You have met the Queen?' Robert put his pencil down. 'Truly? Was anyone else there? Tell me! Tell me!'

'Once and very briefly. Several of the princesses were there as well. The ceremony is very long and one has to stand very still. I spent days practising my curtsy and, despite my stepmother's predictions, managed it without incident.' Phoebe smiled. 'My court dress was very heavy and my headdress pinched. I was pleased to be able to leave and to sit down in the carriage.'

'My mother was once presented at court. I know that.' A frown appeared between Robert's eyebrows as Phoebe went cold. His mother. How was she supposed to obey Mr Clare's orders, if Robert persisted in speaking of his mother? She might disagree with the orders, but Mr Clare's wishes did have to be respected in this. 'She used to speak of it when I was very little. I can remember that. She told me about all the bright lights and how people laughed and laughed.'

'Laughter is what I remember the most about my mother as well. Her silvery laugh.'

Robert picked up his pencil and drew several lines. 'My mother stopped laughing on the day I was born. She told me that once.'

'Your aunt was presented at court. We were speaking of that the other day, the day I decided to come up here.' Phoebe wished her shoulders felt more relaxed and her jaw less tense. Surely her words had been enough to turn the conversation from Robert's mother. And his father. 'We spoke about many things. Your aunt is enjoying London. All the parties, but most of all she likes Rotten Row and its carriages.'

Robert's mouth turned down. 'My mother's name was the Honourable Jayne Northfield and she danced beautifully. She was the Diamond of her season. A Nonesuch. An Incomparable.'

Jayne Northfield. They had been pupils together at Miss Finchley's Academy. Jayne's mother had been friends with Phoebe's stepmother. Jayne

Northfield, the toast of all the regiments in London and Bath. Wild Jayne with her throaty laugh. Phoebe knew bets had been laid at White's as to which Hussar she would marry. But then she had abruptly gone north, never finishing her Season, never returning to London. Phoebe had heard rumours of marriage, but nothing more.

The words died on Phoebe's lips. How the fates must be laughing. She had travelled all the way up here to nurse Jayne Northfield's child. She had never thought to ask Lady Coltonby about Mr Clare's wife, never thought her path would cross with Jayne's. It all made sense now why Mr Clare had had business dealings with her father. Jayne's father had probably engineered it. She should have thought about the possibility before, but it had never entered her head.

'If you were in the *ton*, you must have heard of her. Everyone knew her.' Robert gave her an imperious look and Phoebe knew she had seen the exact same expression on Jayne's face many years before.

'I…I…' Phoebe searched for words to describe their relationship. She could not call it a friendship. *Rivalry* was perhaps a better word, and Jayne had never liked a rival. But that was in the past, and now the poor woman was dead. 'Yes, I did know her.'

'Truly?' Robert leant forward, and the sulky expression vanished from his mouth. 'Was she as beautiful as they said?'

'From what I can remember…' Outwardly she was a beautiful person, but Phoebe had also witnessed the petty cruelties Jayne inflicted on those less fortunate than she. Everyone had expected great things, not least Jayne herself.

Phoebe and several of the other débutantes had danced a little jig when they had learnt that the beautiful Jayne had unexpectedly married a nobody and settled in Northumberland. It seemed poetic justice somehow. It had been wrong of her, but Phoebe's only defence was that she had been young.

She narrowed her eyes and tried to see if Robert reminded her at all of Jayne. His hands and perhaps the way he held his head, but she could see none of the malice in his eyes. Or maybe it was just her memory playing tricks.

'Are you quite well, Miss Phoebe?' Robert asked.

'I am perfectly well, but perhaps a little over-tired, Robert.' Phoebe searched her mind for a polite lie. 'I stayed up far too late last night, reading a novel. Perhaps we can have this conversation another time.'

'But you were my mother's friend?' Robert's

bottom lip trembled and he looked very much like he was about to have one of his fits again.

'I knew your mother.' Phoebe closed her eyes. She could see Jayne's face now, laughing as she confided in the number of beaux she had and whom she had stolen them from. Phoebe shook her head and willed the image to be gone. 'And, yes, she did dance beautifully. Everyone said so, even Mr Brummell and the Lady Patronesses at Almack's.'

Silently she prayed her words would suffice. It was wrong to speak ill of the dead. Wrong. She had never considered Jayne's fate before. Perhaps it showed what a wicked creature she was. She should have cared. From here onwards, she would adhere to Mr Clare's wishes and not speak of the woman. She offered up a promise, if only Robert would change the subject.

'Yes, my mother was beautiful once, but I can hardly remember her face. Sometimes, I worry that I might forget it altogether.' He closed his eyes and gave a wistful smile. His dark lashes stood out from the paleness of his skin. And his long-fingered hands grasped the coverlet. Jayne Northfield's hands. She was sure of it. 'I do not have a portrait of her. I would like one.'

'Surely your father…'

'Papa and I do not speak of it, but I would like one.' He paused. 'Do you think you could ask? He listens to you. I heard Jenny Satterwaite say that. You could make him come up here.'

'Robert, I could not go against your father's express wishes.'

'I suppose you are right, but I still worry. Do you think he will forget me when I die?'

'You are getting better, Robert. And now that you are eating your supper, you will grow big and strong. There will be no question of forgetting as you will be there to remind him.'

Phoebe put her hand to her forehead. The boy needed to be looked after properly. He needed someone who cared about him. She had to hang on to that thought. She swallowed hard and regained control of her emotions. Her responsibility was towards the boy. His mother's identity made no difference.

'Will you show me your picture of the carriage, then? I was in Tattersall's the day before I left. James wanted to look at horses. Perhaps, if I describe it, you might like to sketch that.'

'Do you think Papa might like to see one of my drawings?' A wistful note crept into Robert's voice. 'You could show him one and…'

'I am certain that he would.' Phoebe's neck muscles relaxed. They had safely negotiated the shoals of Robert's mother.

'Will you take it to him tonight?' Robert held out a piece of paper.

Phoebe glanced at the drawing. The temptation threatened to overwhelm her—a reason to see him, rather than send a written report. 'I can do. Soon you will be able to go downstairs yourself.'

'And will you help me get strong enough?'

'I will do my best. Your father will be so proud of you when it happens. We can make it a surprise. One evening, you can just come down with me.'

'That would be wonderful, Miss Phoebe.'

'Yes, it will be our secret.'

A loud cough made her jump. She turned to see Mr Clare standing in the doorway. His hair fell over his forehead, making him look younger somehow, but his eye was shadowed with pain and he leant heavily on the cane.

'Miss Benedict, is the patient improving? You did not come down last evening and I feared the worst.'

'I sent a note. My head pained me slightly… and I understood that you had a visitor.' She hated the white lie.

'It is far from being the same thing.' A smile

tugged at the corner of his mouth, turning him into the near double of his son. 'The chessboard stands waiting.'

'He grows stronger by the day.' Phoebe forced her voice to sound light. She tried not to think of the portrait in the hall of the younger Simon and how he must have turned Jayne's head. She wished that she had known him before. Phoebe glanced up at the ceiling and regained control of her thoughts. 'I am sure you will notice the difference soon.'

'Cook tells me that he has been complaining about the beef jelly again. Robert, I have spoken to you about this before.'

'I dislike beef jelly.' Robert's bottom lip trembled. 'Even when it is hot.'

'We must all eat things we dislike. There is a definite purpose behind beef jelly,' Mr Clare said, his brows drawing together.

'Robert, we agreed. You need to eat it, to keep your strength up…for the carriages.'

Phoebe looked from Robert to his father, and willed him to agree. The last thing they needed was another fit.

'Boys who refuse to eat beef jelly are rarely strong enough to do anything.'

'I will drive carriages when I get stronger.' Robert's expression mirrored his father's. 'Uncle promised. And he is going to get me a horse for my next birthday, if I do well at my studies.'

Mr Clare lifted one eyebrow. 'Coltonby is giving you a horse?'

'And a little pony cart. He promised.' Robert crossed his arms.

'He speaks of little else, Mr Clare.'

She met Mr Clare's gaze and inclined her head towards Robert. Mr Clare's face relaxed, and his smile lit up his face, making it seem years younger. Her heart appeared to have difficulties deciding how it would pound—either it went far too fast or far too slow.

'He wants to drive carriages?' Mr Clare said. 'We shall have to see about it. I have not checked your copy books lately, but a little more application to your studies would not go amiss, young man. You last report was truly awful.'

'But I am learning. I read aloud to Hannibal. He likes stories about battles the best.'

'And does the cat answer back?'

'Papa, you can be so silly. Cats can't talk.' Robert's cheeks became flushed with pleasure.

'I merely enquired. But if you can keep up with

your studies, we shall see. You need to concentrate on the mathematics.'

Phoebe risked a breath. Not an outright refusal. She wondered if Mr Clare knew how much his coming up here meant to his son? It was clear that Robert adored him. She knew the visit would be talked about and mulled over.

'I will, Papa. Because you don't need to eat beef jelly to do well at mathematics.'

'Do not be cheeky, young man. It is unbecoming.' Simon fought against the urge to smile. Despite Robert's illness, the boy had to understand that certain standards had to be upheld. Later he would enjoy the remark, but for now, Robert had to learn the boundaries. Some day, he would be in charge of his father's business empire and he had to understand the importance of getting sums and drawings done correctly.

'I eat it, but I don't like it. There is a difference.'

'I dislike hearing bad reports about you, Robert. See that it does not happen again.'

Robert bowed his head. 'Yes, sir, but it will not make me like beef jelly any better.'

Simon sighed inwardly. He would leave now before he grew exasperated at Robert's obstinacy. He started to make his excuses, but Miss

Benedict's mouth tightened mutinously. She took a half-step forward.

'Perhaps you would like to see the carriage that Robert has been drawing. He is quite skilled at making technical drawings. I have been very impressed.'

Simon paused, one hand on the doorframe, the other on his cane. 'Is he, indeed?'

'Yes, he is. He has spent hours working on them. He likes to get the proportions correct. And the details.'

'Some day I am going to have a carriage made from that exact drawing,' Robert chimed in.

'And here I thought he had been playing with the cat.'

'I have been doing that as well.' Robert's smile echoed his father's. 'Miss Phoebe has given me a bit of string and Hannibal likes to chase it.'

'The drawings, if you please, Miss Benedict.'

Phoebe passed the sheet of paper over to Simon. Their fingers touched and a wave of warmth passed up his arm. He frowned and attempted to concentrate on the drawing rather than on Miss Benedict's lips, turning the paper one way and then the other.

'You want to have a carriage made from this?'

'That's right.' Robert smiled. 'It is bound to be the best carriage ever.'

Simon gritted his teeth. He refused to give Robert false hope. How anyone could say the drawing was skilled! 'Your proportions are incorrect. The back wheels are too large. The carriage would topple over before it went five yards. Redo the drawing and I will look at it again. Then we will discuss about a carriage being made to your design.'

Robert's face fell. 'But, Papa…'

'I know you can do better than that, Robert. I have seen you draw better than that.'

Phoebe watched in horror as tears welled up in Robert's eyes. How could Mr Clare be so unkind? Robert needed to have dreams. She held her breath and waited to see if the St Vitus's Dance would return. However, Robert simply looked indignant.

'I did try. I know the wheels are wrong, but my hand wobbled. It is so hard to hold it still. It trembles.'

'And you can try again. You can do better. There's a good chap.' Mr Clare leaned forwards and put the drawing on the fire. In one brief flash of yellow orange, it was gone. 'I look forward to your next effort, Robert.'

Robert screwed up his nose and his bottom lip

trembled. 'The drawing was meant for Miss Phoebe. She didn't mind that the wheels were wobbly, did you?'

'No, Robert. I didn't.' Phoebe forced her lips to turn upwards and her voice to be light while inside she seethed.

'Miss Phoebe?' Mr Clare lifted an eyebrow. He inclined his head in her direction. 'I do apologise. I thought the drawing was merely a preliminary sketch. A design for *his* carriage. Undoubtedly Robert will do another for you. One with proper wheels. What is the point of producing second-rate work?'

'I will do another one. A better one.' Robert reached for his pencil, but Phoebe took it from him and shook her head. 'You will see! I can draw better!'

'Later. It is time for your rest.'

'I want to draw!'

'Robert wanted to do you a drawing.' Mr Clare's voice held a note of surprise. 'You should see the drawing of the house he did at Christmas. It was truly remarkable. He has the potential to be a great draughtsman when he puts his mind to it.'

'Papa says I might draw.'

'Mr Clare, are you quite finished?' Phoebe

crossed her arms. The man was insupportable. He behaved in such a high-handed fashion. Nearly causing another fit and then indulging the boy. Was it any wonder that the maids and footmen considered Robert difficult? All Robert wanted was a bit of consistency and caring. To think that she had longed to see the man.

'You think me hard, Miss *Phoebe*?' His voice was silken.

'I did not give you leave to use my name.' Phoebe kept her chin upright. 'Yes, life is hard, but do you have to make it harder? Robert is recovering from an illness.'

'I will not allow the boy to become an invalid. Standards must be kept. If you settle for second best, second best is what you get. People's lives will some day depend on Robert. Robert knows this.'

'I do indeed, Papa. The next drawing will be better. I promise.'

Settling for second best. The words pierced through Phoebe as she got the distinct impression he was speaking about more than Robert.

'It is time for Robert's rest. I must insist my schedule is strictly adhered to. Robert, you may draw later, but now you need to rest.'

With a great sigh, Robert put the pencil and

paper to one side and snuggled down in his blankets. 'Do I have to have my medicine?'

'Yes.' Phoebe held out the glass. Robert looked at it and then swallowed it without a murmur of protest.

'Are you a miracle worker, Miss Benedict?'

'Things become easy, Mr Clare, if proper attention is paid. A kind word can do as much as a harsh one.'

'Indeed, and what will you say to the widows and orphans when Robert gets the proportions of the bridge wrong?' His hand was on the door and he turned to go.

'Miss Phoebe, thank you for your story about my mother,' Robert murmured as his eyes closed. 'I like your stories. The Season sounds like a wonderful place.'

Phoebe forced her hands to smooth out the coverlet as she silently prayed that Mr Clare had missed Robert's words.

'Miss Benedict, perhaps you will indulge me with a moment of your time? Once you have settled the patient. I would hate to do anything to break your routine.'

Phoebe regarded him. He appeared the epitome of urbane perfection, but there was a hard glint in his eyes. Her insides trembled. 'If you wish…'

'Papa, Miss Benedict knew my mother. Is that not a wonderful coincidence? I feel certain that she will be able to tell me lots of stories.'

Phoebe looked from Robert to Mr Clare. Her heart sank as Mr Clare's face became blacker. Did Robert know about the prohibition? 'There is a simple explanation, Mr Clare.'

'I will be interested to hear it.' A muscle jumped in his cheek. 'But not here, not in front of Robert.'

'I need to get Robert settled.' Phoebe knew she was stalling for time.

'In my study.' Mr Clare turned on his heel and never acknowledged Robert's trembling smile.

'Miss Phoebe?' Robert said in a quiet voice. 'I am very pleased you are looking after me. You must not be cross. The drawing was awful.'

Phoebe knelt by Robert's bed. 'I am pleased as well. I look forward to the next picture you draw.'

'It will be much better. My father will be proud of me.'

'I know that.' Phoebe gritted her teeth. Something had to be done. Someone had to tell Mr Clare about how much his son needed his approval and how crushing his harsh treatment was. There had to be a way of reaching the man behind the mask, the man who she had glimpsed that first night, the man who had played a game of chess with her and who took pleasure in music. 'Your father is proud of you.'

'If he is so proud of me, why won't he stay and answer my questions?'

Phoebe regarded the closed door. 'That is not something I can answer.'

'And, Miss Phoebe, you are going to stay, aren't you? I would not like it if you left.'

'Why would I go? I gave your aunt my word I would stay until you were better.'

'Papa looked furious. He hates it when I mention Mama.' Tears shone in Robert's eyes. 'I should have remembered that. I don't want to get you in trouble, Miss Phoebe. I didn't think.'

'You did not cause any trouble, Robert.' Phoebe regarded the closed door. 'You behaved perfectly properly.'

'His face looked worse than when he found out that I had run away from school.'

'He is your father. He worries about you. Now go to sleep.'

Phoebe drew the curtains closed, sending the room into shadow. Why did Mr Clare take out his grief on his son? She would not apologise.

Chapter Eight

'Why did you speak to Robert about his mother?' The words were out of Simon's mouth before Phoebe had closed the study door. A tiny frown appeared between her brows. She had stopped to remove her apron, and her dress hung softly about her body, accentuating her curves.

'He asked me.'

Silently he cursed. He had been sharper than he had intended with Robert because he had wanted Miss Benedict to see how well the boy could draw. He had planned to spend the afternoon with them. Throughout yesterday while he was supposed to have been attending to business, he had had a great longing to hear her voice, and to see her smile. And all the while she had been telling tales to Robert about his mother.

His eye and shoulder coursed with pain and he struggled to stand upright. All he had worked for with Robert and his memories of his mother might be undone by a few words. He wanted Robert to grow up without remembering the cruel words his mother had been capable of, or the hurts she had inflicted. Or the part his father had played in the sorry saga. The best he could hope for was that it was a pretty tale for his son and for it to go no further. He had given her a distinct warning. Robert's mother was not to be discussed, but within a few days she had disobeyed him. How much longer could he keep the truth from Robert? And how much longer would Robert be his?

Would Miss Benedict guess the truth and ask the inevitable question? Did she know the tales that had circulated and why Jayne had fled up north? Jayne had never denied her flirtations. She always maintained that she needed them as he was far too concerned with his machines and making sure they were well provided for. Would Miss Benedict see what he feared—that Robert did not resemble him in the slightest? And how could he ask her?

'How well did you know his mother? Do you even know her name?'

She tilted her head to one side. 'Is it important?'

'That is no answer, Miss Benedict, but you appear to have entertained Robert with fairy tales of his mother. Lies.'

'Jayne Northfield was among the débutantes in my first Season.' Miss Benedict's eyes glared back at him as she firmly shut the door. 'We were known to each other from school, but not too close. We were never bosom friends and we never corresponded. I had no idea what happened to her after she departed from the London Season. People speculated, but I was pleased she had followed her heart.'

Known, but not close. Simon regarded the woman. There was more to this story. He could tell from the way her mouth pursed. Had they been close once? Jayne had a great habit of making enemies out of women. She had demanded that all attention be lavished on her and had always tried to cut her rivals down. Simon had done his best, but there was more to his life than dancing on the whims of a discontented and disappointed woman. He had the lives of his workers to consider.

'And what did you tell Robert about his mother? Against my direct orders?'

'I merely told Robert that his mother was a good dancer, a fact that is undisputed.' Her head was up and her gold-tinted brown hair hung about her ears. Defiant. Challenging. 'He asked. I did not volunteer the information. Would you have me lie?'

'I have never disputed it, but why did you feel it necessary to impart this information to Robert?'

'What else should I have said? She was his mother. He asked me if I knew her.'

'Have you often spoken to Robert about his mother?'

'This was the first time. I was unprepared.' She lifted her head and her direct gaze met his. 'You need not worry. I told him pleasant things.'

Simon nodded and longed to ask how Jayne had hurt this woman. He could well imagine his late wife's cruelty. It would have been of the thoughtless kind—a remark over Miss Benedict's height or figure, perhaps. He doubted that Miss Benedict had been a success at the Season, not in the way Jayne had been. Jayne had told the stories over and over again. Jayne had had the ability to be all sweetness and light in public. Her true barbs she saved for those closest to her. 'My wife was unique in many ways.'

Phoebe's smile turned bittersweet and he knew that his wife must have hurt her. Silently he cursed. He had hoped after all these years, he would stop encountering people whom Jayne had been cruel to. He wanted to take the hurt and add it to the blackness in his soul. 'You should have no fear, Mr Clare. I seldom speak ill of the dead.'

'That is good to hear.' Simon regarded the base of her throat where her pulse was clearly visible. He hated that he wanted to crush Phoebe Benedict to him and obliterate all memory of his wife.

'Naturally you wish your son to think the best of her,' she continued on, adopting a faintly pious expression, oblivious to his inner torment.

'You mistake me, Miss Benedict. I would prefer it if Robert did not think of her at all.'

'But she was his mother.' Miss Benedict's mouth dropped open. 'It is only natural that he should wonder. Children need stories of their parents. They long for them. They want to know where they have come from.'

'She was my wife and has been dead for nearly four and a half years.' Simon paused. He ran his hand through his hair. He had no desire to have this conversation with Miss Benedict, or anyone else for that matter. How could he explain about the awful travesty that had been his marriage? How could he explain about the ugliness inside him? The acts he had to live with? 'One must get on with living, Miss Benedict. I wish his face to be turned towards the future and its prospects.'

'I understand.' She stood before him, her hands were pressed together. Her face took on an earnest expression. 'Have you forgiven her yet for leaving you in that way? I doubt she wanted to die. The Jayne Northfield I knew was the essence of life.'

Simon turned away and regarded the embers of the fire. Forgive Jayne for dying? Dying was the least of her transgressions.

God help him, he had thought it a merciful release. It had been something, if he was honest, that he had longed for. The woman he had been infatuated with had vanished a long time before that…if she had ever existed. All that had been left was a bitter husk of a person who took little joy in the world around her and delighted in hurting those closest to her. He knew he should feel more sorrow, more remorse, but it was impossible. His one feeling had been and remained relief. It was part of this great twisted scarring inside him, his great ugliness. He should have been a better husband, a better lover, a better man and maybe none of it would have happened.

And he knew that however much he tried, if he spoke of her to Robert, always the bad would be lurking behind the good. How could he lie to his son? No, it was much easier to pretend that she had not existed. It kept the ugliness inside him, rather than infecting Robert or reminding him of her cruelty.

'You did not know her after her riding accident.'

The flames danced and spun, throwing long shadows against the fireplace wall. Shadowy shapes that reached out with their arms.

'Surely she could not have changed that much. How bad was the accident?'

'She lost the use of her legs. For most of Robert's life, she was incapable of walking, let alone dancing. She was a prisoner in the house. And she hated it.'

'I had no idea.' Miss Benedict's hand clasped her throat. 'We were not close. We never corresponded. Surely it is good for Robert to have pleasant memories of his mother…from a time when she was happy.' Her brow wrinkled as if she had to think of one. 'Jayne had a very pleasing laugh and the most musical of voices.'

'My wife laughed little after her riding accident.' Simon struggled to keep his voice steady. Miss Benedict had such an earnest expression on her face as if the simple memory could undo all the harm. There was no need to explain about the confrontation he had had with Jayne before she had left for riding. How he had demanded an explanation over the indiscreet letters she had sent to that soldier. And how he had taken delight in telling her that the soldier had been captured.

'She must have laughed with Robert.' Miss Benedict's white teeth caught her bottom lip. 'She was his mother. It is unnatural not to laugh with your child.'

Simon's throat worked up and down. He could not think of one instance where Jayne had taken pleasure in Robert. For months after the birth, she had been listless, refusing even to look at her child. Eventually she treated Robert like some sort of exotic pet to be indulged whenever the whim took her and then pushed away. Shortly before Jayne's death, Simon had found Robert weeping about his mother and the way she pinched him. He wanted Robert to have a fresh start and to grow up without the black shadows hanging about him.

How could he explain any of this to her? Miss Benedict could have no conception of the harm Jayne had tried to do. And it was in his past. He wanted to look towards the future. 'As you said, Miss Benedict, you did not know my wife once she came up here to Northumberland.'

'This is true, but…' She held out her hands and her face took on an earnest expression. 'People do not change that much. I know they don't. Jayne's parents had indulged her far too much as a young girl and she was a bit wild, but she loved life.'

Simon forced his shoulders back. She would have to know. He would have to reveal a bit. He braced himself for her recoil of horror. 'My wife died because she chose to sit in front of an open window on a blustery day.'

'Surely it was an accident. An oversight by one of the maids.'

Simon fought to keep the bitterness from his voice. Suddenly he wanted this woman who stood in front of him like some avenging angel to know and to understand.

'I found her drenched and shivering. She had doused her gown with a pitcher of water. She confessed before she died.'

She put her hand to her mouth. 'This explains why you were worried about Robert on the first night. But perhaps it was an accident.'

Simon forced the anger back down his throat. He could not shout at this woman. She understood nothing. Jayne never regained consciousness beyond whispering her damning final confession.

She never saw that it was the young doctor who came. All she had wanted was a bit of male company. To be admired and petted because he could not give her the attention she craved. No man could. 'I had refused to take her other complaint of nerves seriously. She thought she could force me. She did it to punish me.'

He clamped his mouth shut. The last quarrel would haunt him for ever. How she had taunted him about his devotion to machines, and how he had refused to indulge her. She had seen how his father had suffered from lung fever and knew of the epidemic. But still she had insisted and had finally thought to force him. The worst part was that a little piece of him was pleased that her plans had gone far further than she had hoped. In the end, she had looked so peaceful, so like the young girl he had admired before they had married. He refused to think about what had happened two years later when her lover had returned.

'But why does that mean you have to punish your son?'

Simon slammed the door of his memory shut, turned away. 'I am not punishing Robert. I am making things easier for him.'

'He is naturally curious about his mother. Surely

a few light tales about her early life cannot hurt. It will save him brooding.'

'Robert is far too young to brood. If that is your best point, then I suggest our conversation is at end.' Simon made a dismissive motion with his hand. Then he picked up a piece of paper and pretended to study it. Surely Miss Benedict would take the hint and depart?

'Robert is growing up. He wants to know what his mother looked like.'

'I am well aware of how old Robert is.'

Simon eyed her over the paper. Her cheeks had become flushed pink and her eyes full of crusading zeal, impervious to the most crushing insult.

'He is a young man, not a baby. He is your son, Mr Clare. You must do something. He dotes on you. God knows the reason why.' Her hand went out to reach for him, but at his look it fell back to her side. 'Your son. Your flesh and blood.'

Simon turned away from her glowing eyes and her easy words. She did not know how much he wanted to believe her. Instead he forced himself to remember Jayne's final plea to him—look after my son and forgive my sins. Her last little bit of spite. Every day, he watched and waited for Robert to show him the truth, but he only seemed to look less like a Clare and more like the man who lay in an unmarked grave in the churchyard, the soldier Jayne had been planning on deserting him and Robert for.

Simon banished his thoughts and regained control of his emotions. He stood looking at the fire for a long time, willing her to leave him in peace, but she stood there looking at him, her slate-grey eyes smouldering with an intense emotion.

'Robert needs to live in the present and the future. His mother was in the past.'

'How can we hope to live for the future if we ignore the past?' she whispered. 'Please understand that I meant no harm. Children are curious about their parents.' Her eyes became shadowed. 'When I was about Robert's age, I longed to know everything about my mother.'

'And were you told?'

'My stepmother sent me away to school. Miss Finchley's Academy for Young Ladies. Thankfully, my grandmother used to come and visit. She'd spend hours telling me about my mother and how my father married her. A truly romantic tale. They met when he rescued her dog in Hyde Park. It was one of the matches of the Season that year. From the way she told things, I thought all I had to do was to go to London to meet my prince.'

'Did you enjoy your time in the London Season, Miss Benedict, after these pleasant tales that your grandmother spouted? Or did she raise your expectations too high?'

'Some parts of it were very pleasant.' She gave a half-smile and made a helpless gesture. 'You would not know it to look at me now, but Jayne and I were rivals for the title of Diamond during that Season.'

'I had not realised.' Simon regarded her through narrowed eyes. Miss Benedict, a Diamond? He had considered her a bit like Diana—unsuccessful, a wallflower, someone who was far from at ease with society, despite the figure that she tried to hide. Instead, it would seem that she had been a woman who shone in society, Jayne's rival. And Jayne had been the toast of several regiments. But what had happened? She should have married, and married brilliantly. Had she turned up her nose too many times? He wanted to search for the bad points, but his eyes kept returning to her enticing curves.

'My hair has turned a bit less golden with age, Mr Clare, and my figure has become fuller than many would consider fashionable, but I do speak the truth. You can ask Lord Coltonby. He was there. There is a reason why débutantes are in the first flower of their youth.' She gave a small shrug.

Her neck arched slightly and he could detect a small pulse beating at the base of her throat. Her hair sparkled in the fire with rich golden highlights. The blood quickened in his veins but he dampened it down.

'I believe you do yourself a discourtesy, Miss Benedict. Your figure could never be called unfashionable.'

She raised her eyes, steel grey where myriad colours played and clashed. He wondered that he had not noticed before.

'My point is that for some the *ton* is a very pleasant experience—balls, parties and the general gaiety of life.'

'If it was so pleasant, why are you not married? Did you not meet your fairy-tale prince after all?'

'My time in the *ton* ended with my father's death. Have you ever experienced the *ton*, Mr Clare?' She tapped her finger against her mouth. 'I feel certain that we never met back then.'

'My wife came up here to visit relatives. It was a whirlwind romance. Later my sister went to London at my wife's request. Diana found it less than useful. I have no wish for fantasies to fill Robert's head. His place will be here at my side in the north-east. I have built an empire for him.'

'You need not worry about fantasies from me. I have also experienced the cruelty of society. After my father died, the invitations dried up and former friends shunned our door as if somehow we harboured a contagion.'

'I am sorry.'

'It was the worst for my stepmother. She lived for her afternoon visits. Economy came hard to her. For the first time in her life, she had to forgo new ball gowns. My stepbrothers had to be taught by the local vicar rather than at Eton, but even that did not allow for new ball gowns.'

Her mouth was pinched and Simon knew there was a great deal she was not saying. She spoke of hardship to her stepmother, but not to herself.

'And you? What did you give up?' Simon said the words softly, watching her. 'What dreams became dust?'

Her hand went to the door as if she wanted to escape, as if she needed to be away from him. 'Is there anything else you wish to discover or may I return to my duties in the sickroom? Robert may be asleep, but there is plenty to keep me busy. The next time Robert asks me a question, I will tell him, no, his father has forbidden it. I will then check with you to see if the subject meets with your approval. Is that what you are saying to me?'

She was trying to avoid the question. She was trying to hide something. A cold anger filled Simon. This woman was attempting to play games. No one played those sorts of games with him. Simon took a step closer to Miss Benedict. He noticed how her hair curled at her temples in little ringlets. How her breath filled her chest. He wanted to reach out and capture one of the ringlets. His fingers itched to crush her body to him. Simon restrained the urge and contented himself with a nod. There would be no dishonour in this house. Propriety would win the day, but neither would he marry again. Not even for Miss Benedict.

'I would like your report in person, if you please, Miss Benedict. There may be areas that I wish to question you about. A written one is most unsatisfactory.'

'As you wish.' Her words were submissive, but her eyes flashed anger. 'Was there anything else you wished to discuss with me?'

'That will do for the present.'

The click of the door resounded behind her.

'Miss Benedict! At six precisely!'

But the only reply was the sound of her footsteps going up the stairs. Simon put his hands against the mantelpiece and lowered his head to the cool marble. What had he done? What box in his memory had he opened?

'And he asked no more questions about his mother, so your concern appears to have been unfounded.' Phoebe finished her recital of the day's events that evening. Ever since she had left Mr Clare's study this afternoon, all she had thought about was how to make the report right. How to keep her temper. The incident this afternoon was as much her fault as Mr Clare's. She might not agree with his rules, but it was his house.

She needed to be here. There was nowhere else to go. She had to face the cold hard facts, just as she had faced them the night her father had disappeared and she had been the one to discover his final note. It had taken her a long time before she had forgiven him. Even now she doubted if she understood what had driven him that night. Surely he had to understand that people were more important than possessions and nothing mattered as long as they were together. 'His mother was merely a passing topic of conversation. Something to make you take notice. He seeks your regard and if he can't have that, your attention will do.'

'And that makes it right, is that what you are saying?' Mr Clare stood there, implacable.

'You rarely go to see him. He asks about you. He wants your approval. He hungers for it and all you do is throw his picture in the fire.' Phoebe paused and looked him squarely in the face. She had to seize the opportunity. She had to make him aware of how Robert felt about his father. 'Is that fair, Mr Clare? You threw a picture on the fire.'

'He can draw better. Robert is lazy unless you give him tasks. He knows how to draw carriages. I have seen his work before. He needs to maintain standards. Life is very harsh for those who do not measure up.'

'How many drawings have you done since your accident? How many times have you been to the mine?' She placed her hands on her hips and gritted her teeth. 'Robert is a boy recovering from a serious illness. You ask far too much of him. Do you not remember what it was like to be a boy of ten?'

She waited as emotions flashed across Mr Clare's face. When was the last time anyone had really defied him? And what had happened to them? The silence seemed to stretch, but she resisted the temptation to fill it. He had to make a sign that he understood. She refused to back down or give in. She knew that he cared about his son.

'This is why I have asked you for reports on his illness,' he said finally in a low voice. 'Has it ever occurred to you, Miss Benedict, that climbing the stairs is difficult for me? By the time I am in Robert's room, my entire body aches. My temper becomes short. I hate my infirmities, all the more because they are self-inflicted.'

A stab of pity coursed through Phoebe, but she damped it down.

'You are using your injuries as an excuse. How many weeks has it been? Robert needs you to try. Your example will inspire him.'

'Do you seek to lecture me, now? Are you a doctor?' Mr Clare's black eyebrows came down. His face looked so fierce that Phoebe's knees trembled.

'Someone has to!' Phoebe took a step closer. The air between them crackled. Deep inside her, something stirred and sprang to life, threatened to swamp her senses. 'You are like a great black beast who sulks in the corner, threatening people, shouting at them when you do not get your own way. Do you know how many staff changes this house has gone through since I have been here? Your own valet threatens to quit once a day.'

'Ponsby is well paid. He stays with me out of the need for coin.'

'How much better it would be if he stayed with you out of respect!'

'I do not recognise the picture you paint!'

'But it is true. Ask yourself why so many staff leave. It is because you are overbearing and short tempered. Quick to find fault if something disturbs you, but willing to overlook other things that you should be concerned about.'

'How dare you! You overstep the mark, Miss Benedict. What do you know of my staffing problems? What do you know of my situation? Do you know how much my ribs hurt? Or how much my eye aches? I am no martyr, Miss Benedict.'

'But why make others hurt? Why do you allow your fiendish temper full rein? What are you fighting against? You claim to have despised your wife's self-pity, but seem to have no hesitation about indulging in it yourself.'

'Am I a fiend, Miss Benedict? Is that how you see me? It is a wonder you stay under my roof.'

Phoebe put her hand over her mouth. 'I should

never have said that. It was cruel and uncalled for. Pray forgive me.'

'You are quite right to speak plainly, Miss Benedict, I can admire a person who speaks their mind.' Mr Clare's words were easy, but the pain was clear in his eye. Her words had cut him far deeper than she had intended. She wanted to reach out and smooth the creases away. She wanted to feel his warm skin under her fingertips. Phoebe drew in a sharp breath. When had she started thinking such wanton thoughts? She wrapped her arms about her waist and turned from him. Every particle of her being was aware of him as a man. This was not his fault, but hers. She wanted him to notice her as a woman and it frightened her.

'Can we try again please, Mr Clare? I was wrong to criticise.' She held out her hand, but he ignored it, standing there, proud and dignified. The air between them settled. She knew that it should be a good thing, but a stab of disappointment coursed through her. 'It is, of course, your right to have reports about your son. My stepmother rarely came to the nursery after my father died… It is simply that Robert was so pleased to see you in the sickroom. This afternoon he spoke of you with great longing.'

'Has he started drawing again?' Mr Clare's voice was a hoarse croak.

'He refuses to show me the latest one, but he does appear determined. He has thrown away six drawings. Crumpling them up when his hand trembles.'

'He is learning not to accept second best.'

'He could become frustrated.'

'Robert has talent, Miss Benedict. He cannot simply be satisfied with his basic achievements. He is ten, not five.'

'But he could do better with a word of encouragement. There is much to like in his drawings, even if the wheels are slightly off.'

'I do not give false words of praise, Miss Benedict. When he makes sketches of the machines that he wishes to have built they must be accurate. Lives will be dependent on him.'

'When that day comes, I am sure he will be accurate. We are not speaking about a drawing for an engine. We are speaking about a young boy's drawings.'

'They are the same to my mind. He must learn. I did.'

'Is it because it worked for you?' She raised her chin and stared at him. Her heart bled for the boy he must have been. What hard lessons had he been forced to learn? 'Why, then, are you accepting second best with your eye? With your arm? Why haven't you seen a specialist? Why have you given up?'

'My eye and Robert's drawings are two entirely separate matters.' He turned away from her. 'My temper has only become more uncertain since the accident, rather than less. I am not one to bear such things patiently, but neither will I clutch at false hope.'

'You refuse to let Robert give up, so why have you? Dr MacFarlane said—'

He hit his hands together. 'I accept my disability. I can only work with those tools that I am given.'

'It is only because you allow it to be so.' She took a step forwards so that she stood toe to toe with him. He had to listen to her. He could not simply turn away. She refused to let him. 'You have a choice. How can you ask Robert to achieve so much when you refuse to try at all?'

Every particle of her being was intensely aware of him and the power he exuded, but she forced her body to stay in front of his. 'You have allowed your injury to dominate you, rather than working around it. You choose to hug the hurt to you. You make demands of Robert that you do not make of yourself.'

'Will you be silent?' His hands gripped her shoulders. The heat of him burnt through her clothes. 'Or do I have to stop your mouth?'

'Someone has to say these things.' She stared up at him. His mouth was inches from hers. 'You stomp around, and feel sorry for yourself, when it might only take a simple consultation to put things right. What are you frightened of?'

'I am not frightened of anything,' he rasped out.

'Then why won't you? Go on, I dare you! Go, see the specialist. See what he says. Don't give up before you have even tried.'

'And that is all you want? All you desire?' His voice was a soft purr, one that played along her nerves, enveloping her in its silken caress.

'Yes.' She glanced up and saw his face blazing dangerously. She swallowed hard and knew she could not move. His intensity had lit something deep within her. She lifted her face. Her tongue flicked over her lips. 'That is everything I want.'

His mouth swooped down and claimed her, branded her, and she knew her words were a lie. She did want something else. Phoebe stilled as warmth pulsated through her, searing her with its fierceness. She made a little noise in the back of her throat. Then she pushed her hands upwards and against him to save her sanity, her dignity, but his lips called to something deep within her, turning the warmth into a raging inferno. Her hand sank into his hair and held him there.

The kiss lengthened, deepened. Her lips parted and he feasted, devoured her like a starving man. This was no gentle persuasion or chaste kiss, but the sort of kiss a pirate captain might bestow. Plundering and taking. And she wanted more. His arms went around her and held her body against his, her breasts crushed against his chest, her melting softness meeting his hard body. His lips trailed down her throat as he entangled his fingers in her glorious hair. How long it lasted, she had no idea. Time had ceased to have any meaning.

The mantel clock chimed the hour, bringing them back to reality. He stepped away from her, a stunned look on his face.

'Miss Benedict…I…'

Phoebe looked at him, turned on her heel and fled.

Chapter Nine

Phoebe tossed her belongings into her portmanteau. How could she have done it? She had kissed Simon Clare. Not only kissed him, but had pressed her body to his. She was wanton and had abandoned all reason. Was it any wonder that he had looked at her with such a stricken expression? He must have been appalled at what she had done. She was. She had broken every precept of polite behaviour.

She had thrown herself at him. Demanded his kiss.

Her hand flew to her mouth. It was full and slightly bruised, and ached, though not unpleasantly.

She had been kissed before, long ago but never like that. Never with that dark hunger that called to her innermost being. Why had he done that? Had he felt sorry for her? What was worse was that she had responded, behaved like some loose woman. If he had not stepped away, she dreaded to think what could have happened. How could she ever look at him again, knowing what she had done? Phoebe ducked her head, wishing the floor would open up and swallow her. She could no longer remain here. Her moment of madness would hang between them for ever.

'Forgive me, Miss Benedict.' His voice rasped from the doorway of her room. 'I have behaved reprehensibly.'

She froze, with her nightdress half in and half out of the portmanteau. Her other garments lay haphazardly on the bed. She willed the voice to be only her fevered imagination. Then turned slowly and saw him—his face was creased with pain as he again leant heavily on his cane. His breath came swiftly as if he had run up the stairs, had tried to catch her.

'There is nothing to forgive, Mr Clare.' She put the nightdress down and attempted to ignore the sudden pounding of her heart. He had come up here. And the aching need inside her grew. She had thought herself safe for a few moments, and that she would find in those few moments enough strength to walk away. It was far too soon to confront him. 'Pray do not dwell on the matter.'

His good eye had become like smooth green

glass. 'That was not meant to happen. It will not happen again. My touch no doubt repulses you. My injuries have rendered me into a fiend, as you so rightly called me earlier. There are times when I no longer recognise myself. I should never have touched you. You had the right to be safe in this house without fearing for your honour.'

'It is not that.' Phoebe concentrated on the pleats in her skirt and tried to think how to put it, how to describe this dark desire that seemed to have infected her. She had behaved inexcusably and without proper decorum. She knew if she stayed that she would want it to happen again, and that was impossible. She had no expectations of marriage and she refused to bring shame on her family.

Surely he could not think himself a fiend? It made no sense. With a start, she realised that she had stopped noticing his scar days ago. There was much more to Simon Clare than what his face looked like. Or how he carried his body. All she noticed was his raw masculinity.

'You need not feel ashamed. I know what my injuries have turned me into. I have been told...'

'Who told you that?' Phoebe crossed her arms. 'A friend or a foe? From what I understand, your scars came honourably. Your outward appearance has nothing to do with your inward character.'

'A young lady of my acquaintance—the Honourable Miranda Bolt.' His mouth twisted. 'She made a pointed reference to it. Several references. It was made very clear that, despite my wealth, she could not bear the thought of me touching her.'

'She should learn to keep her mouth shut. And since when does one foolish woman's opinion hold sway over others? Let yourself be judged by your actions, not your outward appearance. You obtained those scars honourably.'

'My scars came from my own arrogance, Miss Benedict. I have never sought to disguise the fact. It was only through the grace of God and Coltonby's quick thinking that I was not killed. I thought I could control my travelling engine, but I couldn't.'

'And what happened?'

'The boiler exploded because the pressure was too high. I was thrown through the air as boiling water spewed everywhere. No one was killed, but Coltonby's horses had to be put down. Very expensive horses they were, too. I compounded the problem by attempting to oversee the removal of the engine. One of the belts slipped and, without thinking, I rushed forwards to steady it. If it had swung loose, I dread to think of what could have happened to the men and the reputation of the mine. I have no one to blame except my over-whelming hubris.'

'None of this makes you a fiend. It simply makes you injured in a terrible accident. Thankfully it was not worse.' She stared at him. He could easily have died. Either time. 'You have not lost a limb. You retain the function of your brain. It is better than many hope for. The streets of London are becoming littered with the poor soldiers from the war.'

'You know nothing of my injuries.' His hand gripped his cane until the white of his knuckles shone. 'Nothing of what I have suffered. I did consult doctors in Newcastle at first. They tell me there is little hope. My injuries are a judgment, a warning not to meddle with forces that I don't understand.'

'I do know that you have not been made into some sort of "hell-born imp" who must be kept away from society. And maybe you ought to make sure you know the exact forces before you experi-ment, rather than afterwards.' She put her hand to her mouth. There was something about Mr Clare that made her speak far more plainly than normally. It was far easier to speak plainly than to give in to the temptation and to beg for his kiss. 'Now if you excuse me, it is best that I finish packing. I wish to be gone as soon as possible. It is for the best. Every time we encounter each other, we…fight.'

'We were not fighting in my study.' He ran a hand through his hair, making it stand on end. Her hand curled around the nightdress as she fought the urge to bury her fingers in his hair, to smooth back that white blaze. 'I behaved most inexcusably and must beg your humble pardon.'

'There is nothing to forgive, Mr Clare,' Phoebe said when she finally felt in control of her emotions again. Mr Clare apologising! 'I have been kissed before. Several times. I knew what I was doing and I know how to avoid such things. It is best not mentioned again, that is all.'

She straightened her skirt and reached for her handkerchiefs. It was best not to mention that the kisses she had endured before had been nothing like his soul-drugging touch. Neither did she expect some sort of offer because of the kiss. She had voluntarily gone into an unmarried man's house to look after his son. That fact alone put her outside society's precepts—something that she did not need her stepmother or anyone else to tell her. She had played with fire and, thankfully, only her fingers had been singed.

He had moved inside the door and the walls seemed to close in around her, pushing her towards him. She bunched a handkerchief up and threw it into the portmanteau.

'Is there something else you wish to say to me? This is my bedroom. Hardly the proper place to conduct a conversation.'

'There are things that need to be said.'

'I think we have done all the speaking that we need to.' She glared at him. She had little doubt about what was coming next. She could hear it all now. About how sorry he was, and what a mistake it had been, and how they both should forget it ever happened, but wouldn't she please leave? Or, worse yet, would she like to become his mistress? She had not sunk that low. She refused to drag her family through the mud. 'This is hardly an appropriate place for a conversation. Gentlemen do not barge into ladies' bedrooms.'

He withdrew his pocket watch. 'You have ten minutes to refresh yourself, Miss Benedict. If you do not come down, I will be quite happy to have the conversation here, but I will not be held accountable for the consequences.'

He gave a pointed look at the bed, and then left the room, closing the door behind him with a distinct click.

Simon paced the floor of the drawing room. Would she actually appear? It would not have been seemly to stay. The bed was far too tempting. Two steps more and he would have kissed her again. Thoroughly this time. Without stopping, without pausing to ask if he might. He would have given full vent to the dark passion bubbling up inside him. He could not remember when he had desired a woman so much. He would have made her his.

He also knew who she was. He could not plead ignorance. She had a good family name. His sister had sent her to look after Robert on the understanding that Miss Benedict would be treated properly. And he had given in to his passion, come close to ruining her. The time away from her had only increased his desire for her. He was left with no option. He had to act.

A soft rap made him look up. Miss Benedict stood in the doorway, bonneted and enveloped in her travelling cloak. Her portmanteau was clutched in front of her. The harpy had returned. Simon gave a half-smile.

There was only one course of action he could take.

'Miss Benedict, you are a minute late.' He replaced his watch in his pocket and gestured towards the sofa. 'Come, take off your bonnet and cloak. You are safe.'

'I will save you the trouble of asking me to depart, Mr Clare.' Her eyes blazed unexpected defiance. She ignored the armchair and her hands kept tight hold of her portmanteau. 'I will leave voluntarily. You may arrange for a coach. Or else I will take the mail coach. I am not fussy. You may explain to Robert that I have gone back to see his aunt. The tale will have to suffice. In time, he will get better. He is out of danger and one of the maids can look after his needs. He appears to like Jenny Satterwaite. I suggest her.'

'Depart? I never took you for a milk-sop miss who ran at the first sign of trouble. Hear me out.' His insides twisted and cracked. Leaving? She had not even waited to hear his proposal. His plan. He was not a cad. He knew full well what he had done and what he wanted to do. And that he could never treat a lady like that. Miss Benedict above all things was a gently bred lady. He was prepared to accept the consequences of his actions. How could she think otherwise?

'I will listen and then I will leave. It is for the best.'

'Robert remains an invalid.' Simon kept his voice steady. 'You will be breaking your promise—to him, to Diana…to me.'

Phoebe moved away from him. 'He is well enough to cope. Time is a great healer. The change within him over the past few days is astonishing.'

'You offer the flimsiest of pretexts. You sought a reason to depart, simply because you did not get your own way over my seeing a specialist.' His gaze narrowed on her. 'I did apologise, Miss Benedict. It was most reprehensible of me to behave in such a fashion.'

'I have no doubt you will find someone else, someone more amenable to your way of thinking. Someone who did not know your wife and can tell no tales to Robert. Someone who will not badger and bully you…' Her voice faltered and faded.

'What if I don't want anyone else? What if I want you?' Simon's whisper echoed throughout the room. He willed her to understand what he was asking. Until that moment in the study, he had planned on remaining a widower for ever. All that had changed. He had to do the honourable thing, but he also had to keep her safe. He refused to repeat his past mistakes.

'I beg your pardon.' Miss Benedict shook her head. 'Surely you must understand why it is impossible for me to stay. We cannot go on as before.'

'Before you came, the household was a shambles. Now, I get hot water for my shave on time. Cook made execrable meals that are now more than edible. Jenkins appears to be in a happier frame of mind. And the change in Robert has been nothing short of a miracle. Why would I want to throw that away?'

'I hardly think your shaving arrangements have anything to do with me.' Her knuckles were white against the dark leather handle of the portmanteau. 'And no one will know about what just happened here. You must forget it. I already have. Please allow me to retain a little honour. I can be no man's mistress.'

As she said the words, she knew she lied. The searing kiss would be played over and over in her mind. She wanted to feel his lips against hers again, his hands entangled in her hair. But she also knew it was wrong, and she would be branded a disgrace to her family. It certainly wouldn't help her stepbrothers' careers.

'You call me stubborn. It is the perfect solution. I need a housekeeper, and Robert needs a mother. You need a home. You would not have proposed this solution to my sister if you had another place to go.' His eyes raked her form. 'You are well on the shelf and are unlikely to be called a Nonesuch even if you do re-enter the Marriage Mart.'

'Marriage Mart?' Phoebe shook her head as the room reeled. She had to have heard incorrectly. He did not want to marry her. Men like him did not marry <u>impoverished spinsters</u>, even when they had kissed them. She swallowed hard and tried to rid herself of the giddy feeling. 'What precisely are you asking me, Mr Clare?'

'Is it not obvious, Miss Benedict? I am asking you to marry me. You are hardly mistress material.'

'Marry me?' Phoebe whispered, staring at Simon Clare. Of all the things she had guessed that he might wish to speak about, she had never considered a proposal of marriage. He had no need to make the offer. Society would not expect it. 'What sort of <u>fustian</u> nonsense is this, Mr Clare?'

'A practical solution to the situation we find ourselves in. I require a housekeeper and a companion for my son. I believe you will do both with great skill and efficiency. I am full of admiration for what you have achieved in the short while you have been here.'

Phoebe pressed her lips together. Marry for duty and responsibility. Somehow she doubted that his proposal to Jayne Northfield had been this matter of fact. It had probably been full of romance, going down on one knee while music played softly in the background and the stars twinkled down on them. Some people's lives were made for romance, while others worried about the cleaning and the mending.

Phoebe swallowed, trying to rid her throat of its sudden lump. She had wanted romance once. Wanted it still.

It bothered her that she begrudged the dead woman so many things—her son, and most of all her husband. Jayne had belonged somewhere and Phoebe belonged nowhere. Nobody would mourn her if she was gone. She wanted to think that she was a better person than that. Her grip on the portmanteau became so tight that she wondered the handle remained whole as she tried to think of a reason to refuse.

'You make the marriage sound practical, a business arrangement. You are seeking to employ a housekeeper.' She forced her voice to be light.

'There are any number of women I can recommend. Shall we advertise for one?'

'You mistake me. I am asking for a wife. That kiss should never have happened. I pride myself on being an honourable man. There are many who would say that I took advantage of you and your position in this house.'

'No, I think I understand you very well.' Phoebe shuffled her portmanteau into her other hand. 'Marriage for me must mean more. It must mean mutual understanding and admiration.'

'Love?' His lip curled around the word.

She hated how her insides trembled as his face grew colder and more remote. All around her the clocks sounded louder, echoing in her ears, somehow making it worse. 'That would be pleasant.'

'You have not been married before, Miss Benedict, so I forgive you your ignorance,' he said, finally breaking the terrible silence. 'What you describe is infatuation and rarely lasts a week. I no longer believe in it. I am sorry, but I have no heart to offer on a silver platter. There will be no declarations of undying devotion. I have gone beyond such things. I offer comfort and security. Do you think my offer is in jest? I can assure you that I am all seriousness. To whom should I address the offer, or are you capable of answering for yourself?'

'I am twenty-seven, Mr Clare. Long ago, I stopped asking for my stepbrothers' approval on anything. I have no fortune, so no one is interested in what I do.' She hated the truth in her words. She hated feeling that Sophia and Alice would be pleased to have her off their hands. One less problem. And James, once he received his commission, would not be interested in her. And Edmund would not make a fuss. He would think about how much Mr Clare could do for him. 'It will be me who makes the decision.'

'Then I shall make my address to you.' He put his hands behind his back and began to address her in much the same manner that she imagined he presented at a business meeting. 'Quite simply, Miss Benedict, it has come to my attention in recent weeks that this household is in dire need of a feminine touch. A person of the fairer sex. There is much that could be done here. I need someone to organise my menus and my staff and to look after my son when he is at home. I do believe you could fulfil that position. Admirably.'

Phoebe put a hand to the side of her face and sank down on the sofa. He was deadly serious.

The room spun slightly. Her head remained giddy from the kiss earlier. Perhaps somehow she was suffering from delusions. Something was not right. She should grab her portmanteau and depart. But he had just proposed. She wanted to be married to him. But more than that, she wanted him to kiss her again. She wanted to feel that raw hunger inside her. That crackle in the air between them. She wanted a passionate declaration.

'You seem surprised, Miss Benedict. I only state the truth. I am in desperate need of help. You have shown me that. I had planned never to marry again. And your antecedents are such that I would have naturally ruled you out…if this incident had not taken place.' She watched as Simon Clare sat down, then stood up again like a restless cat. 'My opinion of the nobility is not high.'

'Am I to be flattered that you are making an exception? Like you, Mr Clare, I had little say in my ancestors. I can only make my own way in life. But I do remain proud of their achievements.'

He put his hands behind his back. 'You are making a moot point. I kissed you. Some would say I ruined you. You need a permanent place to live and I need someone to look after my house and Robert. I do like neat solutions, Miss Benedict.'

'Nobody saw us. My reputation is safe. I am well on the shelf.' Phoebe regarded her hands. 'After my father died, my eligibility became negligible anyway. There is not much opportunity to meet appropriate suitors when one is taking care of one's stepbrothers… I am not one to cry over roads not taken. I am content with my life.'

'If you marry me, you will be mistress of your own home. I will keep you in comfort, Miss Benedict. All I ask is that you look after the boy and my house.'

Phoebe nearly asked him why he called Robert 'the boy', but held back the words. This was not about Robert. It was about her and the rest of her life. Either she continued existing on the edges of society or she could become Simon Clare's wife. Phoebe put her hand to her throat. It was surely better than being his mistress. But he was right. She had gone beyond the age of romance, though it did not stop her from wishing for it at odd moments. The life of a spinster was a lonely one and she did want to hold her own children in her arms. She knew she could love Robert as her own. He cried out for love. 'All that you ask?'

'Isn't that enough?' He captured her hand and lifted it to his lips. His tongue touched her palm briefly, sending a spark shooting through her. 'You wish to spend your life in service to others? Solitary and alone?'

Phoebe put her hands on either side of her head, blocking out his words. Was it enough? Most women would agree with him.

'It is not that simple. I do my duty. It is expected. My family needs me.' Phoebe forced her voice to sound strong. Did her family truly need her or was she merely the encumbrance that Sophia claimed? 'They depend on me. James. Edmund.'

'Your stepbrothers are grown men from all that you have said. They will do better if they have me as a brother-in-law.'

'But…but…' Phoebe stopped.

How could she explain that she desired affection? That she wanted a marriage like the one her parents had enjoyed. She longed to be the centre of a family, its hub. She needed to matter to another person. The worst thing was that she was attracted to Simon Clare. Was it right to marry a man for the wrong reasons? To live in hope that somehow he might come to care for her?

'Robert depends on you.' He held out his hand. 'Please think of that. You do not wish to break the boy's heart. You are important to him.'

Robert. She could do this for Robert. He did need a mother. Maybe that would be enough. It would have to be. She wanted to matter to another person. And where else did she really have to go?

'I will accept your offer, Mr Clare.' She stood up and held out her hand.

'I believe you may call me Simon.' He looked down at her hand and then back at her face. He bent his head; his mouth brushed hers. Lightly and possessively, but without the hunger or passion of earlier. It was the work of an instant. Then he stepped away. Phoebe tested her lips with her tongue. 'Say my name. Say it now.'

'Simon.' She tried the name. Rolled it around on her tongue. It suited him—a forthright name for a forthright person. She stood a little straighter. 'I will call you that.'

'I should like that…Phoebe.' He said the name softly as if it held promise.

'As you say, it is to be a practical marriage. It would be foolish to pretend emotion where there is none. You were right to make the offer. It was just…unexpected.' She hated the way her voice stumbled over the last few words.

'I would not dream of having any other sort.' He turned away from her and stared out of the window at the snow-bound landscape. 'Soppy sentimentality has long gone from my life.'

Phoebe waited. There was no need for him to explain when it had gone out of his life. Obviously first the illness, and then the death of his wife, had affected him badly. She could see the pain etched on his face and longed to find a way to wipe it clear. All she knew was that forgetting the past was not the answer.

'And what happens next?' she asked into the silence, seeking to bring him back from wherever he had gone.

'I will arrange for the banns to be posted.' He looked at her under hooded eyes. 'I have business that will take me away to Yorkshire for a few weeks.'

'Business?'

'A new investment for me and possibly a new buyer for my coal. It is what provides for this house and my lifestyle. If I remain in this house, I reckon on becoming a recluse or worse. Yorkshire and its cotton mills may prove valuable in time. Did you not give me a lecture on this the other day?'

'It was wrong of me.' She glanced down at the portmanteau. 'Might Edinburgh be on your journey? Might you take the time to see a specialist?'

'Yorkshire is to the south and Edinburgh to the north. Is geography not a strong point?'

'I merely enquired.'

'When I return, we can be married quietly. I will ask the vicar to read the banns in the old church. Not many are in church at this time of year. I will inform Robert as well.'

'Quietly? A hole-in-the-corner affair?' She shook her head. 'Is that what you mean? I had always imagined that my family would be at my wedding. Surely there must be friends and colleagues that you want to invite. And then there is your sister. Surely you wish to wait for your sister.'

'I once had a large wedding, Phoebe.' The furrows in his face became deeper, harsher. The door into his heart slammed shut, reminding her that there were places where she was not welcome. 'It is something to be endured rather than to be enjoyed.'

'I understand.' Phoebe pressed her lips together. He wanted nothing to remind him of Jayne. She hated herself for being jealous that his heart belonged to one woman, and had been buried with her. 'I will inform my family of the intended marriage. There should be no objection. Relief, I expect. Alice will undoubtedly make much of your connection with Lord Coltonby. But I doubt she is up to such a long journey. She prefers to stay in semi-retirement. I believe they were planning to go to Bath.'

The fact that she needed to give excuses depressed her. She wanted Alice to be there. She wanted Edmund and even James if he could make it. She wanted to feel for once that she was part of a family.

A silence fell over the room. He regarded her with speculation in his eyes. Phoebe played with the button of her glove. Why should the mention of her family cause him concern? Did he think she would use them as an excuse?

'If you like, Phoebe—it makes no difference to me.' He gave a slight shrug as if the matter was not of the least import. 'I am marrying you and your good sense, not your relations. Your lack of a settlement is not important. You will want for nothing.'

The use of her name sent a warm pulse down her back. She liked the way it rolled off his tongue. But his words made her start. She was a pauper, dependent on others. When Charles had been alive, he might have been willing to make some sort of settlement, but Sophia would never agree to it now.

'I had never considered settlements. There may have been something in my father's will. I will consult his man of business.'

'I leave it to your discretion, but I assure you it is entirely unnecessary. I will arrange an adequate allowance for you. You will take your place in the Tyne Valley society.'

Phoebe knew her cheeks burnt. Her throat closed and she seemed to be gasping for air. 'I should go and check on Robert.'

'Always the practical one.' He caught her hand and brought it to his lips. His mouth lingered there for a moment longer than necessary. Phoebe kept her body perfectly still and ignored the warm pulse that ran up her arm. 'Far be it from me to keep you from your duty.'

'I always try.' She moved away from the enticing warmth of his body.

'Wait!' He twisted off his signet ring and put it into her palm. She closed her fingers around the still-warm band of metal. 'Wear this and know my intentions are honourable.'

'I never felt they weren't.' She slipped on the ring. It felt large and unwieldy, weighing her hand down. Reluctantly she took it off. 'I will lose it.'

His fingers curled around hers, keeping the ring in her palm. 'Wear it on a chain, if you like, but it is a symbol of my intentions.'

'I will remember that.' She opened her fingers

and looked down at the heavy gold signet ring. His initials were entwined on the face. Somehow she wished that he had kissed her again.

'When I return, we will marry, Phoebe. I have given you my promise.' He raised her chin and looked into her eyes. Her lips grew heavy and full as if he had touched them. Then he let her go and stepped away. 'You will not suffer any dishonour at my hands. You will be my wife before we share a bed.'

Chapter Ten

The days and weeks that Simon was away passed far more slowly than Phoebe had thought possible. The snows melted, and the ground became a sea of mud punctuated by groups of white snowdrops and the vivid yellow of winter aconites. Robert's hair grew back in black and thick, making him resemble his father more by the day. It was not so much in his face, but in the way he held his head and gestured with his hands.

Phoebe wrote to Alice and Sophia, but received a terse reply. The delights of Bath were far more preferable than her impending marriage to a coal-mine owner, however well connected he might be. Phoebe had burnt the letter in the fire, taking delight in seeing it dissolve into a pile of ash.

The conversation in Simon's study took on an

unreal air. Every morning she would go in and stand there for a few minutes, reliving it, fingering the ring she wore about her neck. She had convinced herself that the kiss had not happened. But late at night, with the sound of ice cracking on the river filling the room, she would wake with her mouth tender and her being filled with an aching longing.

Had he done as he had promised and contacted the vicar? She resolutely stayed away from church. And the other servants made no mention of it. Phoebe concentrated on the tasks at hand, rather than worrying about the what-might-have-beens. She thought that he might have written, but she received no post from him.

Hannibal developed the proportions of a young cat with an appetite to match. Robert spent several hours a day playing with him. When the cat tired and slept in his box, Robert concentrated on his school work. He would speak longingly of a carriage and horse and how one day he would make carriages work without horses.

'The master's carriage has turned into the drive!' The call reverberated through the house three weeks after Simon had left. Doors slammed as the servants scurried to open the shutters and remove the dust covers in the drawing room.

Phoebe snapped her book shut and went over to the steamed-up window. With her hand, she made a circle on the glass and was able to see the dark carriage pulling up. She watched Simon's black boot as he started to emerge from the carriage and then drew back, heart thumping in her ears.

Rapidly she pinched her cheeks and smoothed the wrinkles from her gown, but she could do nothing about the sudden trembling in her stomach. Thankfully she was wearing her pale blue-grey gown with its Tudor lace collar, a combination that brought out the color of her eyes and hid the floridness of her complexion, according to Alice. Sophia would roll her eyes and exclaim that nothing could hide the floridness of her complexion except a heavy dowsing of powder.

'Your father has arrived home.'

Robert dropped the string that Hannibal was batting and shuffled through his drawings. He held up one. 'He will be proud of this engine. I have drawn it perfectly. It was in that book you brought up from the study.'

'I feel certain he will be, but the important thing is that you are proud of it.'

Robert's lashes fluttered and he reluctantly put the drawing on top of the pile. 'I suppose so. When Papa…'

His voice trailed away and Phoebe understood the unspoken fear—Simon would not come up to see him. Or, if he did, it would be towards the end of the day.

'Shall we go down and greet your father? I am certain your legs are strong enough to climb down the stairs. You made it down yesterday without any help.'

Robert's hand plucked at the coverlet and his face shone. 'I think I can do that. I know my legs can carry me.'

'Your father will be very proud to see you up and about. It will be quite a welcome gift, far better than any drawing.'

'Do you think so?' Robert put his head to one side, an exact imitation of how Simon held his head when they played chess.

'I know so. Your father wants to see you strong and well. Why else would he have sent for someone to take care of you?'

Phoebe held out Robert's dressing gown and the boy gave her a grateful smile. 'I will walk down the stairs on my own, Miss Phoebe.'

'And I will be right behind you.'

Phoebe allowed Robert to walk slowly ahead of her. She kept a careful eye in case he should stumble, but he moved at a slow but steady pace. They were halfway down the corridor when Simon appeared at the head of the stairs—booted and still wearing his travelling cape. He carried his cane lightly in his hand, but no longer leant as heavily on it. Phoebe halted, drinking in how he looked. The scarring had faded slightly and the blaze in his hair stood out clearer. Her pirate captain had returned. And some day soon, he would be her husband. The very thought made her heart leap.

Dimly she heard Robert greeting his father and knew she ought to say something as well.

'Well, I have achieved a cherished ambition. I have rendered Phoebe speechless.'

'We were on our way down,' Phoebe said, forcing the words out, aware that her cheeks burnt. He had no right to look like that. His breeches were light tan and moulded to his thighs. The eyepatch merely served to make him look more dangerous, someone to be tamed, rather than pitied.

'I came up,' he purred.

'Obviously.'

He held out his good arm and Robert hurried

over to him, moving quicker than she had seen Robert move. Simon spun him around, his frock-coat billowing out. Man and boy. Phoebe felt a lump rise in her throat. They looked so happy. And yet she wished that he had greeted her with a kiss. She wanted to be part of that circle too. The thought bothered her and she pushed it away, concentrating on the joy Robert displayed.

'There is no use asking if your health has improved, young man. Soon the roses will be back in your cheeks.' Simon put him down.

'I can walk the entire length of corridor, Papa, without Miss Phoebe's help.' The pride was evident in Robert's voice. Silently Phoebe prayed that Simon would recognise the immensity of the accomplishment. When Simon had left, Robert had struggled to make it to the sickroom's window.

'And whose idea was this?' Simon's eyes met hers over Robert's head.

'We planned it. It was a surprise,' Robert said stoutly. 'Do say that you like it.'

'I am pleased that you give Miss Phoebe some credit.'

'Robert really did do it on his own,' Phoebe protested. 'It was his sheer determination and strength of will, something he shares with his father.'

'You mean stubbornness.' A strange smile quirked on his lips. 'Or perhaps simply bad temper.'

'If you want to call it that.' Phoebe crossed her arms and turned her attention resolutely away from Simon's smile and the way it changed her insides to jelly. A practical marriage was what he wanted.

'I shall get strong again. I am quite determined.' Robert's bottom lip stuck out resolutely. 'Only sometimes, I find it hard to catch my breath.'

'And a very good surprise it is too. Jenkins will be up in a moment with the surprises I have brought for you.'

'Papa, your arm. You are not holding it awkwardly any more.'

Phoebe looked and saw that Robert was correct. Simon was using his arm, a bit stiffly but without much hesitation.

'Yes, my arm is improved. MacFarlane said it would heal in time.' He gave a little shrug. 'I was far too impatient. I should have believed him. And you, Miss Phoebe.'

Phoebe examined the hall carpet. Was it an apology? Whatever it was, she was pleased he had decided that somehow it was no longer a punishment sent from God. It was a step in the right direction.

She wondered if the scars had begun to heal on the inside as well. 'Perhaps you are being forgiven?'

'I have never asked for it.'

'You brought me things,' Robert said. 'What sort of things? I have drawn you an engine. One for a Loco Motive. It will not blow up. I read about high-pressure engines in the book Miss Phoebe found.'

'Have you, indeed?' Simon lifted an eyebrow.

'He was beginning to be bored drawing carriages. I thought you would approve.'

'Can I see the drawing, Robert?' Simon's face gave nothing away.

Simon and Robert returned to Robert's bedroom, and Robert held out the picture with a trembling hand. Phoebe silently prayed that Simon would not spoil the moment. That he would be sympathetic.

'This one has a higher smokestack than the one in the book,' Robert explained. 'So it can pump out steam better. It will be safer as it will not explode as quickly.'

'A higher smokestack is an intriguing proposition. It could solve several problems.' Simon looked at Robert, impressed, and his smile touched his eyes. He put the drawing inside his frock coat. 'I will investigate the idea. But you should get back in bed. Else this cat of yours will miss you. And I should hate for that to happen.'

Phoebe listened to Robert's excited chatter and Simon's deeper voice as Simon led him back to bed. She leant against the corridor wall and closed her eyes, giving father and son time alone. After a few moments, Simon came out. His face appeared excited.

'Robert's idea about the smokestack has some merit. I wonder that I had not considered its length before. He appears to be engine mad. I have yet to figure out if this is a blessing or a curse,' he said, giving a laugh. 'He asked so many questions.' He put a hand on her shoulder. 'Shall we go downstairs?'

'If you like…' Phoebe attempted a normal voice as the heat from his hand seared through the cloth of her dress. The ring about her neck seemed heavier than ever. It was one thing to agree to his proposal and quite another to have him close and real, not a figment of some dream. 'We did not expect you back so soon. The house is in the midst of spring cleaning!'

'And here I was about to apologise for taking such a long time. It seems like I was away for an age.'

'Three weeks.'

'Three weeks, then.' He inclined his head and

she saw the crinkle in the corner of his eye. 'Did you miss me? I thought of you and Robert often.'

'Robert missed you a great deal.' Phoebe lowered her eyes and prayed that her voice would not give her away. All the while his words 'a practical marriage' kept echoing in her brain. He was simply being polite. But her heart wanted to store every scrap. She wanted to hear the words.

'Robert appears much improved. I would hardly recognise him as the same boy.' His hands turned her towards him. His eyes searched her face as if he was looking for something. Phoebe forced her features to remain impassive. 'Do you remain of the same mind?'

Phoebe moved away from him. In another instant she would forget herself and demand a taste of his lips. 'I have written to my stepbrothers informing them of the change in my situation. Edmund has replied. James has left to join his regiment. Lord Coltonby was as good as his word.'

'My brother-in-law is a man of action. I expected no less. My sister wrote to me about it. She wanted to make sure you arrived safely and all was well.'

'I did write to her.' Phoebe kept her head high. She refused to beg for more intelligence about what Lady Coltonby had written. Did she know about the proposed marriage? Was she returning for the wedding? How did she feel about a penniless woman marrying her brother? 'About Robert…not about our proposed marriage. I thought you had best inform her.'

'I have written to her.' Simon's brows drew together. 'Diana has definite views on the subject. She married for love, you see. And thinks everyone should. I, however, remain to be convinced that such a thing truly exists except for those very lucky few.'

'I see.' Phoebe pressed her lips together as a pang went through her. She wished she knew more of Lady Coltonby's story. She knew her cousin had once been considered a rake and many women had tried to capture him. 'Certainly she and her new husband appear very happy.'

'Does your stepbrother raise any objections?' Simon gave her a dark look and she could see that the subject had been very firmly changed.

'He…he sent my settlement along with his regrets.' Phoebe felt a tightness in her throat. Surely her impending marriage was more important than a trip to Bath, or a trip to some barrister's house in the pursuit of his pupillage. He had never bothered to send her trunks. She kept telling herself that it was only natural that his studies should come first, but she wished that for once someone would put her first.

'Your settlement?' Simon's face became stern. 'I told you there was no need. I am marrying you for other reasons…'

'No Benedict bride is married without a settlement,' Phoebe said firmly. She had not known whether to be annoyed with Edmund or not. His heart was in the right place, but the offering was entirely inappropriate and possibly in poor taste. She had shed a few tears when it had arrived. 'Wait here and you will see.'

'You intrigue me greatly.'

Phoebe walked rapidly to the tiny room near Robert's and plucked the piece of parchment from her chest of drawers. 'Here it is, such as it is. Possibly not even worth the paper it is written on, but it is my marriage portion.' She gave a wry smile. She could not say what else Edmund had written. About how marrying a man like Simon Clare would do wonders for his own credit in London. She was positive that Edmund had meant it in jest. 'He thought you might find it useful as you were involved in business.'

'What did he send you? Hand it here, Phoebe. I refuse to allow your stepbrother to upset you. There are tears in your eyes.'

'The shares in the Peruvian silver mine. They are worthless, but it is what my brother could afford.' Phoebe gave a slight shrug. She had wept over the letter earlier, but now she could see the amusing side of it. Several years ago, those shares were worth a small fortune and now they were probably only fit for lighting a fire.

His fingers plucked the piece of parchment from her. A deep frown appeared between his brows and then he pocketed the paper. 'I will look into it for you. You can never tell. Sometimes mines come good. I do have connections.'

'I am sorry it is not more.'

He put his finger under her chin and raised her face. She could see the lines about his eyes and how smoothly shaven he was. The faint scent of shaving soap intermingled with something that was indefinably him reached her. Phoebe's mouth went dry. His eyes searched her face. Then he let her go. Her body protested at the sudden air that rushed between them.

'I will take this as a sign that your family approves. My wealth is more than enough for the both of us. I will keep you in style. My wife and her appearance reflect on my business. I would not have anyone say that I am a miser or that my business is failing.'

'They regret they are unable to attend the wedding.' She forced her lips to smile. 'If you are of the same mind, it only remains to set the day and time. I am sure your well-wishers will pack out the church.'

She hated to think of the contrast between his side of the church and the emptiness of her side. She had always thought that when she married, the church would be filled to the brim with her friends and family. But now it appeared they had turned their backs on her. They must blame her too. She would be truly alone.

'The sun is shining. I have spoken to the vicar. We can marry this afternoon.'

'But…but I am not dressed for the occasion.' Phoebe wet her lips. Her stomach had knotted. Marriage today? There were a thousand things she had to do.

'I am marrying you and not the gown. It is a pretty gown. I have seen far worse. The shade matches your eyes.'

'Even still…'

'It will be a quiet wedding. The vicar's wife and his curate will act as witnesses. I don't want to wait for some extravagant dress that you will wear only once.'

'And Robert?'

'I will inform him while you change. I take it that he knows nothing.'

'I was worried that you might alter your mind.'

He gave a small shake of his head. 'I suspect that Robert will be very happy.'

Phoebe put a hand to her throat and struggled to breathe. It was all going too fast. When she'd awoken this morning, the last thing she could have imagined was that she would be married before three o'clock. She smoothed her skirt, refusing to feel pity for herself and her childish dreams of an extravagant wedding. She had agreed to this arrangement. 'I will fetch my bonnet and gloves.'

Simon said the words of the marriage ceremony, looking down in Phoebe's face. Her eyes shimmered and her full lips were eminently kissable. Simon knew if he touched her more than briefly, his dark passion would be unleashed. He wanted her. There was no longer any reason to wait. If he had delayed, she would have proved too tempting.

And he refused to dishonour her in that way. He refused to have society whisper.

This wedding day was as different from his previous one as he could make it. No society wedding, nothing special, just Phoebe standing there. Even the church was cold and damp with grey light filtering through the stained glass windows. It was rarely used these days, as most preferred the newer church in Ladywell with its majestic wood carvings.

It was impossible to explain his choice of church to Phoebe. He was not ready for that. His first marriage and all the mistakes he had made were going to stay in the past. All the hurt and the ugliness would be gone. There was no need to enlighten Phoebe about what had gone on. He had learnt his lessons. Caring too much led to heartbreak.

He kept all emotion from his voice as he said his vows. When he bent to kiss her, his lips barely grazed hers. Cool and impersonal. And ultimately unsatisfying. Her mouth, ripe and full, remained turned up to his. It was an enticing morsel and one which had invaded his dreams nightly on his recent journey. Inwardly he groaned. He wanted to devour her, but he also had to honour her as his wife. He laid his hands on her arms and put her away from him.

The vicar's voice flowed around him and he realised with a start that the closing words had been said. He handed the vicar an envelope with a hefty donation to church funds. The vicar bowed slightly and his wife simpered about how lovely Phoebe looked as a bride. Simon concentrated on keeping his face impassive.

'There, the deed is done.' He tucked Phoebe's hand into his arm and smiled down at her. 'Cook will have prepared the wedding breakfast by now. I left strict instructions. It always amuses me that, no matter the time of day, the meal after a wedding is called a breakfast.'

'There was no need to go that trouble.' Her nose wrinkled delightfully. 'Do we really need such a thing as a wedding breakfast? It is not as if we have many guests to feed.'

'The servants will expect it. I hate to think of disappointing them. You are my wife and I will have you treated with the respect you deserve.' He noticed that she stayed silent. She had to understand that her status in the house and the neighbourhood had changed. As Mrs Clare she would have duties to uphold. He cleared his throat and tried again. 'Robert will enjoy it. I have asked Jenkins to install him downstairs when he wakes from his nap. He and one of the footmen can carry the boy.'

'He will want to walk down the stairs on his own.'

'Jenkins will catch him if he falls.' Simon forced his voice to sound light as a stab of fear went through him. He had thought it would be a pleasant surprise for Phoebe, but she seemed intent on pointing out all the flaws. 'Robert will enjoy the fuss.'

'You appear to have thought of everything.' She took her hand from his arm. Her lips turned upwards in a smile that did not quite reach her eyes.

'I have tried. It is the appearance of the thing that is important.'

'If you say so…'

He reached out and straightened her bonnet so that it was sitting more squarely on her face. His knuckles brushed the silky smoothness of her cheek. A little gesture, but one that made him crave more, that called to the darkness that he kept under control. He tightened his grip on his cane and forced his voice to sound casual. He did not want to see the pity in her eyes. 'When Robert has recovered and is back at school, I thought to have a wedding trip….possibly to Edinburgh.'

'To Edinburgh?' Her eyes lit up. 'You could go and see the specialist.'

Silently he cursed. He had put the eye specialist from his mind. On his recent trip to York, he had found that he could see dim shadow with his bad eye but that was all. It made his head pound to use both eyes.

'No, there is no point.'

'I am sure I will enjoy the wedding trip wherever we go.'

'Is there somewhere you would have preferred?' Simon kept his voice even.

'No, I had not really expected a wedding trip at all.' She turned so that her bonnet shadowed her face and she played with a button on her glove. 'Anywhere you want will be fine. It is not as if we have a love match.'

Simon stopped and put his hands on her shoulders. He could feel her flesh tremble slightly. Had she lied? Did he repel her? It worried him that the passion in him threatened to overwhelm his rational side. He wanted to honour her, and not to take her without consideration. 'It is to be a proper marriage, Phoebe. In every sense of the word.'

She scraped her toe along the path and her cheeks became flushed.

'I should not have said that. It is just that I would like some more time.' Her voice faltered on the last word.

'More time for what?' Simon fought to control his impatience. He had stayed away from her. They were married. There was no longer any reason to wait.

'More time to prepare. Marriage is a big step.' Her voice was barely audible. 'An unknown.'

A slight shiver went through him. Could it be that his new wife was untouched? Her kiss had been passionate. He had not looked for that. She had travelled in the same crowd as Jayne once upon a time. Maybe she was a tease like Jayne. All fiery heat outside and ice cold underneath.

'Has anyone spoken to you about such matters? What passes between a man and his wife?'

'I am twenty-seven, Simon, and have raised several brothers.' The words were swift, but her mouth had become pinched. 'I was in the *ton* for several years. I do know what passes between a man and a woman, even if I have never experienced it.'

'But has anyone discussed these things with you?' he pressed. Could he trust her? Jayne had sighed and declared that he was the only man for her, but she had been hiding a secret.

'I and several of my classmates bribed a maid at school. She was reasonably forthcoming on the particulars.' She kept her head high. 'I only hope that I will not disappoint.'

'You are my wife. How could you?' Simon opened the carriage door and helped her in. A light drizzle was falling. Today was turning out to be the complete opposite of that fateful day over ten years ago. His hand tightened on the carriage door. He would make it different.

The carriage ride from Ladywell Old Church was short, but Phoebe sat hunched in one corner, trying to keep her body from sliding along the horsehair seat and into Simon's. Her lie seemed to grow with each turn of the carriage wheel. She had pretended that she knew something of passion, but she knew next to nothing of what happened behind closed doors between a man and a woman. A few stolen kisses when she was a débutante, but nothing exciting, nothing that had sent her pulse pounding in the way his kiss that day in the study had. Alice had been very careful to keep a good eye on her, not letting her associate with any man who was not safe in a carriage. Jayne Northfield had run wild and Phoebe had envied her freedom. And now what did he expect? What did he want from her? Would he compare her to the other women he had experienced? Would she be found wanting?

Phoebe regarded Simon from under her lashes. His face was all planes and shadows. What would he be like as a lover?

'You are not paying attention, wife.'

Phoebe started with a jerk. 'Wool-gathering. One of my worst habits. I was thinking…about the spring cleaning and whether or not the linen cupboard had been properly cleared out.'

Her voice trailed off and she knew how pathetic it must sound. Linens on a day like today, after what had just happened. Surely he must guess what she was thinking about. His countenance did not change, but remained the same impassive mask it had been since the vicar had pronounced them man and wife. She was tempted to say that he was indifferent, but every so often out of the corner of her eye, she would catch his intent look and knew that behind the mask lurked a danger- ous man, one who set her pulse racing.

'I merely pointed out that we had arrived back… home.'

Home. The very word sent a shiver down her back. Northumberland would be her home now.

The house in the spring sunshine with its new grass and haze of bluebells was a complete contrast to the austere house she had first encountered. But she still felt like an impostor, like she did not belong.

His hand encircled her waist. 'Go on, they are expecting you to say a few words.'

'Welcome back, ma'am,' Jenkins boomed out.

The servants were arranged in a row. As she walked through the door, all the maids curtsied. Jenny Satterwaite came forward with a posy of bluebells. Phoebe stumbled through a few words, painfully aware that they were hopelessly inadequate. She wished Simon had thought to inform her earlier of his intentions to have a formal welcome with the staff, to have given her a few moments to prepare something. When she had finished, the servants burst into applause.

'I knew you would find the right words.' Simon's hand guided her towards the drawing room.

'When did you arrange all this?'

'You do not have all the managerial skill in this household. I sent orders several days ago that I wanted a feast to be ready on my return. I requested that Jenkins keep it a secret.'

'It is the best we could do, ma'am, but we are

right glad that you are to be the new mistress,' Jenkins said.

Phoebe nodded back, noting that she had gone from Miss Benedict to ma'am, her old position in the house gone for ever. 'Thank you. I shall do my best.'

'And now to see Robert…' Simon put his hand about her waist and shepherded her into the drawing room where Robert lay on the sofa, swathed in blankets. Robert's freshly washed hair spiked upwards and his face was bright pink after being too close to the fire.

Swiftly Phoebe went over, took two blankets off him, and kissed him on the cheek. Robert curled his arm about her neck and hugged her close.

'Are you pleased?' she whispered.

'Yes, it means that I do not have to give Hannibal up.' Robert's eyes danced with mischief. 'Papa explained everything.'

'You and that cat.' Simon sighed. 'I wonder that he is not here with a large bow to welcome Phoebe.'

'He prefers my room.'

'Hannibal is allowed to stay in Robert's room as long Robert attends to his mathematics,' Phoebe said in an undertone as she busied herself with straightening Robert's remaining blankets. He might be able to walk down the stairs on his own, but she had no wish for a relapse. 'That way you can have no objections to Hannibal staying here.'

'I must protest. I did not object precisely. I was bemused as to why anyone would want to save such a bedraggled creature. But I am grateful if it means Robert will be more attentive to his schooling.'

'If that is what you call not objecting, I should hate to see you in a bad temper.' Phoebe gave a little laugh, but her unease increased. Simon's sense of humour was so dry that it could easily be mistaken for other things. She wanted this encounter with Robert to go well. She had been a little younger than Robert when her father had remarried, but she could still remember vividly the awkwardness of the first meeting.

'Ah, but I have a hunch that you would stand toe to toe with me and argue.'

'I only argue what for I believe in,' she answered slowly.

His eyes searched her face. 'It is good to know.'

'Where is this wedding breakfast you promised? I am famished.' Phoebe blinked rapidly and hoped that Simon would understand why she'd had to change the subject.

'Do weddings make you hungry?' Simon drawled. 'I had not considered it.'

'Sometimes.' She put her hand to her stomach. 'I did not have much for breakfast, and then have missed lunch. I was a bit frightened that my stomach might gurgle in the middle of the ceremony.'

Robert put his hand over his mouth, stifling a giggle. Phoebe allowed herself to smile. The dangerous moment had passed.

'Shall we make sure we get your new mother fed?' Simon's eyes danced and the hint of a dimple flashed in his cheek. It was clear where Robert had received at least some of his mischievous streak from. 'After all, we do not know how long it will be before her stomach rumbles. Or how much indignity she will suffer.'

Robert gave a hiccupping laugh as his face lit up.

Phoebe was stunned. A joke from Simon? They had made progress. Perhaps the bringing together of father and son would be easier than she had imagined.

'Must I call her Mother? She isn't, you know.'

'You should speak politely, Robert.' Simon frowned. 'I expect better of you. Manners show what kind of man you are. Treat your new mother with respect.'

Robert hung his head. 'I know that. It is just… just that Miss Phoebe is not my mother. She never will be. My mother is in heaven. She left me to go there, despite what you said.'

'Phoebe is now my wife, Robert. I thought you understood.'

Tears welled up in Robert's eyes. It was all too easy for Phoebe to remember when her father had introduced Alice into the house. She had wanted so desperately for Alice to like her for her father's sake, but had felt that if she did not keep doing things for Alice, then she would be excluded from the family.

'I would like to be your friend,' she said quietly. 'I think we are friends, Robert, and I intend to stay here and look after you whatever you decide to call me. My father called me Phee—perhaps that will suit.'

'Phee. Yes, I should like to use that name very much and Hannibal will as well. He plans to be a mouser when he grows up.'

'A talking cat, whatever next?' Simon lifted an eyebrow.

'And what will you be, Robert?' Phoebe asked lightly before Simon could make a disparaging remark and ruin Robert's fancy.

'A carriage driver,' came the ready reply.

'He will be taking over the family business, Phoebe.' There was no warmth in Simon's eyes and the air crackled. 'I am counting on being able to spend time with you, when Robert is a grown man.'

Robert swallowed hard and examined the carpet.

'I am sure you can be both. My stepbrothers all love to drive, but they also do other things.' She was amazed how steady her voice was.

'Papa is right.' Robert's voice was high and shrill. 'I will be working with him in the family business with all the accounts and ledgers. But sometimes he builds machines and engines.'

She reached over and gave Robert's hand a squeeze. 'Now, shall we go in and see about this breakfast that your father has had prepared.'

'It is the proper name for it,' Simon replied. 'It is important to maintain civilities.'

'I have seen the jellies and pies,' Robert whispered. 'And there is a cake. The poppy seed one that my uncle likes so much as well as a proper fruit cake. Jenny told me all about it while I waited.'

'It sounds delicious, but far too much.'

Phoebe forced a smile on her face as she listened to Robert's excited chatter during the meal. It would be hard to guess that this boy was the same one from a few short weeks ago. The change was absolutely remarkable. Even more remarkable was the thought that when Lady Coltonby…Diana saw him, she would never realise how ill her nephew had been.

'What is the point of a feast if it is beef jelly and congealed rice pudding? Don't you agree, Robert?'

Robert nodded enthusiastically.

'And will your sister be annoyed about the wedding?' she asked her new husband.

'If she had wanted to be here, then she should have come up to Northumberland. The Thames is clear, and the packet boats are travelling. She has chosen to stay in London.'

'She has a reason.' *A far better reason than Edmund.* Phoebe found it impossible to stifle the thought. 'But will she approve of me?'

'Diana rarely does anything that she does not want to do. I'm sure we would have heard if she had not thought you appropriate.' Simon reached for another piece of seed cake. 'You must try this seed cake. It is superb.'

Phoebe drew in her breath. Would Lady Coltonby understand why she had married Simon? Looking across at him and the way his hair curled ever so slightly at the nape of his neck, she was not sure practical reasons were even a consideration. She still did not feel like she belonged here.

Chapter Eleven

'I think you have been long enough, Phoebe.' Simon's low voice carried across the sickroom. 'Robert is sound asleep. I can hear his snoring halfway down the corridor.'

Phoebe glanced up from where she sat reading a book. Simon's shape loomed in the doorway, large, dark and dangerous. His neckcloth was undone and she could see the hollow of his throat. Hurriedly she glanced down at the book, but the print blurred in front of her eyes.

Robert's gentle snoring filled the room. Here she had nearly convinced herself that this afternoon had been some sort of pleasant dream and that nightfall would never come. Or, if it did, she would simply slip back to her old room as if nothing had changed. And yet everything had.

'It has only been in the last few moments that he started snoring.'

'If you say so…' A sardonic smile touched his lips. 'I have been watching you for a while now.'

Phoebe resisted the urge to begin tidying the room. 'Watching me? You should have said something.'

'I had no wish to disturb you. You looked so peaceful. And totally absorbed in the book. Is it worthwhile?'

'Tremendously. It has had me enthralled all evening. Robert enjoyed it as well.'

'Truly?'

'It put him off to sleep.'

She gently closed the book on sermons and blew out the candle. The words had long since ceased to have any meaning and the only thing she could think about was how cool Simon's lips had felt against hers in the church and what the night might hold. She knew he was doing this out of the need to provide Robert with a mother and not out of any true desire to have a wife. It was her fault that the kiss had ever happened, and Simon was far too much of a gentleman. She had taken advantage of him.

Her eyes looked up and she saw him regarding her with a thoughtful expression. He must have been truly handsome in his youth.

'I hope he will have a good night's sleep tonight. Today has held quite a bit of excitement for him. It is not every day that a child acquires a stepmother.'

'It is not every day that I acquire a wife.'

'A big day for all of us then.' Phoebe wished she could say something more profound or witty.

'He will not need you to sit by him any longer.' Simon held out his hand. 'Come with me now. Your duties here have ended for the night. There are other places for you.'

And my other duties? What will they be like? Are you looking forward to them? Or is it something that you have to get through? The words rose up within her, but she couldn't say them. How could she accuse him of anything? She had known what the marriage was going to be like when she'd agreed to it. It was no good hoping that it would be different now.

Phoebe ignored his hand, but she walked out of the room, carefully closing the door behind her. The dim light in the corridor made Simon's face all mysterious planes and shadows. His broad form seemed to fill the hall, blocking her way. She took a step backwards and encountered the wall.

'And who is going to take my place beside Robert? What will happen if he calls out?' she asked to cover her nervousness. She did not want to think about Simon doing his duty. Or pretending that she was another woman. Or all the other thoughts that had run through her head. All she knew was that she was not his first choice. Dimly she realised that he was speaking to her about Robert in a concerned tone. And that somehow made it worse. She knew he cared about Robert.

'And did he take his medicine, Phoebe? He seems to be sleeping peacefully enough just now. Before you came, his sleep was often restless. I thought today maybe that the Robert I knew was coming back.'

'He did. He made a face, but he took it. He wants to get well…Simon.' She said his name hesitantly. 'He wants you to like him.'

'How many times has Robert woken during the past three weeks?'

'He has slept through, but that is not the point. Someone needs to watch.' She waited with bated breath for his agreement. She wasn't refusing his bed, but simply postponing the inevitable disappointment.

'It is your wedding night.' The words sounded like a death knell. 'Jenny can watch Robert. She is a sensible girl. I have been very impressed with her.'

'Ours is not a normal marriage. It is a practical marriage. A marriage forced on you by your sense of duty.'

'It is still a marriage.'

'Tonight or tomorrow night will not matter. A postponement. It will give me time to prepare.' Phoebe clamped her mouth shut, aware that she was babbling.

Simon reached out and his fingers encircled her wrist. Strong and firm. 'I will not have anyone say that this is not a normal marriage. Your things have been moved to my room. There are two dressing rooms. One for your use and one for mine.'

To his room. Phoebe's mouth went dry. She noticed the power in his shoulders and his long fingers. 'My parents never shared a bed.'

'I will not enquire where you were conceived.'

Phoebe's cheeks burned like she had stood for hours in front of the fire. 'That is not what I meant. They had separate bedrooms. It was the done thing.'

'Ah, but I am not an aristocrat, wife. My parents did share a bed. It makes for…a better marriage.'

'Does it?' Phoebe hated the way her voice squeaked. She had avoided thinking about the marriage night except in her dreams when she would wake, filled with a nameless longing.

'I will give you some time to get ready. Do you need any assistance?'

'I have been able to manage on my own for the last few years.'

'Nevertheless, you shall have to hire a lady's maid. It would be unseemly for you not to have one.' He paused and his shoulders became tense. 'I can perform the function for you tonight if you wish.'

Phoebe kept her back upright and drew her gaze away from his hands. 'I am fully capable of dressing and undressing myself. It is a skill I acquired through necessity.'

'Then I shall leave you to it. Will a quarter of an hour suffice?'

'It will be more than enough.' Phoebe forced the words around her tongue. A quarter of an hour to prepare! The time at once seemed to stretch endlessly and to shrink to nothing.

Simon made a bow and walked away. Phoebe stared after him, uncertain if she should call him back. She had thought all this would be easy, but it was so much more difficult than she had imagined.

Simon doused the candle as he regarded the bedroom door from his dressing room. He had given Phoebe enough time to ready herself, more than enough time. He had discarded his coat and shirt but kept his breeches on, unlike his usual habit of sleeping naked. He would go slowly and treat her with care. She deserved that. This time he was no callow youth. He had seen how impatience and unbridled passion could ruin everything. He knew how disastrous his last wedding night had been.

He slowly opened the door, hesitating as it creaked slightly. He moved by stealth and memory.

Silver moonlight flooded into the room from a window. He frowned as he saw the figure in white standing, staring out at the moonlit scene. She was unmoving with her hair rippling down her back. Her thin nightdress hinted at the curves that he was sure lay beneath. His body hardened while his fingers itched to caress them and to take possession of them. The last few weeks, his dreams had been plagued with erotic images of her, long limbs spread wide to welcome him, and he intended to see if he could make them a reality. The dark passion inside him demanded it.

'You should be in bed. Your feet will get cold.'

She continued to look out of the window at the moonlit landscape. Her neck and back appeared to tense. Simon knew if he touched her, she would shy away like an untamed animal. He would have to take it slow and coax her into trusting him.

'What took you so long? I have heard the clock sound at least twice.'

'I was looking at the drawing Robert did earlier of the travelling engine,' he murmured, choking back the truth. 'There may be something in his idea. I had not thought of it before. I lost track of time. Forgive me.'

She did not move from where she stood. 'Robert will be pleased. He spent a great deal of time making sure that everything was perfect.'

'And who found him the book? Did he go downstairs on his own?' Simon kept his voice soft. It seemed odd to be speaking about Robert on his wedding night, but it also seemed natural. He knew Phoebe loved the boy and he hoped in time she would come to care for her husband.

'I did. I thought he would enjoy drawing something different.' Her voice was no more than breath.

'He seems to have quite a talent for mechanical drawing. Perhaps he might like to see a real engine.'

'When he is better, I should think he would like it very much. They appear to have captured his imagination.'

'It is odd what little things can do.'

He walked several steps closer. The hem of her nightgown grazed his foot. He reached forwards and touched her shoulder. She held herself rigid, but her flesh quivered slightly. Her soft scent rose, surrounding him in its embrace. His body reacted instantly to it.

All of his boyish illusions about women had been ground to dust long ago. But here in the starlight, he found that he wanted those illusions to return. He wanted her. His body reminded him of how long it had been since he had cradled a woman in his arms.

'Your hair is loose.'

'I can't abide caps. It is one of my many failings.' Her voice held a small catch. 'No doubt you will discover them all in time.'

'It surprises me that you wish me to know them.' He watched her breasts rise and fall under her nightdress. Simon sought to retain control. 'But we shall keep all secrets in the past if you like.'

'It is easier to explain than to hide. My sister-in-law always complains that a truly well-bred woman wears caps to bed.'

'As much as I am sure your sister-in-law is a worthy woman, I must disagree with her. Your hair ripples down your back in waves.'

He took a step closer and lifted her hair off her shoulder, running the silky softness through his fingers. It revealed a tiny patch of skin, just above where her nightdress skimmed her throat. She shivered slightly, but did not pull away.

'What did I say? The night air will give you a chill,' he whispered against her ear lobe, tasting its smoothness with the tip of his tongue 'Shall you come to bed? Or shall I find another way to warm you?'

Phoebe nodded slightly. His hands were warm on her shoulders, burning through the thin material. His tongue made pulses of warmth dance through her body. She struggled to hang on to her decorum. How could she explain to him her fear that he would come to her and then, as the time slipped away, that he wouldn't. And now he was here, behind her, with the heat rising off him. 'I was waiting for you.'

'I am sorry that I took so long, then.'

His hands turned her towards him. In the silver light, she could only see the barest outline of his face. His eyes appeared dark. She inhaled, savouring his scent as a deep ache filled her body. With a trembling hand she touched his lips. He opened his mouth and suckled the tip of her finger. She started to pull back, but his hands held her there, drawing her slowly towards him.

He lowered his mouth and his lips brushed hers with no more than a butterfly's touch. She lifted an arm and put it around his neck, holding him there. She would not be able to bear it if it was the same impersonal touch he had given her at the church. Instantly the kiss deepened, becoming darker and more insistent.

His tongue traced the crease of her lips and found the tiniest of partings, demanding entrance. Hesitantly she opened her mouth and allowed him in. Their tongues touched.

She drew back in surprise, but his hands cradled her face, holding it there as his lips began to move over her face. Soft kisses rained down on her eyelids and her temple. Then he returned to her mouth, and this time she did not draw back. The kiss deepened, causing heat to shoot through her body. She arched forwards, seeking the warmth of his mouth, and found her soft curves meeting the hard planes of his body. It was so very different with only the thinness of her nightdress between them.

He shifted his hands and suddenly she was lifted into the air.

'Are you sure you can hold me?'

'For this short a distance, yes. I have no wish for your feet to get colder.' His voice rasped in her ear. 'It would be a dreadful thing if you caught a chill.'

'I am a very hardy person, my stepmother has always said. Others might fall ill, but never me. It is my lot in life to nurse.'

'Allow someone else to look after you for a change.'

He covered the distance to the bed in two strides, placing her on it before she had a chance to protest further. Phoebe pressed her lips together and tried to think clearly. He had to understand that she didn't need looking after. It was not the way the world worked. Early on she had learnt that things became easier to bear if she concentrated on someone else. It made it feel like they actually wanted you there.

His hands captured her foot and held it to his cheek. His lips nuzzled the instep. 'Don't move. It is very cold.'

Simon leaned over her. His skin had taken on a blue-silver tinge in the moonlight, making him seem more like a gilded statue than a living man. Phoebe licked her lips and tried to hold still, but the gentle pressure on her foot was doing strange things to her insides. It was opening up a deep ache within her. She moaned slightly and pulled her foot away.

His hand brushed her hair back from her face. He was warm and inviting and she knew he was no dream.

'May I?' His fingers touched the top button of her nightdress. 'You are overdressed.'

'I am?' Her eyes flew to his face.

He gave a wicked smile. 'Most definitely. You see my shirt is off. And you are wearing a nightdress.'

Her tongue wet her lips and she wished she had the courage to touch his skin. He was tantalisingly close.

'If you say so…'

'I do indeed.'

His fingers pushed at the button and worked it free. Then went to work on the next one. When they reached a third button, he swore under his breath, grabbed the material and there was a great ripping sound as the nightgown was split down the middle, exposing her body to his gaze.

'What are you doing?' Hastily she moved to hide her body.

'I am useless with buttons. My hand remains clumsy from the accident.' He gave a self-deprecating smile. 'It seemed the most efficient way.'

'But that was my only nightdress!' Phoebe struggled to hold the two sides together. She thought that he might simply lift her gown, not expose her body to his scrutiny. She knew her stomach and breasts were larger than they should be. Sophia had remarked on that the last time they had spoken. How she was becoming matronly. And now they were open to Simon's gaze. She tried to cover them with her hands, but he shook his head.

His hand clasped both of hers and held them above her head. 'Why don't you let me worry about that? I can afford plenty more…if you truly want one.'

'But…but…' Phoebe tried to think of all the reasons why he should not have done that, but the only thing she seemed capable of concentrating on was the way his breath felt against her skin, hot and sultry.

His other hand parted the material and revealed her breasts. The nipples had curled into two tight peaks. He grazed them with his knuckles and they became even tighter. Then he lowered his head and teased a nipple with his tongue. First one and then the other. Swirling and suckling. White-hot jolts went through her.

A moan escaped from the back of her throat and

her body lifted off the bed, arched towards his questing mouth.

His mouth descended on hers as he lowered his body on to her, covering the length of her. His arousal pressed against her through his breeches. She squirmed slightly as he feasted on her lips. Her fingers touched his waistband. The material was taut against her fingertips. She drew in a sharp breath. She wanted to get this right, and to show him that she was sophisticated, not a fumbling amateur. 'Are you perhaps overdressed now?'

'I might be.' He lifted up and quickly took off his breeches. She drew in her breath. She had seen her stepbrothers when they were little boys, but nothing had prepared her for the magnificence of this man.

'Will it be all right?'

'Trust me.' He pushed her hair back from her temple. 'I will go slowly.'

His hands trailed her body, stopping to cup her breasts, but then moving on. A finger entangled itself in her curls, sending the ache inside wild. Her body arched upwards, demanding more.

'So impatient,' he murmured.

Her hand reached out and touched his chest, found his flat nipples and mimicked what he had done earlier to her. He raised an eyebrow.

Emboldened, she allowed her fingers to slide down his smooth skin.

Using his knee, he nudged her thighs wider apart. Positioning his body between her legs, the tip of him touched her crease, probing along it, slowly and steadily.

Her hands clawed at his shoulders. Then, without warning, he eased himself into her. An unbidden cry emerged from her throat. Where it had been a pleasant ache, it was now burning. 'Please, please,' she whispered.

He froze, then withdrew. Simon lay on his back and tried to regain control of his body. Phoebe was truly a virgin! After his experience with Jayne, he had scarcely allowed himself to hope.

A virgin. And he had nearly taken her with an urgent callousness. He could not do that. He could not bear the thought of her looking at him with injured eyes. He had given his promise to go slow and the warmth of her response had enticed him onwards. His dark passion had nearly destroyed everything.

He forced his breathing to relax. Give her time, he thought. But he willed her to turn to him.

Phoebe knew she should simply lay back and allow him to proceed, but she also wanted to go back to what they had shared before. She hated that she did not have the words to explain. Tentatively she put out her hand and reached for his fingers. 'Simon.'

The bed creaked as he moved away. Her insides twisted. She had done everything wrong. This was supposed to be the start of the marriage and she had promised to be a good wife. It was as her step-mother had often whispered, about men taking their pleasures elsewhere. The only thing she knew was that a cold marriage bed was not what she desired.

'Simon, I am sorry, so sorry,' she called out, fighting to keep the rising panic from her voice. 'I didn't know what to do. I have ruined every-thing. I will be better next time.'

'Here, this might help.' He laid a hand on her shoulder. Tender, warm and soothing. 'Drink. You have done nothing wrong.'

'It tickles my nose.' The fiery liquid burnt a trail down her throat. She sat up, but his hands eased her back down amongst the pillows.

'There is time enough to speak of that later. I want to look after you now.'

'Look after me?'

'There may be blood. Allow me to look after you. Please?'

It was that one word. Her pirate was asking, instead of taking. She had not thought it possible. She gave the tiniest of nods.

He placed a damp towel between her legs. Held it there firmly against her. His hand reached out and smoothed a curl away from her forehead. Cold replaced the burn. Gently he moved the towel. Back and forth. Sliding it over her, giving sweet relief to the ache.

'Will it always be sore?' she asked in a small voice.

'Not always. It is only the first time, but you may ache in the morning.'

He gave a slight smile as he continued to press the cloth against her. She noticed how the nature of the movement changed. It became slower and more languorous, rubbing in small sensuous circles. It began to call to a deep growing ache within her.

Her hips lifted in time to the movement of the towel. The fire within her began to consume her, blocking out everything except the need to experience this. A deep burning desire built within her again, fiercer this time. Bolder. Her hips thrust upwards.

He replaced the towel with his fingers, sliding down her pink folds and into her. Back again.

Slowly, carefully. Her body buckled and the warm pulses exploded into white heat. She moaned, wanting something more.

She knew she needed him, needed him inside, and was prepared to risk the memory of the pain. She drew his body towards her.

This time, her body opened up, and took him fully inside her. There was a brief moment of pain, but then he began to move and the world came down to just one thing. This time her body matched his, and when the shuddering overtook him, it claimed her as well.

Much later, Simon propped himself up on the pillow and watched Phoebe's face soft with sleep.

He had not expected this, this all-consuming need. He had known that he wanted her, but had not expected to feel such a desire for her, such a longing to unlock her hidden depths.

Gently he eased his body away from hers. She murmured slightly and moved to the spot he had just vacated, seeking his warmth.

Simon watched her, and then turned away. He had neglected his drawings and plans for the travelling engine for far too long. It would give him something to do, a reason to keep away from her, to keep her firmly in a compartment of his life.

He had risked his heart once, and he refused to do that again. He took one last look at the figure in the bed, her hair spilling over the pillow, her mouth moving softly in sleep, and forced his fingers to pull the door closed behind him.

Chapter Twelve

Phoebe woke to an empty bed and sunlight streaming in through the window. The room was large and masculine, but devoid of life. She sat up with a start, discovered she was naked and dived under the covers again.

She lay there, body flushing with shame, trying to make sense of what had happened in the night. She had half-expected that last night had been another of her dreams, but seeing the ripped nightgown, the indentation in the pillow next to her and Simon's room around her, told her that it was very real. Everything.

She wished Simon had stayed until she woke. Maybe then this feeling of being vulnerable, of not belonging, would have vanished. But it washed over her again, threatening to swamp her senses.

The clock chimed ten. Phoebe put a hand to her

throat. Not even when she was a débutante in London had she slept this late. She hated to think of all the things that needed to be done. Simon had not married her so she could spend the day lazing about. He had married her to have a housekeeper and a mother for Robert.

Hastily she dressed, twisting her hair up in a simple knot, and hurried down the corridor to Robert's room. Robert should have had his medicine two hours ago.

There she discovered Jenny tidying the room, but no Robert. Hannibal gave her a baleful look, opening one green eye before he settled back down in his basket.

'Has something happened to Robert? Where is he? Why did no one wake me?'

'The master has taken the young master for a ride in his carriage,' the maid said as she smoothed the coverlet. 'He said that you were to sleep. Undisturbed, like.'

'I am awake now.' Phoebe picked up the discarded pens and pencils and began to put them back into the case. Simon had taken Robert off. This was a good sign, but somehow she could not rid herself of the nagging sense of disappointment and the stab of jealousy. She wanted to be the one who Simon wished to spend time with. She wanted him next to her when she woke.

The pencil in her hand snapped in half and she hated her perverse jealousy. She had worked so hard for Simon to take note of Robert. She should be pleased, but the hurt rose up within her. 'It was just I never expected to sleep so late.'

Jenny nodded. 'If I might be so bold, ma'am. You will be needing a woman now. Someone who looks after your clothes and your hair. I am willing to learn and I have nimble fingers. Me mam always says that. And shy bairns get naught.'

Phoebe opened her mouth to refuse, but saw the pleading in the young girl's eyes. The maid was correct and Simon was right, she would need a lady's maid. It would be tempting to think about being wealthy and getting a French maid, one of the luxuries she had dreamt about when she was a débutante. But what use would Phoebe have for a French maid up here? It would be far better to train a girl up. It made practical sense. 'Yes, that will be fine. I am sure I can put your fingers to good use. I suspect my wardrobe will need some updating now.'

The maid let out a breath. 'Thank you, ma'am. I won't let you down. And I can sew a fine seam.

Me mam used to be a seamstress for the Dowager Lady Bolt and she could sew ever so fine.'

Far away, Phoebe heard a door open. She hurried out into the corridor, hoping that Simon had returned, but Jenkins appeared, carrying several cards on a silver platter. 'Lady Bolt and her daughter are here to call, ma'am. Are you receiving visitors?'

'Is it me that they wanted to see? Not Mr Clare?'

'They did request to see you, ma'am. Mrs Clare. Lady Bolt was most definite about it.' Jenkins shook his head. 'Most irregular, that. And the master left without issuing orders. I had to ask. Not worth my job to make decisions like that.'

Phoebe understood the butler's dilemma. The situation was not his fault. No orders. But if she sent Jenkins back with a polite 'not at home' she risked offending the callers. She knew too little of the politics of Tyne Valley society. This was where she lived now, and she could not risk having anything held against her.

Her gown was serviceable, but several seasons too old. It would have to do. When her trunks arrived from London, she and Jenny would set to work altering things. The wife of a prosperous businessman needed a very different wardrobe from that of an impoverished spinster.

'Very well, Jenkins, I will see them in the drawing room.'

'I will inform the ladies you are at home.'

Phoebe pressed her lips together. How many years had it been since she had received callers? Six? She would have to get back into practice. She would make Simon proud. A small step towards starting to belong in the neighbourhood.

'Keep your scarf up,' Simon said, looking down at Robert.

'But I want to see. Is this the engine? The engine…that did, you know…explode?' Robert's voice trailed off as his eyes grew large.

'These are the remains of the engine. Iron and other bits and pieces can be salvaged from it.' Simon regarded the lump of metal with its twisted and buckled casing. It seemed such a long time ago, that morning back in the autumn, when it had exploded. But he supposed it was really not so long ago.

The colliery looked as it ever had with the pumping engines going full blast and men and carts moving about the place. It was good to be here, to remember the things that were important in his life and why he was for ever scarred.

And yet he looked down at Robert's shining face and it was good to see the place with different eyes. The superficial scars did heal. The engine could be made better. But was it too late for him?

'Are there any other working engines?'

'There is the pump engine. I can have Smith show it to you.'

'I want to be able to draw one for Phee.'

Phee. Phoebe. Who with any luck should still be asleep, her lips softly pursed and her hair spilling out across the pillow.

Resolutely he turned his mind away from his wife. He wanted to keep the evil part of him from seeping out and infecting her. He could not bear it if she saw him for what he was, if she knew what he had done. He knew what he was capable of. Yesterday when they had left the church, he had glanced over to where Jayne's lover was buried, unremarked and forgotten. How could he confess to Phoebe his hand in that death? He had been provoked, but that did not end the guilt. Would Phoebe understand? Or would she turn away from him?

He would allow Robert a little while longer with the engines and then they would return home…the long way. 'I will be over by the carriage when you are finished, Robert.'

'Mr Clare, thank God, you are still here.'

'Is there a problem, Dodds?' Simon asked his foreman.

'Fire damp, down in the third tunnel about halfway along…'

Fire damp—the very words sent a chill through his bones—pockets of gas underground, waiting for the inattentive miner and the open flame from the miner's candle. He hated to think of the number of lives destroyed in explosions. Some called it a disgrace that no one had found a solution, but there were always other more pressing problems. And, once known about, fire damp could be avoided.

The last thing he wanted was another explosion at Ladywell. Even if no one was injured, miners were notoriously superstitious and he would have trouble retaining the good ones. The entire notion was too horrible to contemplate.

'Can it be bypassed?'

'I think so. A candle flickered. And Smith did not like the look of it.' Dodds appeared unhappy. 'It will take a few weeks, mind, to get a new tunnel down to that seam. We need it now that there is the order from Yorkshire.'

'Is there any way we can keep it working until the new tunnel is dug?'

'There is the tunnel you closed afore you left for Yorkshire. You know, the one where Tommy Jameson spotted the water coming in and we propped up them timbers. You said it was to be used in emergencies only…'

'It is better to be cautious. The fire damp may or may not go away of its own accord. But I can't lose that order. I want a full survey on my desk by this evening and I want all suspect timbers replaced.' Simon put his hands behind his back. Here was an answer to his prayer—a problem to be solved. It would not take very long. In all likelihood, Phoebe would not miss him.

He would solve the problem now, and then, when he returned, he would be able to concentrate on his wife in the way she deserved. It was unfair to return to her with his mind full of colliery problems. He winced, remembering that he had once used his work as an excuse. Jayne had thrown it in his face any number of times, but this was different. It had to be sorted now or he risked an even bigger problem. 'No one is to go down into the fire damp tunnel, unless they have my express orders. Is that clear, Dodds?'

His foreman gave a nod. 'I understand, but what about them timbers?'

'I want to see them for myself. Now.'

'And the young master?'

Simon turned to where Robert stood, happily chatting to several coalmen. It was good that he seemed to enjoy this place. It would be his responsibility in years to come.

'The brakeman can look after him for a few moments. He will be fine.' The pain intensified in Simon's head. Phoebe would have to wait; first he had to see to the colliery's safety. Safety and his men—it was where his responsibility lay. Phoebe would understand.

'Pray forgive the intrusion,' the well-upholstered lady dressed in an elaborate puce carriage dress boomed out before Phoebe had reached the final step. 'Mrs Fletcher, the vicar's good wife, told me the news in the haberdashery this morning. Miranda and I had to hurry over. We wanted to be among the first to welcome you to the neighbourhood. It all does seem rather sudden. No one had any idea.'

'Very sudden, Mama.' The Honourable Miranda Bolt echoed her mother's tone, but dropped a slight curtsy. The brightness of her evening primrose gown made Phoebe's eyes water. 'It will be the wonder of the neighbourhood. Maybe even the entire county. Mr Clare has taken a wife at last. Who would have thought it? And to a woman outside the neighbourhood. It is beyond imagining.'

'How pleasant to meet you both.' Phoebe kept her voice calm, her movements contained. She would write to Edmund today and demand her trunks be sent, instead of a letter promising their impending arrival. She would also see if there were any lengths of cloth about. She would hate asking Simon for money, but she desperately needed new gowns. 'So kind of you both to call and to wish to make me feel welcome.'

'The pleasure is all ours, Mrs Clare.' Lady Bolt was the sort of woman she had encountered many times in London—completely convinced of her own superior social status and importance to the world. 'Were you married by special licence? I do not recall hearing the banns read at St Aidan's.'

'I believe the banns were said at the Old Church.' Phoebe pasted a smile on her face.

'I told you, Mama, that we ought to go there. Mr Gough often preaches there. He needs to get practice with his sermons,' Miss Bolt said, fluttering her eyelashes.

'I suppose it does depend on the church you frequent.' Phoebe used her best society voice, the one she saved for aged duchesses and Lady Patronesses of Almack's. The two women stared at her. Phoebe kept her head up. She refused to feel awkward and at least her guests kept her from wondering where Simon and Robert were, and why Simon had not bothered to greet her this morning. 'I have asked Jenkins to provide tea in the drawing room.'

'We can only stay a moment. I do not suppose you have poppy seed cake.' Lady Bolt smacked her lips.

'Mama is partial to poppy seed cake.'

After the tea was served, the questioning began. Lady Bolt's bonnet positively quivered with excitement. 'And where are your family from? To which Benedict are you related? Mrs Fletcher is so forgetful on such matters. And I find it best to get connections straight in my mind at the outset.'

'Mama is interested in where people have come from.' Miss Bolt's face took on a studied, but pious expression.

Phoebe took a sip of her tea, and took a small amount of pleasure in prolonging their agony. She had little doubt that Lady Bolt had decided that she was some vicar's daughter, or an upstart governess, someone who could be subtly helped or, worse, made into a project. But definitely somebody entirely dependent on Lady Bolt's good will. 'My elder brother was the Viscount Atherstone.'

Lady Bolt's mouth snapped shut and her cheeks reddened.

'That means Mrs Clare is at the very least an Honourable, Mama, doesn't it?' Miss Bolt rocked back and forth on the sofa with ill-concealed mirth as her mother's discomfort increased. 'Mama is most particular about getting titles correct.'

'Hush, Miranda, do not be impertinent.'

Phoebe regarded the younger woman with more interest as Lady Bolt snapped her fan open and shut.

'I have heard of them,' Lady Bolt pronounced finally. 'I understand the Viscount is currently unmarried.'

At the word, unmarried, Miss Bolt sat upright and her face assumed a hopeful expression. 'Shall we be seeing your brother here? An unmarried viscount would be a great addition to the neighbourhood. Do you not think, Mama? Perhaps it is a good thing that Mr Clare married.'

'I doubt that the current Viscount Atherstone is looking for a wife.'

'But he must be.' Miss Bolt widened her eyes.

'Unmarried titled gentlemen need wives. It is a well-known fact. How else would the succession carry on?'

Phoebe knew she should not give in to temptation and should feel some pity for Miss Bolt, but she remembered the words Simon had said. Here was a woman who had called him a fiend. She forced her face to be perfectly bland. 'My nephew is but a little over a year old. He was born two months after my brother died.'

Lady Bolt turned the colour of mottled purple, matching exactly the colour of her dress as Miranda Bolt sharply drew in her breath. 'Daughter, learn to look at *Debrett's* before you open your mouth.'

'Yes, Mama.' Miss Bolt had the grace to hang her head.

Phoebe politely but firmly moved the conversation on to the weather.

'I shall cut through the pickles and smoked gammon, Mrs Clare,' Lady Bolt proclaimed, setting down her tea cup and declining a scone. 'We have come about the Grand Allies ball.'

Phoebe tilted her head. The words meant nothing to her. 'I am sorry…you hold the advantage.'

'Surely your husband has told you about the

Grand Allies, the coalition of Northumberian coal-mine owners?'

'I fear such subjects have not been discussed. My stepson has been ill, Lady Bolt.' Phoebe did her best to keep her temper. The woman was obviously of some importance in local society and she had no wish to make an enemy of her, not at this early stage. But equally she refused to be pushed around. Northumbrian society would be a scaled-down version of London's.

'I did send a fruit basket.' Lady Bolt gave a harrumph as if sending a fruit basket was guaranteed to make anyone feel better. 'Perhaps Mr Clare did not think to mention this as he has been remiss about the Grand Allies as well.'

'What do the Grand Allies have to do with me?'

'A ball is held every year at different houses. This is to ensure no one gets precedence or is burdened with too much preparation. The Baileys have had to withdraw after Mr Bailey senior died from the typhoid. It falls to me to organise it again this year and I wished to ascertain if you will attend.'

'I will have to discuss it with my husband.'

'Mr Clare is sure to be there.' Lady Bolt waved a dismissive hand. 'He always attends. It would not be done for Mr Clare to miss such a thing. He entertains us all with his latest schemes for a travelling engine. The problem of the opening quadrille concerns—'

'The opening quadrille? I do not understand.' Phoebe concentrated on the teapot. She wished now that she had simply taken their visiting cards. Matters were clearly far more intricate than she had considered possible. She had seen wars waged over less. Slights could be remembered for years. 'What precisely is the problem?'

'Your marriage, to be frank.' Lady Bolt tapped a finger against her cup. 'The opening quadrille is normally led by the host and hostess, except when one of the masters has just married. And Miranda has been desperately looking forward to it. Her conversation revolves around it. She has been practising her dance steps for weeks. We ordered a new gown, specifically with the quadrille in mind.'

'Gold net over ivory silk to show off my colouring.' Miss Bolt fluffed up her curls and batted her lashes.

'I did not know the tradition.' Phoebe shifted uneasily on her seat. She should have guessed that it was a possibility. Most balls opened with some sort of dance performed by newly-weds. She had not danced for a few years, but she was certain that she would acquit herself well. She had to pray that her gown would be up to it as well. Northumberland might be a backwater, but she could tell from the two ladies in front of her that costume was up to the minute. 'Thank you for being so kind and telling me about it. I will make sure both my gown and my steps are up to the challenge.'

'Our Miranda was promised the quadrille this year as brides were distinctly lacking on the ground.' Lady Bolt's expression became more severe.

'No doubt her turn will come.' Phoebe forced her lips to smile. So this was what the visit was all about. They thought that they could browbeat her into giving up her place. Simon was sure to know about the slight, if she did give in, and Phoebe discovered that she did not want to. As Simon's wife she would have standing in this neighbourhood, and would not have to defer to Lady Bolt. 'You could hardly be asking me to stand aside, Lady Bolt.'

'On the contrary, I simply wanted apprise you of the situation and allow you to make the choice.' Both the Bolts adopted self-satisfied expressions.

'More tea, Lady Bolt?' Phoebe held up the pot, hoping that Lady Bolt would take the hint and cut the visit short.

Lady Bolt defiantly held out her cup as Miranda played with the pearl button of her glove. Phoebe concentrated on pouring out the tea as she vowed that she would dance the quadrille. She refused to give way. Declining another serving of tea, Miss Bolt asked in low voice, 'Did you happen to see Mr Gough, the curate?'

'A tall man with light brown hair and a shy smile.'

'Yes, that is him.' Miss Bolt's cheeks coloured faintly. 'He was not at church on Sunday and I had hoped that he was well.'

'He seemed in good spirits. He was one of the witnesses to our marriage.'

'I had wondered. I considered sending him a fruit basket. If you do see him, please give him my regards.' Miss Bolt straightened her bonnet and then continued in a louder tone. 'Still, a curate is not the same as a red-coated soldier, and I do adore the way soldiers look in their coats.'

'One of my stepbrothers has become a soldier.'

'Ah, he sounds more promising and is connected to a title. Mama has promised me a Season in London if necessary.'

'Seasons can be a tremendous trial. I suffered through several.'

'But you were not an Incomparable.'

Phoebe replaced the teapot. 'Actually I was. These things are much easier if you have the proper breeding behind you.'

Lady Bolt's mouth opened and shut several times, giving her a distinctly codfish-like look. 'You must understand that we came out of concern and a desire to be helpful.'

'I understand precisely what drove you to come.' Phoebe inclined her head. Lady Bolt and her daughter reminded her of some of the more sycophantic types in the London Season, the type of people she had sworn to avoid if at all possible. 'It is wonderful to find such sterling manners up here in Northumberland.'

Two red spots appeared on Lady Bolt's cheeks.

'We have said our piece, Mrs Clare. Should you require anything, please call on me. It can be difficult dealing with another's child. I have often warned Miranda about the dangers of marrying a widower.'

'Indeed, Lady Bolt, I had not noticed. Robert is a perfectly charming child.'

Miranda Bolt choked on her tea.

'I do believe it is time we are going. Delightful to have met you, Mrs Clare.'

'Do call again. I plan to be at home on Wednesdays.'

Phoebe waited until the pair had left, then she flung open the spinet's cover and attacked the keys. Music flowed from her fingertips, loud, violent music that gave vent to her feelings. The sort of music that Sophia had always derided as having far too much passion. She had hoped it would revive her spirits but, somehow, it left her feeling emptier than before.

'Are we late, Papa?' Robert asked Simon as they entered the house. 'All the lamps have been lit.'

'A bit later than I planned. Things took longer at the colliery. After the fire damp was sorted, other problems arose.' As Simon said the words, he knew they were excuses. 'Hopefully Phoebe will forgive us.'

'She is bound to. Phee is like that. She forgave my untidy bed yesterday.' Robert gave a small smile. He had had a brief sleep in the carriage, but otherwise he appeared fine. Simon wished that he had the same easy assurance that Robert possessed.

Robert's reaction to the colliery pleased him immeasurably. The various engines and pumps had entranced the boy, and Robert kept asking questions about how this or that worked. But Simon found it difficult to be as enthusiastic; his thoughts often circled back to Phoebe and how she had looked in the early morning light when the dawn had kissed her bare shoulder.

He'd had to go, or else he would have woken her. And he could not bear to see her eyes, accusing him.

'Mrs Clare is in the drawing room,' Jenkins said, taking Simon's hat and gloves. 'The spinet has a lovely sound. Peaceful.'

'Thank you.' Simon ignored the sudden tightening in his shoulder. Exactly what would Phoebe be like today? He had hoped to be back before she woke, but it appeared she had spent the day playing music. A good sign or a bad one?

Robert raced on ahead, calling for her. And shouting about the engines he had seen.

He discovered them in the alcove of the drawing room. The spinet was open, but no music lay on the top. She glanced at him with her grey eyes, one delicate eyebrow raised. Her hair was simply dressed in a top knot. Several tendrils softly curled around her face. Simon sucked in his breath and wondered how he could ever have left her, and then knew why he'd had to. She was far too tempting. If he had stayed, she might have sensed that twisted part of him, and he could not bear to see her eyes when that happened. He had no wish for her to turn from him like Jayne had done.

'You are up and dressed for the afternoon.' He forced his voice to be even.

'I did not spend the entire day in bed.' She crossed her arms and frowned at him. 'I have never spent an entire day in bed.'

'We must make arrangements some day…' He lowered his voice, but there was no answering smile on her face and her cheeks did not flush with colour. Simon's heart sank slightly. He had hoped to avoid the recriminations that had marred his wedding morning all those years ago by taking Robert away for the day, but perhaps he had made a mistake. 'But you should have rested.'

'You left before I woke.' The words grated over his nerves and he braced himself for the recriminations and the subtle anglings for a treat, a way to assuage his guilt. Everything, in fact, that he had hoped to keep away from.

'Someone needed to look after Robert and this appeared to be the ideal opportunity to take up your suggestion. He enjoyed his journey to the colliery far more than I thought he would.'

'I was quite willing to look after him. It is why I am here.'

Simon bit back the words explaining that she was now his wife and here for an entirely different purpose. 'You looked so peaceful that I didn't have the heart.'

'But you took him to the colliery…'

'To see the machines. I am only following your orders, attempting to spend more time with Robert.' He ruffled Robert's hair. 'He acquitted himself admirably. If he behaves, he may have another trip, before he returns to school. At the rate he is improving, it won't be long.'

Phoebe sat with her back perfectly straight. She had played music until it seemed that all the emotion was wrung out from her. Simon had never said that it would be a love match. It was a practical marriage. She had to be content with that. A tight hard place developed inside her. She refused to let him see the hurt.

'Robert has dark shadows under his eyes,' she said as she put her hand against his forehead. Cool, but fevers could so easily return. She hated feeling cross and out of sorts, particularly as Robert appeared so happy, but she wished that she had been consulted about the outing. 'I should not like to think about his fever returning.'

'But he is happy, aren't you, Robert?'

Robert gave a quick nod and started again on the engines and about how Simon promised him that he could do the drawings for the new engine. It bothered Phoebe. Simon and Robert had been having a marvellous time while she had endured Lady Bolt and her daughter.

'You have said your piece, Robert, and now it is best if you return to your room.' Phoebe heard the sharpness in her voice and cringed. She stood and reached over, whispering in his ear, 'No doubt you will want to tell Hannibal all about it.'

'Yes, I have promised Papa that I will go straight to bed, but playing with Hannibal would be better.' He gave a cheeky smile and hurried off. 'To think engines could be that big and that noisy. Wait until the boys at school hear.'

The door closed with a loud bang and his steps echoed on the stairs. Phoebe regarded her hands. It was obvious that his day out had done Robert a world of good. Phoebe wanted to be unselfish and be pleased for him, but she wished that Simon had kissed her good morning, or showed in some way that last night had meant something to him.

'Shall I see that Robert is settled?' she said into the silence. She did not want to stand there, awkward. How did one greet one's husband after he had deserted one's bed? What was the proper form of etiquette? She wanted to pretend that it meant nothing, but his actions had hurt her more than she thought possible.

'No, leave him. He is a big boy. I trust him to do as he is told. I want to hear about your day.' He made no move to take her in his arms, but simply looked at her. It was disconcerting to see him looking at her with both eyes, without his eye patch. 'Did you sleep well?'

His voice played over her skin like a caress. Phoebe resisted the temptation to lean her head against his chest. Instead she rearranged the folds of her gown. 'Lady Bolt called. No orders were left with Jenkins and so I felt I had to receive her or risk giving offence.'

'Lady Bolt has a very thick hide.'

'Simon!'

He hung his head. 'You must know that I did not expect any callers today. I would never have left you to face Lady Bolt and her daughter without an ally. They are an acquired taste.'

'I am used to receiving callers. The niceties of society are not beyond me.'

Simon lifted an eyebrow and he shifted slightly.

His eyes became a fraction cooler. 'Was there something in particular she called about?'

'To congratulate us on our marriage and to explain about the Grand Allies ball.'

'Lady Bolt's ability to garner news never ceases to astonish me. If Wellington could somehow figure out her secret, this detestable war with the French would be over and grain prices would be back to normal.'

'She met Mrs Fletcher at the haberdashery.'

'Ah, all is explained. The haberdashery. I had wondered what her secret was. Lady Bolt seems to know the news before anyone else. She takes great pride in her ability to discern the gossip.'

'Apparently Miss Bolt is to have a gold net over ivory silk gown. It was described in great detail. She had plans to be in the opening quadrille.'

There, she had said it. Simon should know what she was talking about. She assumed he was familiar with the operations of the Grand Allies ball.

'I had quite forgotten that was coming up.' Simon's face was a bland mask. 'Do you want to go? My sister used to avoid balls if she possibly could. I have always gone. It is terribly bad form if one does not go. It is in four weeks' time. There is an invitation somewhere on my desk. Under the latest survey of Ladywell Main, if memory serves.'

'I presume it is the done thing for all colliery owners and their wives to attend.' Phoebe hated the cold sound of his voice. Did he not approve of her mingling with the county set? She wished he would say something kind, be the way he was last night. 'There is the question of the ball gown. All mine are several years old and cannot compete with gold net over ivory silk. But I am quite quick with my needle if a length of cloth could be procured. I used to make over my stepmother's gowns after my father's death. It solved many problems.'

'I refuse to have anyone saying that my wife is not properly clothed. You must see a modiste without delay. You only had to say, Phoebe.'

'I did not like to ask.' Phoebe plucked at the folds on her gown. 'I am hoping that my trunks will arrive soon. I have written to Edmund for the third time. There is a rose one that can be made over if everything falls into place…'

Her voice trailed away at his intense gaze.

'You will have a generous allowance, Phoebe.' He reached into his coat pocket and withdrew several large bills. 'I refuse to have my wife in a made-over gown at the Grand Allies ball. There is a little French woman that Lady Bolt uses in the village.'

'It is no bother, I assure you. The ball is not for several weeks. A length of cloth will suffice. Jenny assures me that her mother is a seamstress, if I need any help.'

'It is best if you have some money,' Simon continued as if she had not spoken. 'I always insist that seamstresses and tailors are paid promptly. It saves a great deal of bother. I have seen far too many good men go under because a few aristocrats failed to pay on time. I must insist.'

Phoebe backed away from the money and from his cold assessing look. After her father's death, she had been appalled at the tradesmen's bills and how Alice would never look at them, but somehow the money in Simon's hand seemed to imply that he did not trust her to be sensible. It was not how it was done. She was the daughter of an aristocrat. She never paid hard coin for anything. Tradesmen sent their bills. The thought of doing otherwise made her feel dirty.

She raised her head and stared back him. 'I am quite happy to have the bill sent to you.'

'There is no need for me to check on how much you spend. It seems barbaric. I trust you to be sensible.' He held out the money again and then added another bill. 'Have gold net if you prefer. I fancy this will cover it. As long as you keep within the budget, we will get on. I do not want to have to deal with false tears and protestations when suddenly your millinery bill is twice what was expected.'

Phoebe regarded Simon. He had wilfully mistaken her. She hated the thought that he was handing her money. 'I was not asking for a more elaborate ball gown. I was merely pointing out the practicalities.'

'And I will not have it said that my wife is not properly clothed. It would reflect badly on me if you wore less than the latest fashion. I allowed Diana to do as she wished, but my wife must be up to the minute. Now, come along and take the money. The French modiste will suffice. Newcastle is too far away for fittings.'

Phoebe stared down at the money and then back at her husband. He wanted her to look pleasant for the sake of his business. She supposed it was accurate. 'I will try to be sensible.'

'I never doubted you would.'

'If you will let me, it is time that I made sure Robert was in bed and asleep.'

'If you wish…' He paused as if he would say something more, but was uncertain how to put it.

She knew she was being a coward. But she could not stand the thought of being rejected. He had made no move to touch her. She had hoped for something more. The money he had handed her made her feel dirty, as if it were a payment. She had asked for no payment. She had not married him for his money.

'And when you are finished, you may join me for dinner.' His voice was clipped and precise. 'There is no need to change. Your gown is quite acceptable.'

'Yes, then we can discuss precisely what my duties will be.' Phoebe refused to let her smile waver. She drew on the lessons she had learnt about being cordial and charming. He would never know how much he hurt her. 'I have no wish to make a false step.'

'And tomorrow, I will take you visiting. It will save the neighbours calling and making a nuisance of themselves.'

'You don't have to if you have other things to do.'

'I refuse to allow the Bolts to hold the advantage. It is far better this way.' He paused, but his face held no warmth. 'The thought of ravening hordes of women descending on this house fills me with terror. We will go out and face them together.' He picked up a pile of letters and she knew she had been dismissed. He had dealt with a domestic crisis and had now turned his attention elsewhere.

Phoebe forced a smile on her lips. The promise of visiting was kind, but he seemed to really mean it. That he did want her to belong. Or was it simply for show? And would she end up feeling more alone than ever?

Chapter Thirteen

Simon's smile ached and his patience was stretched to breaking point as they said their final farewell. How Diana could have stood it for all these years, he had no idea. But he could finally begin to understand why she had always returned in a bad temper. Several of the women could drive a man to drink.

He had lost count of the number of houses they had visited. Mostly they had simply left cards, but at several of the grander houses, they had gone in and had yet another cup of lukewarm tea. A mind-numbing act of boredom, repeating the same words over and over again. He was certain that the words were engraved on his forehead. He could only bear the experience once. Phoebe would have to cope on her own from now on.

He looked at her sitting opposite him, her straw

hat with its blue ribbon sat squarely on her head and her gloved hands folded primly in her lap. She had sat by Robert's side for most of the night and he was uncertain if it was the marriage bed that she was trying to avoid, or just him. He would know by the end of the journey. He had promised himself that when they started out. It was why he had chosen the closed carriage, rather than the smarter open one.

'We should have started with the elder Mrs Sarsfield,' Phoebe remarked as the carriage drew away from the house.

'Why is that?'

'It seems to be the furthest out. I will remember for the next visit. It will save time if I get John to drive me here first.' She tapped her finger against her full lips.

'I have my reasons. Trust me.' Simon propped his cane against the door and pulled his gloves off. 'But when you are alone, of course, you must do as you see fit.'

She played with the button of her glove, revealing the cream of her wrist. 'I shall. It makes the most sense.'

Simon leant forwards. His leg brushed against hers and sent a warm pulse through his body.

Resolutely she looked out of the carriage window, ignoring his advance. He rubbed his chin, trying to decide on his next move.

The carriage went around a sharp bend. Phoebe slid into him, her body colliding with his. Breast hitting chest. She drew her breath in sharply. His good arm went around her and kept her there. He heard the sharp intake of her breath and forced his arm to loosen, giving her the choice.

'I should not want you to fall. You had best sit beside me rather than opposite.' He made a little more space on the seat.

'I am fine,' Phoebe lied as tingles went through her. She hated the way her voice quavered. She forced her body upright, intending to move away from his warmth, but his scent was like a drug and she wanted to stay there as long as possible. 'I did not expect the carriage to sway like that.'

'The road is a bit bumpy from here on out. You will need to be careful that you do not fall.' His arm cradled her a little closer. The temptation to place her head on his chest nearly overwhelmed her. She forced her back to be rigid.

'Do you travel this way often?'

'I have been on this road enough times,' he purred in a thick rich velvet voice that seemed to belong more to the night than to a closed carriage in the afternoon.

'I thought the tea at Mrs Sarsfield's was particularly good.' She strove for a normal tone, ignoring the way his fingers ran down the back of her neck. 'Green tea is supposed to be very good for the digestion.'

'Is it really? I have never investigated the matter.' His breath tickled the curve of her chin.

She wet her lips, intending to make another pleasantry, but he lowered his mouth to hers. Hot and insistent.

'If you speak about tea any more, I shall go mad,' he growled against her lips.

'I won't,' she whispered back, her mouth aching. 'It is just sometimes I can't help myself. There seems to be a void that needs to be filled and tea is a suitable subject. It is like the weather. Pleasant, and something on which one can safely have an opinion.'

His fingers gently removed her bonnet and placed it on the seat beside his hat. 'I would not want this to get mussed.'

'It is an old bonnet.' The words were difficult to say and she was aware of her pounding heart. Surely she was safe in a carriage. Nothing ever happened in carriages, not between married people.

She would keep to safe and appropriate subjects. 'Shall we speak about the state of the road?'

'Your hair is like silk.' He cupped his hand at the back of her head and tilted her face, raining small nibbling kisses on her eyes and her cheeks. 'I have wanted to do this all throughout the visit to the Ortners and the Sarsfields. I was bored by talk of tea.'

A warm curl wrapped itself around Phoebe. She raised her arm to put it around his neck and held it there. Her heart soared. She had not repulsed him. Here in the dim light of the carriage, he had to know who he was kissing. It was not like the darkened bedroom. He was kissing her because he wanted to kiss her, not because he was pretending she was someone else.

She pressed herself closer and gave her lips up to his. He took small discreet nibbles, nibbles that did strange things to her insides. Cautiously she parted her lips. Instantly the kisses changed, became harder, more insistent. His tongue demanded entrance and she willingly parted her lips, tasted him with a faint hint of coffee. It was a feast.

Then she pulled back slightly as the carriage rounded another bend. 'We shouldn't.'

'Why not? The driver is paid to keep his eyes on the road and not to worry about what is happening inside the carriage. He cannot hear what is going on.' He ran a hand down the length of her neck, making her tremble. 'Lots can happen in a carriage if you are with a willing partner.'

'Am I?' A deep ache filled her as she remembered what it had been like to be in his arms.

His fingers worked on her pelisse, undoing several buttons, revealing the depth of her gown and piece of lace that went around its neckline.

'I like to think so, but tell me if you become uncomfortable. We go no further than you wish.'

She gave a nod.

He slipped a hand between her lace and skin and cupped her breast. His thumb flicked her nipple, making it grow tight. Gently he eased the material down and revealed its rosy hue. The cool air caused her nipple to furl tighter. His hot breath touched it, warming it. Intense waves flooded through her. Her back arched towards him. He raised an eyebrow. 'Shall I or shan't I?'

'What are you doing?'

'Teaching you about why we are going the long way home. About what can be done in carriages when you are not quite alone,' he murmured against her breast before he suckled. 'Do you want to learn more?'

'Yes.'

The rocking of the carriage threw her against him and her body rose to meet his. The apex of her thighs met his hard arousal. And she knew that she wanted him, wanted to experience again that deep hunger. Her hands pulled at his head, raised his mouth so she could devour it. Her hands clung to his hair, holding him there.

'Feel, feel what are you are doing to me.'

He captured her hand and put it on his breeches. She felt him straining against the material. Her fingers fumbled with the buttons, slipped inside. She hesitated, then touched the pulsating steel. Silky soft and yet so hard. Alive.

His fingers lifted her skirt and pushed the material of her drawers away. Parting her curls, he found the edges of her sex and stroked. A deep shuddering went through her. She clutched his shoulders.

'Have I convinced you yet?'

She gave her head a little shake as his fingers continued their play. His mouth pressed kisses on her face.

'Perhaps this will help you make up your mind.'

He lifted her and settled her down, wedging her thighs wide. The tip of him nudged her. She started, remembering the pain, but his arm held her in place, kept her meeting him.

'Relax. Let the carriage do its work. Feel its movement. Enjoy it.'

She nodded slightly as the horses surged forwards, sending her body against him, again and again. Her body opened up to him.

The movement of the carriage echoed the movement of their bodies and a great shuddering came over her. Over them both. She placed her head against his chest and listened to his breathing. It was as if they were in a private world, a place remade just for them. A place where she belonged.

'We have nearly arrived back, Phoebe,' Simon's voice whispered in her ear.

Phoebe opened her eyes, astonished. The trip seemed to fly by. His arms held her against his chest. 'But…but…'

'It is a pleasant way to pass the journey, isn't it?' His eyes twinkled down at her.

She moved away from him and started to straighten her hair and rearrange her clothes. The pristine appearance was now hopelessly rumpled. Two buttons had come loose from her pelisse and the lace around the top of her gown sagged.

'You look delectable.'

'I may look several things, but delectable is not the word that springs immediately to mind.' She tried to put her hair back into order, but she had lost several of her pins.

'No one will mind.' His thumb traced the outline of her lips. 'You simply look thoroughly kissed, and we are just married. The servants will forgive you this once.'

The experience appeared to have left no mark on him. She wished that his neckcloth was more mussed or his breeches creased, but he appeared just the same as when he had stepped into the carriage. Not quite the same, as the watchfulness had gone from his mouth.

'I suppose you are right.'

'I know I am right.' He laughed and ran his hand along her shoulder. 'There is nothing wrong in enjoying your husband, Phoebe. We shall have to wager properly when we next play chess. What new torments can I devise?'

'You will be home this evening?'

'If my business allows me to be.' He gave a sigh. 'You must understand, Phoebe, there are other claims on my time. I will be there if I can be.'

The air abruptly left her lungs and she was left

gasping. How to answer him without revealing her growing feelings for him? She wanted to be with him. She wanted to share all of his life.

'I need to check on Robert.' She walked quickly away from him into the house, trying to compose her face. It would be so easy to fall in love with him and she knew that he had no heart to give her back. He had made that quite clear. She wanted to be in all parts of his life, to feel like she was truly a part of him. But that was impossible. Shadows remained between them, secret places that he refused to share.

She was grateful that he made no attempt to catch up with her. Or to hold her there. Once she was inside, she'd be able to catch her breath and to make sense of what had just happened.

'And what have we here? Is that my little cousin I see before me?' A lazy masculine voice resounded as she came into the hall.

Phoebe started and turned to face the impeccably dressed man coming down the stairs. 'Cousin Brett, I did not anticipate that you would be calling today. I thought you and Lady Coltonby remained in London.'

Her cousin smiled as he studied her face and the twinkle grew in his eyes. 'Have you had a rough ride?'

Phoebe glanced down and saw that she had mis-buttoned her pelisse.

'We were out visiting,' Phoebe said with as much dignity as she could muster.

'So I am given to understand.'

She inclined her head and wished the ground would open and swallow her. If she had but known of her cousin's arrival, she would have made sure that she was appropriately dressed. She would never have permitted what had just passed between her and Simon. A trembling filled her. But what was worse, a large piece of her was pleased with what they had done. 'Is Lady Coltonby with you?'

'Diana is upstairs visiting her nephew. Once she knew the danger had passed, there was no holding her back. She was determined to come.'

'I will go to her immediately.'

'If you like, but I suspect that she would rather see her brother. She has a few words which she wants to say to him.' He quirked an eyebrow and Phoebe knew her cheeks were scarlet. 'Simon's actions were rather unexpected.'

'Coltonby, I had no idea you were arriving today,' Simon said, coming up to put an arm about Phoebe. 'This is indeed a pleasant surprise.'

'I understand you were out visiting. You and

your *wife*. Diana was quite taken aback to learn that you already had a wife. She swore through our journey that you would never marry without her.'

'We married two days ago…in church. Quietly. Simon thought his sister was otherwise occupied,' Phoebe gasped out. 'No one was there, not even Robert. Simon felt it best. My family could not come either.'

Phoebe pressed her lips together and hoped her cousin would accept the explanation. Otherwise the relations between the brother and sister might be strained. And she did not want to cause that. Families were important.

'Gretna Green?'

'Ladywell Old Church.'

'Admirable, but I seem to remember you were the one who insisted on a large wedding for Diana.'

'I wanted our wedding to be quiet. It was a second wedding, rather than a first.' Simon stood completely still. 'I wanted it to be completely different. Unassuming.'

Phoebe's insides twisted. Completely different. He had insisted that Diana have a huge wedding, but he had opted instead for a quiet one for her. He had only married her for honour after all.

'A hole-in-the-corner marriage? I thought you

thoroughly disapproved of such things, Clare. I seem to remember a lecture you gave Diana but a few months ago…' There was laughter in her cousin's eyes and he appeared to be enjoying Simon's discomfort. 'Or perhaps there was a reason why you had to get married, Clare. Were you caught in a compromising position? It is good to see you do have a spark of initiative in you.'

'You should watch your words, Coltonby!'

Simon's hands clenched at his sides. Phoebe took a step forwards. 'I will not have brawling in this house.'

'The lady has spoken.' Her cousin inclined his head. 'I do apologise, Clare. My remarks were in poor taste.'

'You are lucky you are my brother-in-law, Coltonby, and I hold my sister's happiness close to my heart.'

'It makes a change, Clare. I did not know you had a heart.'

'How is your wife?' Phoebe asked quickly. 'Did she find the journey over-taxing? How goes her confinement?'

'We took it in easy stages by coach.'

'A packet boat is far quicker than a coach.' Simon's scowl increased. 'My sister should know better. It is her own fault then that she failed to make the wedding.'

'Diana did not think the sea would do her stomach any good,' her cousin replied. 'Her safety is my primary concern.'

Simon nodded stiffly. 'Where is she?'

'Up with Robert. I thought they needed some time alone together. She kept demanding the horses go faster. It is a hard job keeping that woman safe. Sometimes, I wonder if I should wrap her in cotton wool. There are so many dangers lurking out there.'

'That is the only reason I tolerate you, Coltonby. I know you love my sister.'

'That is beyond dispute.'

Simon gave a distinct nod and moved up the steps, his frock coat flapping. Phoebe was unable to keep her heart from leaping. His injuries had improved so much over the past few weeks that it was truly astonishing.

Brett Farnham gave a laugh, before he raised Phoebe's hand to his lips. 'You are wearing your most severe frown, Phoebe. I do hope you forgive me, Cousin, but it was priceless to see his face. It will do him good to have a set down from Diana. He gets away with far too much.'

'Is Lady…is my sister-in-law very upset?' Phoebe withdrew her hand. She had always enjoyed her second cousin on the rare occasions that they met, but now she disliked the way in which he teased Simon.

'She lost her wager.' Her cousin gave a self-satisfied smile. 'I told her that he wouldn't, but she was certain her brother would wait. I suspect not being able to drive for the duration of her confinement will bother her far more than Clare's marrying you. Above all she wants her brother to be happy.'

'You wagered on my wedding?'

'A friendly sort of wager. It pleases me that I understand my brother-in-law and his considerations.' Her cousin gave a languid shrug. 'It will do Clare good to be married again. Marriage is a highly agreeable state and I can wholeheartedly recommend it. Of course, the Clares are a bit stubborn…'

'You are speaking to one.'

'Ah, but to one by marriage. You were my cousin first.' He reached out and gave her a kiss on the cheek. 'Remember that. I know what Clare can be like. Bossy. Arrogant. Far too used to having his own way.'

'A bit like you then.'

'Touché, sweet cousin.'

Phoebe kept her lips tightly pressed together. Exactly how much did her cousin know or guess? 'I know what he is like as well. Our marriage is not the same as yours to Lady Coltonby. It is not…a love match.'

Brett raised an eyebrow and his gaze travelled slowly down her figure. 'I will take your word for it. My brother-in-law may be many things, but he is no fool. He had no reason to marry unless he desired it.'

'If you will excuse me, I had best change. I did not think to meet anyone and I do want to look my best for Lady…for Diana.'

'You will need what is in the drawing room, then. Your brother has sent your trunks and a letter.' Brett reached into his frockcoat and pulled out a sealed letter.

'Edmund sent my trunks with you?' Phoebe hated to think how paltry her possessions must seem. Only a few dresses and trinkets. And her grandmother's pearls.

'He knew we were coming and wished to save money.'

'That sounds like Edmund.' Phoebe gave a short laugh as she opened the letter and rapidly scanned it. Her heart sank as she read his brief note. He hoped she did not mind, but he had discovered her pearls when packing up and had needed the money for his pupillage. Her grandmother's pearls. She had carefully saved them for emergencies. He had no right. It was not the way a brother—even a stepbrother—behaved. She could never see Simon behaving in that fashion. And what was worse, she knew that Edmund would never have behaved that way towards his mother or Sophia. It was only her that he treated in such a cavalier fashion. She glanced up at the ceiling and bit her lip, crumpling the note in her hand.

'Not bad news, I hope.'

'Typical for my brother.' Phoebe forced her lips to smile. She would decide the exact wording of her letter later. All she knew was that she had given him a chance and he had behaved terribly. He had taken advantage of her. It was not something that families did. She felt dreadfully alone. 'He sends salutations and he regrets that he could not come up here himself, but is otherwise detained.'

'What do you think of your new mother?' Simon heard Diana say to Robert as he stood in the corridor. Diana's voice was light, but he could hear the stern note behind it.

'Phee is not my mother.'

A sharp intake of breath from Diana as she absorbed the knowledge. 'Who is she, then? Your nurse?'

'Phee. Just Phee. She brought me Hannibal.'

'Hannibal?'

'My cat.'

'Your cat? Really, Robert, I do not intend to play a game of questions with you.'

'I used to enjoy them, Aunt Diana.'

'I have missed you, Robert Clare, but not your questions. Truly not your questions.'

'Phee encourages them.'

Simon entered the room and saw Diana kneeling beside the bed, holding Robert's hand. There was a sort of glow about her that he had not seen before. Her hair appeared glossier and she carried herself with more assurance. But he could also see the puzzled frown she wore between her brows, the same expression she used when Robert's pronouncements became too much for her. 'Marriage suits you, Diana.'

'Do you think so?' His sister spun around. 'I wonder if it suits you, Simon.'

They chatted with Robert for a few moments longer before leaving him to sleep.

'He is so pale, Simon,' Diana said the moment the door closed. 'And thin. I could see his bones under his nightshirt. Is he being fed properly?'

'He is far better now than before Phoebe came.' Simon closed his eyes, thinking back to the dark days. 'You showed uncharacteristic good sense in sending her. She is an admirable addition to the family.'

A hurt expression crossed her face. 'You married her. Married her without me being there. And you insisted on being at my wedding.'

'I wanted my second wedding to be very different from my first.'

'Simon! I am your sister! You could have waited.' Diana crossed her arms and glared at him. 'I even wagered with Brett that my brother could not be so cruel and unfeeling.'

Simon stared at his sister, surprised at her reaction and the look of hurt in her eyes. He had thought that her mind would be far too full of Coltonby and the impending birth of her first child to risk returning here. He had thought that he no longer mattered. There was no point in waiting for someone who would not appear. He had misjudged his sister.

Had Phoebe wanted her family there? Perhaps he should have offered to pay for them. He rejected the notion. Phoebe would have told him if money was the problem.

'Have you returned to Northumberland for good?' he asked.

'It is our home—Brett's and mine. I always planned on coming back here. Once I heard about your impending marriage, I moved heaven and earth to get up here. You had to know that I would.' Her hand plucked at her skirt and she resolutely refused to look at him.

Simon sighed and regarded the ceiling. Pregnant women often took strange notions into their heads. 'You will like Phoebe once you get to know her. Blame me, not her.'

'I would have been here sooner, but Brett insisted that we take our time. Some days he acts like I am made of spun glass rather than the hardy Northumberian that I am. He has even forbidden driving. Women have been having babies since the dawn of time.'

'He loves you, Diana.'

Her cheek glowed and she lowered her gaze. 'But that does not make it any easier. I suspect you were cross when Phoebe arrived, though. I had to do something. I could not just leave you stranded. You sounded so desperate in your letter.'

'Robert's condition frightened me.'

'But it worked out. If he is looking better, I dread to think what he must have been like before.' Diana raised a handkerchief to her eyes. 'You must forgive me. My condition means I cry at practically anything. I dare say that I am driving Brett mad. He is very good. He simply keeps handing me fresh handkerchiefs.'

Simon shifted uneasily. His sister knew him too well. And he was pleased with how she had blossomed. The marriage to Brett had all the hallmarks of being a success. He had known that his marriage to Jayne was a failure before the first week was out.

'Did I say I was unhappy about Phoebe's arrival once I became used to the idea? I merely said that you failed to arrive when requested. There is a difference.'

'Do not split words with me, Simon Clare.' Diana shook her handkerchief at him. 'You did not want me at your wedding. And that hurts.'

'I never meant to hurt you, Diana. You know that.'

She gave a small sniff and seemed mollified. 'Well, I've lost my wager with Brett that you wouldn't. Now I shall have to submit to his rules about driving.'

'Ah, this is all about you losing a wager, rather than your brother marrying without you.' He shook his head as she hung hers. 'Admit it, Diana. You wanted to win.'

'I was certain this time that I had won. And I did love driving the curricle. Now I shan't. He won't even let me drive the pony cart.'

'It bothers me that Coltonby shows more than a modicum of common sense.'

'Well, he did marry me.'

'Yes, he showed a bit more decorum about that than you. How does it feel to be an honest woman?'

'I like being Brett's wife very much.' Diana leant forwards and gave him a hug. 'And what about you? I thought you had vowed never to marry again. My proud independent brother. I wagered with Brett on that one, too. It should have been one wager I won easily.'

Simon carefully shrugged a shoulder. He was not about to start explaining his reasoning to his sister. She was so happy, so convinced of the validity of true romance. Seeing her and how she had changed, he was tempted to believe that for her it was the case. For him, he would have to be satisfied with a simple regard. All-consuming love too often turned into all-consuming hatred. 'Marriage became a necessity.'

'Did you compromise the girl? How could you, Simon? I trusted you.' Diana wiped her hands against her gown. 'I would never have sent her up here. I thought you would not be tempted at all. Brett said that he was not surprised. She had a reputation for being a beauty when she was younger, and he maintained that her figure was still exquisite and that you would have to be dead not to notice.'

'I am not prepared to discuss my private life with my sister. I married Phoebe because it made sense. I could not allow things to continue in their current state. The house was going to rack and ruin. You would not come back. Robert was going to be impossible when Phoebe had gone.'

'You did not marry for love.'

'Phoebe understands. There is no pretence between us. I made no false promises. I want a marriage on a secure footing.'

'What could be more secure than marrying someone you love and who loves you back?'

'Once I married for infatuation, Diana. It was not a success.'

'Not all marriages are like that. You were unlucky with Jayne. But marriage is far more pleasant when there is a certain regard between partners.' The corners of her mouth twitched. 'I suppose there are compensations. You could have married the Honourable Miranda. I would never have forgiven you for that.'

'Please credit me with some sense. I pity the man who becomes involved with her. She cannot look beyond a man's face or title.' Simon fingered his scar.

Diana sobered. 'I hope you are wrong there, Brother. She once said something important to me, and perhaps one day she will surprise us all.'

'Now come and meet your new sister. And be pleasant.'

'First, tell me how much she knows about your first marriage? About Jayne? About Robert?'

'They were débutantes together, Diana. But the past is past, and it is the future I am concerned about.'

'She doesn't know, then.' Diana put her hand to her throat. 'I will allow you to tell her, but you had best do it before she hears a tale from the gossipmongers. You know some people have long memories.'

'What am I supposed to say to her? How can I explain? I shall wait until the moment is right and trust the gossips to be concerned with other matters.'

'I do hope you know what you are doing, Simon Clare.'

'You should trust me, Diana. When have my schemes ever gone wrong?' Simon ignored her pointed look at his scars. Once he was sure that he could trust Phoebe, he would confide in her, but for now he wanted to keep his marriage secure.

Chapter Fourteen

'Seeing you side by side makes me realise how much the Clares look alike.' Phoebe looked from Simon to Diana when they met on the landing. Even if she had not known they were brother and sister, she would have guessed the family connection. 'Your chins and eyes are the same. All of you.'

'All of us?' Simon's eyebrow lifted, intrigued. 'How many of us are there?'

'All of you, even Robert,' Phoebe explained.

Phoebe noticed Diana gave Simon a significant look. There was something there. Simon gave a little shake of his head. Diana shrugged.

'I had always considered that Robert looked far more like his mother,' Diana said before Phoebe was able to ask. 'But now that you mention it, perhaps there is a bit more Clare in him than either Simon or I thought.'

'He looks like his mother, I will grant you that,' Phoebe said, remembering the pure golden beauty of Jayne Northfield. 'But his eyes, his hair colouring and the way he carries his head—those are pure Simon.'

'If you wish to mention his temper, I will agree with you.' Diana's eyes danced. 'The pair of them are enough to drive anyone to the madhouse. I must confess that I used to escape out to the summerhouse whenever the devilment and the incessant questions became too much. I wonder, knowing them, how Simon ever managed to make you agree to the marriage.'

'Your brother can be very persuasive at times.' Phoebe resisted the temptation to pull the neck of her gown higher and wished she had met Diana after she had changed rather than before.

'You mean he bullied you.' Diana cupped her hand around her mouth and raised her voice. 'I know where the blame for the quick marriage lies and it is with my brother, not my new sister.'

Phoebe struggled to keep a straight face at Simon's expression. She had always wanted a sister and perhaps in time she and Diana could become friends as well. Sophia had seen Phoebe as some sort of rival for Charles's affections and had resented any time that he had spent with his stepsister.

'There are a few reasons, Diana, why I was pleased you went away,' Simon remarked in a dry voice. 'The house was so…much more peaceful. You must not go telling stories. The memory my sister has for slights.'

'But there are others why you are glad that she has returned,' Phoebe said quickly in case Diana somehow misinterpreted the remark. 'He has moved the spinet back into the drawing room.'

'You have moved the spinet back.' Diana clapped her hands.

'Phoebe plays,' Simon replied. 'It has been a long time since this house has had music. I had quite forgotten what it was like.'

'Your hand appears better. You used to play such lovely tunes when I was growing up. So I imagine Phoebe will be fighting with you for time on it.'

'And then there were those saucy songs at Cambridge,' Brett remarked, coming to the bottom of the stairs to join in the conversation. 'I have a certain recollection of a few of them.'

'Your recollections of Cambridge are bound to

be hazy, Coltonby,' Diana said quickly to the general laughter.

Phoebe stared at Diana in astonishment. Simon played the spinet? It was Simon's and not Jayne's. The bubbles that had been fizzing along her veins since the carriage ride popped all at once, leaving her feeling flat. He had not lied to her exactly, but he had kept it hidden. Why? Did he think she would have forced him to play? Or did it go deeper than that? Whatever the reason it hurt, it hurt more than she thought possible. 'I did not realise that Simon played.'

'He used to…until the accident.'

'I gave it up before that, Diana. Long before that. Stop causing mischief.' Simon frowned. 'My hand has little to do with it. My life started to revolve around other things. There was no longer the time. I doubt I could even play the simplest melody.'

'But you used to love it,' Diana persisted. 'I have a distinct memory of you sitting with Robert on your knee as you played a little march for him. This was long ago, Phoebe, before I left for London. Jayne was away somewhere and we were having tea in the drawing room. You do remember, don't you, Simon?'

Simon stood with a tightened jaw and squared

shoulders. His voice had become clipped. 'I have some small recollection of it.'

'I should like to hear you play one day,' Phoebe said as Simon glowered at his sister. Simon had obviously played with his son once upon a time, but what had happened? And why did the memory of it make him so upset? 'It might even strengthen your wrist if you played.'

'I doubt I can remember how.'

'Such things never go away. We could play a duet some evening.'

'Yes, that would be pleasant.' Simon's voice was as cold as ice. 'I shall look forward to it.'

Phoebe's throat closed. He would not do it. He would have never told her if Diana had remained silent. Music was so important to her and he could not even share the fact that he used to play. He would have never let her know. A small fact like that would have given her pleasure and he refused to share it. It was like he wanted to keep her locked in a box, away from everything in his life, things that his sister knew. Hurt stabbed through her. It was as if he had put her in one place and meant to keep her there, and the rest of his life was closed to her. Hurriedly she made excuses and hoped that no one noticed the sudden tears in her eyes.

Simon watched her go and silently cursed. He saw now that he had been wrong. He should have explained about the spinet, but she had taken such pleasure in it. He had wanted to surprise her when he could play back up to his old standard.

'Thank you, Diana.'

'What have I done?' His sister's eyes widened with mock innocence. Simon ground his teeth. She appeared determined to make him suffer for not waiting. With her careless words, she could have ruined everything. He had hoped by ignoring that part of him, it would go away. He had even begun to wonder if it had already gone. 'How was I to know that you had never bothered to explain to your wife that you played the spinet? What other subjects are forbidden? I did warn you to beware of the secrets that you keep.'

'Do not cause mischief, Diana.'

'And here I was, thinking you were content with your marriage of convenience. Do you want something more? Do you care about your wife's regard?'

'You are the one who used those words.' Simon glowered at his sister. 'Simply because you were not here for the wedding, do not seek to drive a wedge between my wife and me. You are my sister, but I will not have my marriage turned into a battleground.'

'Perish the thought.' Diana clapped her hand over her mouth. 'Oh, Simon, I am so sorry. I am such a beast. But I do want you to be happy without the shadows in your eyes. Phoebe should know about your past.'

That was exactly what Phoebe should *not* know. One tiny slip and the whole ugly truth would come out. It might have been fine before, but Simon knew that he wanted to see admiration in Phoebe's eyes, not the horror and disgust that he saw each time he looked in the mirror. He needed her touch. What was between them was too frail and new to withstand his past.

'Diana, I know what you want for me, but what you and Brett have is unique.'

Her husband approached them and she slipped her arm through his. 'Simon thinks what we have is unique. Do you agree, darling?'

Coltonby dropped a kiss on his wife's upturned face. The easy intimacy bothered Simon. He was happy for his sister, but it made him all too aware of how much his life had been lacking until Phoebe had come along, and how much he wanted to hold on to her.

'I will not be drawn into a dispute between brother and sister. I am bound to lose.'

'Your sense continues to astonish and astound me, Coltonby.'

'The letter Phoebe received from her brother today contained bad news. She went pale,' Coltonby said.

'Oh, no!' Diana cried. 'And here I was worried that I had upset her and that was why she rushed off suddenly. I am truly a beast.'

'It could be anything. Phoebe will tell me if there is any problem.' Simon regarded the door. He wanted to rush upstairs and demand Phoebe's explanation. Was it her brother or his failure to confide in her?

'Her other brother James asked me to keep an eye out for her before he left with the regiment. He worries that Edmund might be easily influenced.'

'I know the type—aristocratic waster.'

'Your words, not mine.' Coltonby inclined his head. 'But I would give the same assessment. James knows what he owes to Phoebe. He told me the night before he left to join his regiment. On the younger brother's own merit, I would not lift a finger to save him, but your wife's coming up here meant the world to Diana.'

'Phoebe's coming up here meant much to me as well.'

'Indeed, but I did want you to know the situation. Both brothers are able bodied and quick witted when they choose.'

'But like many sons of aristocrats, they refuse to do an honest day's work.'

'I don't think that is the case. James's colonel wrote me a glowing report. He expects great things from the man. Rather I think life has been made too easy for them.'

Simon put his hands on the mantelpiece. He understood Coltonby's unspoken warning. As he suspected, Phoebe had made it too easy for her stepbrothers. She had not allowed them to grow up. 'James is settled and that leaves Edmund, the one who wishes to go into the law.'

'I saw no such inclination when I met him. He seemed more intent on drinking the Thames dry.'

'Indeed.' Simon waited. Coltonby's words were not simply an idle way to pass the time. 'What else has my new brother-in-law done?'

'He sold Phoebe's pearls to me. They belonged in my family once. He claimed that she had given them to him. Somehow, I don't think she would. If she had wanted to, she would have used them to purchase James's commission and saved herself a trip up to Northumberland.'

Simon silently swore. It bothered him that Phoebe's trust in her stepbrothers had been misplaced. She had given up so much for them and with so little back. 'Have you brought them with you?'

'You understand my motives.' Coltonby withdrew a slim box from his coat. 'I did not want to risk the possibility that they might go out of the family, waiting for your instructions.'

'I will write you a banker's draft.'

'There is no need.' Coltonby pulled at his cuffs and his face assumed its usual arrogant expression. 'You once tore up my draft. I would do the same to yours. Think of it as a wedding present.'

'But…'

'The money will see him through, but you will have to think what to do when the next request comes, because there will most certainly be one.'

Simon stared at Coltonby. At Cambridge, he had thought him insupportable, but the man had changed. Simon had not expected the kindness, or the concern. 'Thank you for letting me know.'

'Do you have a plan?'

Simon regarded the embers of the fire. Phoebe had to be protected. That much was clear, but equally, the brother would just keep coming back. He would solve the problem simply—get the man where he could keep an eye on him.

'The only thing I can do is to wait and to watch, to see what she does next. I will not have blood-sucking relatives going behind my back, bleeding me dry. For some misguided reason Phoebe feels that she needs to support men who are fully capable of supporting themselves. If she asks, I will tell her so.'

'You are a hard man, Clare.'

'A fair one. I am giving her the opportunity to turn to me.'

'Then you had best hope she takes it.' Coltonby swung away and began talking to Diana.

'More than you realise,' Simon said softly. 'More than you realise.'

'You never said that you could play the spinet.' The words finally spilled out of Phoebe halfway through their chess match that evening. She hated the petulant way they sounded, as if she was a child, but she had waited until Diana and Brett had left and the words just bubbled out of her.

Simon's hand paused momentarily on the bishop, but then he moved with a graceful ease.

'You never enquired. It is not a dark secret, Phoebe. My hand remains stiff. I cannot play. I will not play until I can play as before.'

Phoebe put her lips together and concentrated on the board. It was not what she had meant. And he knew it. She had given him everything and he had held back even the smallest most insignificant details from her. The hurt welled up inside and threatened to overwhelm her. How could she even begin to explain about Edmund when he refused to share even the smallest detail of his life with her?

'Are there any other talents you have kept hidden? Anything else I should know about?'

Simon stilled, took another sip of port. 'What do you mean?'

'Things I should know. Things that are general knowledge, but which you have neglected to tell me. I really know very little about your history. About your business. About your life. I am your wife. I have the right to know.'

She waited, remembering the look Simon had given Diana earlier. Surely if there was a question about Robert's heritage, Simon would have said something. He would not leave her simply to discover it.

'The past is the past. My face is towards the

future. You need not worry about your reputation becoming soiled because of something I did. You do not see me quizzing you on everything that has happened in your life.'

He leant forwards as if he expected her to answer with some great insight.

Phoebe shrank further back into the armchair. She should have brought up Edmund's letter before now, but she refused to ask Simon for the money to get the pearls back. How could she explain what the pearls meant to her? And that she longed to have them back? He had already done enough. She did not even know where Edmund had sold them. 'My life is very simple. You know what has happened to me, why I married you.'

She prayed that he would end the conversation and she would not have to confess that she was coming to care for him. And how it had come about before her family had washed their hands of her and not after. She was not clinging to him because she had nowhere else to go. It would be too humiliating since he obviously did not care enough about her to confide in her.

'So I know every last thing about you?'

Slowly Phoebe shook her head. His lips curved

upwards in a sarcastic smile. 'I thought not. Shall we leave it there?'

'But do you intend to play the spinet again?' Phoebe pressed. She might not know about the past but she could influence the future. There was no need for him to give up something he loved. 'I would want to do a duet with you. Your hand does seem to be improving. Even if it's not a complicated piece, it could still be amusing to play together.'

'I have tried, Phoebe, but what is the point if I can't play up to my old standard? I would always be making the comparison.'

His words hit her like a blow. He would not share his past and he did not particularly want to share his future. He was not even willing to try. Why? What had he done? What did he think he had done?

'I think you are using your hand as an excuse. I think you gave up playing long before the accident. Diana's tin ear was simply an excuse as well. Why did you give up, Simon?'

'You don't understand. I had to.' He raised his face to the ceiling. 'I couldn't. It would not have been right.'

Not right? What had he done? This was not about burying his heart, Phoebe suddenly knew that. There was something much more. Something that had to do with the look Diana had given Simon when she'd mentioned how Robert looked like him. She had to continue or she could not live with herself. She pressed her hands together and held them up under her chin. 'But why? Surely Jayne would not have asked you to give up such a thing that you loved? Why are you punishing yourself?'

His gaze became cold like green-sea glass. 'You are overly tired, Phoebe. It has been a long day. It was wrong of me to entice you into this game of chess.'

He was going to walk out and she would have lost him for ever. She had to try. She rapidly rose and went towards him with her hands held out.

'I forgive you,' she said before her nerve failed. She made sure that her words were loud enough for him to hear, that there could be no mistaking them.

He tilted his head and his face became hewn out of rock. 'Forgive me for what?'

'Forgive you for whatever you have done that you think is so terrible. I know you are a good father to your son. A good employer. A good man. Why are you afraid to admit it?'

She stood there, stomach in knots as he watched her with an ever-hardening expression. She willed him to understand. Somehow he had to see that she wanted to help, that she believed in him. He took a step towards her. She lifted her hands, raised her face. 'Simon.'

Simon turned on his heel and went out of the room, slamming the door behind him.

Phoebe regarded the chessboard with its pieces. Everything had soured from this morning. She had felt in the carriage that they had turned a corner, but now they appeared further apart then ever. And it was her fault for wanting more. She wrapped her arms about her waist and rocked back and forth, desperately trying to hold back the sobs.

'Will you require a clean shirt, sir?' Jenkins asked. 'Only, the valet enquired.'

Simon stared at the mass of drawings on his desk and then down at his once pristine shirt—a variety of inkstains now covered it. He had always had trouble keeping his shirts clean, which was why he kept a supply of clean ones in his office and at the colliery as well.

Dimly he was aware of the passing time. The early morning light shone through the curtains. He ran a hand through his hair. 'What is the time?'

'It is nearly seven in the morning, sir.'

Simon glanced up at the clock. 'So it is. An idea took hold of me and I worked through the night.'

Simon stretched. Far easier to say a white lie, than admitting the truth. He had worked because he was afraid of going into the bedroom and seeing Phoebe. Or of not seeing her. He had come so close to blurting out the truth, to revealing the existence of that twisted piece of him. In many ways he wished that Diana had not come back. He was happy to see her, but there was so much that was unsettled between Phoebe and him. He was pleased that Diana looked happy and contented, but it brought his relationship with Phoebe into sharp relief. He wanted it to be different. He cared about Phoebe, but he feared the look in her eyes when she knew the truth about him. He feared that somehow he might change her, and he needed her to be who she was—strong and ready to tilt at windmills.

Simon took Jayne's miniature from the drawer and held it in his hand. Slowly he slipped it into his pocket. Somehow, he would find a way to make this marriage different.

'And will you be breakfasting this morning?'

'There are things I need to do at the colliery. Business has called me away. Please have my regrets conveyed to Mrs Clare.'

Jenkins's face revealed nothing.

Simon wished there was something more that he could do. But he had learnt a long time ago that working on his machines helped to keep the terror and the ugliness at bay. Now more than ever, he was going to have to work at it. Phoebe was his wife and she deserved a better husband than he.

He wanted to concentrate on being that better person, and forget his old self with the horrid twisted part. But every time he tried, it came back— that awful night when Jayne's lover had returned, demanding money for his silence, and Simon had been unable to restrain his temper. He had beaten the man, but he had left him alive and breathing. Someone else had stabbed him in the road.

Would Phoebe understand that? She had said that she forgave him, but she had no idea how great his sins were. Would she forgive him if she knew the truth?

'What is the news in the neighbourhood? Something always happens in the Tyne Valley and it seems like I have been gone an age. I never thought I'd miss it as much as I have.' Diane leant forwards with an eager expression. She had arrived early this morning, just after Phoebe had finished a solitary breakfast. 'Simon said that you went visiting yesterday, so I know you will be up on the latest. I do hope you don't mind me coming across, but Brett is going over the house plans with the builders and I wanted to get to know my sister better.'

'I am pleased you came by. Robert is having a nap and I too would like to get to know my sister.'

Phoebe finished pouring the cup of tea and then began relating everything she had heard yesterday. Diana nodded, commenting on the birth of yet another Sarsfield, and exclaiming about the younger Ortner girl's marriage to an officer in the Fusiliers. All the while, Phoebe tried to keep her voice light and pleasant. She longed to ask Diana about Simon and what he thought he had done, but would Diana actually tell her?

'There is the Grand Allies ball in four weeks' time.'

'Truly? That time has come around again?' Diana's nose wrinkled. 'I am pleased to be in confinement. The company is much more pleasant.'

'But there will be dancing.'

'Good luck if you can get my brother to dance. He does it under protest. I even made him have lessons for my wedding. He wanted to refuse on account of his injuries, but I said no—I was going to waltz with my brother on my wedding day, even if only a few steps. He managed it…with ill-concealed disgust and plenty of sighing. He swore it made him worse, but I suspect that is balderdash. He should never have been there when they moved that engine.'

'Has he always hated dancing?'

'Before his marriage, he adored the dance floor. My brother is stubborn. Do not let him neglect his duty.'

'Your brother knows how to waltz? James taught me last summer. I had not realised that it had reached this far north.'

Diana's cheeks reddened slightly. 'Let us just say that I came late to the merits of waltzing. But Miranda Bolt will not be pleased that you know how as well. She likes to keep the waltz to a select few.'

'It will be a pity to disappoint her.' Phoebe kept her face totally straight as a shiver went down her spine—waltzing with Simon.

'What is the state of your ball gowns?'

'Excuse me.' Phoebe nearly choked on her tea. 'The state of my ball gowns?'

'If you don't mind me asking…' Diana leant forwards again and lowered her voice. 'Because it is no good going to the French modiste in the village. She will simply do you up a ball gown that is exactly like any number of other ladies, and there is not time for you to go into Newcastle, not when Robert is still recovering.'

'Simon suggested the modiste.' Phoebe thought about the pile of notes lying beneath her handkerchiefs. She hated the thought of going to the ball wearing the same dress as half a dozen other women. She wanted something special.

'Simon knows very little about women's clothes. He might know all there is to know about travelling engines or the inner workings of a coal mine, but he has no taste in clothes. He wears whatever the tailor produces.'

'Then I shall have to ensure that the tailor produces something that suits him.'

'I knew I liked you, Phoebe.' Diana touched Phoebe's hand. 'It is a pity that Rose is away on her wedding trip or I would have had her make you a ball gown from the silk in the attic.'

'There is silk in the attic?'

'Lengths of cloth that I purchased when I was a débutante. There is a jonquil, and a puce, and…' Diana clapped her hands. 'Better yet, there is a length of Pomona green silk that I bought when I was in London. It would suit your complexion best, I think. The yellow apple green will help bring the gold highlights of your hair out. It would be far more flattering on you than me. Rose thought it made me look queasy, but I like the colour. So bright and cheerful.'

Pomona green, one of her favourite colours. She had an afternoon dress made out of the colour some years ago and had worn it until it was good for little more than the rag bag. Phoebe bit her lip. 'Jenny Satterwaite and I could manage it. I suspect her mother would help. She used to sew for the Dowager Lady Bolt.'

'If you want the cloth, it is yours. There is some Belgian lace that could be used for a trim.'

Phoebe closed her eyes. She could readily imagine dancing in apple green. But more than that, Diana had actually offered her something, had thought about her. 'It is such a generous offer, Diana, far more than I expected.'

'You are my sister-in-law. Who better to use it?' Diana patted her stomach and her expression was beatific. 'I will have no use for silks and ball gowns for at least a year. And you must allow me to pay Mrs Satterwaite, so it is truly a gift. I want the dress to be a wedding gift to my new sister. It is the least you can do as Simon neglected to let me enjoy the wedding.'

'It is good to have a sister.' Phoebe reached out her hand and hoped Diana would understand.

'I feel the same way.'

Phoebe leant back against the sofa. She knew exactly the style that she would make. It would be based on a picture she had seen in one of her step-mother's magazines. A half-dress over a cascade of white silk. 'Think of how Simon will look when he sees me.'

'You love my brother very much, don't you?'

Phoebe clung on to her teacup. The question was so unexpected. The words had slipped out from her. There was no point in lying. Not to Diana. Not after they had decided to be sisters. 'Does it show that much?'

'Only to someone else who is in love with her husband. I know the look.'

'Our marriage is not a love match.' Phoebe swirled the tea in her cup. How could she begin to explain the fight of yesterday or the fact that Simon did not even come to bed last night? To say it out loud would be to truly admit it. 'Simon was most definite on that. He asked me to marry him for other reasons. He did not ask for my…infatuation.'

'My brother can be particularly dense at times.'

'There are times when I feel like I am competing with a dead woman. That he looks at me and sees Jayne.'

Diana tapped her fingernail against the side of the fragile porcelain cup.

'He dislikes speaking about anything that happened before.' Phoebe tried to keep the desperation from her voice. 'Even asking about the spinet…'

'That was wrong of me. I should never have teased Simon. If I have caused problems, I am sorry.'

'You have not caused problems. You were not to know.'

Diana shook her head. "No, I will not break confidences, but sometimes, it is best to face your past. Brett taught me that.'

'I will let him tell me about it, then.' Phoebe placed her tea cup down, suddenly confident about what she had to do. She had to let Simon tell her in his own time. She had to be patient. 'I know my stepmother used to worry my father on and on about my mother, so I had not wanted to say anything…in case I seemed to be opening up old wounds.'

'I have no advice to offer on that, except that it

is Simon's story and not mine. Listen to him and not the gossips.'

'Yes, I know that. I intend on doing that.'

'I love my brother dearly, even with his faults,' Diana confessed. 'My brother never apologises, not with words. Remember that. Jayne found it very hard as she needed to be constantly reassured and admired. There was fault on both sides, but Simon is rather hard on himself at times.'

Phoebe forced a smile and firmly turned the conversation towards the ball gown and its possible shape and style. Silently she resolved to find out from Simon the truth, before it destroyed both of them. She had to know that he trusted her enough, and that he wanted to tell her. Suddenly it mattered very much to her.

'Papa! Papa! You are back!" Robert's excited voice greeted Simon when he returned two days later. 'Phee was worried, but I told her not to be, that you often have to go away suddenly.'

Simon regarded Robert with pride. Robert was beginning to grow into a fine man. 'You did right, Robert.'

Simon knew he should have given Phoebe more of an explanation than a simple note, but he had needed to think. His business in Hexham had merely been an excuse. He had no wish to return to the ways of his first marriage. Hopefully, Phoebe would understand and they could begin again.

He reached into his coat pocket. 'I have something for you, Robert.'

'From the colliery? From Hexham?'

'I brought you something from Hexham, but this is more important.'

'More important?'

'It is from your mother.' Simon handed the reframed miniature of Jayne to Robert. 'I thought you were old enough for this. Your mother would have liked you to have it. I had the framer in Hexham put a proper frame on it. A boy should have a picture of his mother.'

'Thank you, Papa.' Robert stared at the miniature for a long moment, fingering the gold gilt frame. 'I will keep it on my mantelpiece, but will it be possible to get a miniature of Phee as well? Just in case she goes away?'

'Phoebe is not going anywhere. She will stay here with us.' A cold chill went through Simon. Was he too late? Had she already begun to pack? He wanted to beg her to give him another chance. Simon forced the concerns from his mind. He had to believe in Phoebe. 'But I plan on having her portrait painted and we can have a miniature done at the same time. I made arrangements when I was in Hexham.'

'Thank you, Papa.'

'I think it is best if we see Phoebe now.'

Simon adjusted his stride to keep pace with Robert.

Phoebe heard the rise and fall of their voices. Her heart swelled. Simon. She only had a moment to put aside her sewing and smooth her gown before the door burst open.

'Robert, where are your manners?'

'Papa brought you something.' Robert held up a box.

Phoebe looked over Robert's head and saw Simon give a slight nod. 'Go on, open it.'

She undid the ribbon, opened the box and saw a magnificent pair of tan gloves. She fingered the fine leather. 'Thank you.'

'Hexham tans. I was in Hexham earlier today on business and saw them. Do they fit?'

'Perfect. I have heard of Hexham gloves and it is good to own a pair.' The words were hard to say around the lump in her throat. She did not want presents. She wanted answers. She wanted him to explain. She wanted him to trust her.

'Up to bed now, Robert…or else.' Simon's face showed mock severity. A tiny place in Phoebe ached. He was able to joke with Robert now. It was clear to see that Robert adored his father.

Robert made a slight face. 'Papa brought me a riding crop. He means for me to learn, really learn. Wait until Hannibal sees.'

'And what else?' Simon asked. 'I believe I gave you something more important than a riding crop.'

'He gave me my mother's miniature. And he says you are to get your portrait painted.'

'He is getting stronger,' Simon said into the sudden suffocating silence after the boy had rushed off. 'He deserves a treat. If Coltonby teaches him, I am sure he will be fine. I do want the best for him.'

'I didn't doubt it.' Phoebe brushed the bits of thread from her skirt. He intended her portrait to be painted. Why? What was his game this time?

'Do you like your gloves?'

'They are very pleasant.'

'I saw them and thought you would like them.' He ran his hand through his hair. 'They are a peace offering, Phoebe.'

'Are we at war?'

'Don't make this more difficult.' He ran his hand through his hair again. 'I brought you a pair of gloves. I have arranged for your portrait to be painted. The least you could do is to be grateful.'

'I wasn't trying to be difficult, Simon. I do like them. And I will sit for my portrait.' She drew a breath. She had to say it or something inside her would grow bitter and twisted. She had to fight. She had to make him understand that it was not possession that she wanted, but answers. She had to take the risk. 'A pair of gloves or a picture gives me no clue as to why you gave up playing the spinet.'

The silence was deafening. Phoebe was certain that he was going to walk out on her again. But he stood there, clenching and unclenching his fists. She resisted the overwhelming urge to say something to fill the void. She simply looked at him.

'Because I had to.' His hoarse whisper echoed around the room. 'And it was nothing to do with my hand. That was an excuse.'

Phoebe forgot to breathe.

'The day Jayne died, she and I quarrelled bitterly. I should have checked on her, but I was playing on the spinet, letting the music flow over me. If I had gone earlier, I might have saved her.

She might not have contracted lung fever. By the time I discovered her, it was too late, far too late.'

Phoebe closed her eyes. 'But…but you did not want her dead. You would have saved her if you could have.'

'I don't know what I wanted. All I know is that I couldn't save her.' He regarded the spinet. 'I thought giving up music would make amends.'

'I would love to hear you play.'

Simon gave a crooked smile. 'Phoebe. You are good. You are always seeking to see the best.'

'I am not.'

'Do you know why Jayne married me?'

'I assume it was a love match,' she whispered.

'Jayne was quite the most enchanting creature I had seen when she came up here. We seemed to get on. I proposed marriage within a week of meeting her. I was head over heels in love and did not even stop to question until it was too late. Jayne had fled from London because she was pregnant and the man refused to do the decent thing. I gave her the respectability she craved, nothing more.'

Phoebe put her hand to her mouth. How that must have hurt Simon. 'Not Robert?'

'She lost the child two months later. Our marriage fell apart. I retreated into my work and she accused me of ignoring her. She had flirtations, one after another, each one more blatant than the last. She wanted me to notice her, and be consumed with jealousy. But I found it easier to spend more time at the colliery and with my other business interests. Eventually I stopped going to her bed.'

'But you had Robert. Surely you must have found a way.'

He gave a bitter smile. 'There was one particular Hussar, the younger son of a baron, the sort of man I despised. Jayne glowed and delighted in his attention. The gossip grew to a crescendo. His price for leaving was a better commission in a more fashionable regiment. After he had departed, I confronted her and we quarrelled. An ugly argument. I took her into my bed. The next morning, I was disgusted with my behaviour and never went near her again.'

'But surely Robert is yours?' Phoebe whispered, her heart breaking for both Simon and Jayne. Their marriage had been a mess.

Simon took a long time before he spoke. 'Robert was born eight months after the quarrel. Jayne always swore he was early, but I did not know what to believe and had no desire for scandal.'

'Is there anything else?' She kept her hands in

her lap. Simon had to tell her everything. She had to know.

'On the morning of her riding accident, I found her half-finished letter to her former lover. Life with me was intolerable, and she begged for his help. She was planning on leaving me. I was going to confront her, to let her go if only she would leave Robert. But she returned injured. I had to do my duty and look after her.'

Phoebe closed her eyes. Her heart bled for Simon and for Jayne. She reached out her hand, but he ignored it.

'In the moments before she died, Jayne confessed that she did not know who Robert's father was. She was not sure, but she begged me to look after him like my own. I tried.

'About two years after Jayne's death, her former lover turned up, wild with drink and blame. His family had disowned him after some business of cowardice in London. He wanted money. He threatened to blackmail me. I refused. He flew at me and I lost my temper. That is my only excuse. I beat him with my fists to within an inch of his life and then kicked him out. He swore vengeance.'

Phoebe stuffed her hand into her mouth. It was far worse than she had imagined. 'What happened?'

'He was found dead on the road a day later by Dodds, my foreman. He had been knifed and his money stolen. I arranged for the body to be buried quietly. He lies in the churchyard, near Jayne. But I was glad. Robert was mine and no one would question it. Then the doubts came. Had I caused the death of Robert's father? Could I have done more? I found it impossible to have Robert near me, in case somehow he guessed my part in his parents' death.'

'You said he was attacked on the road. You had nothing to do with him once he left. You must stop blaming yourself,' Phoebe protested. Simon's face was tormented. She wanted to take his demons away.

'If I had not beaten him, he could have fought back. The man was a trained soldier and could fight, I will give him that. His blood is on my hands.'

'You did what you could.' Phoebe's heart turned over. 'You did not ask for his death.'

'I have never told anyone else the full story. I could not even tell Diana. Robert had to be looked after. But Diana guessed, confronted me and I told her some of the tale. She thinks my notion is fustian. I let it go and we agreed to differ. She has no idea about the grave in the churchyard. She had been away visiting relatives when he appeared and I have kept it as my burden.'

Phoebe laced her fingers together as her heart turned over. All these years and he had carried this inside him. She wished she could do something, anything. 'But Robert is yours, not just in his looks but in what he is. What he likes. He is even learning to play chess. There is more to being a father than simply…'

'I hope you are right, but I fear the look in Robert's eyes. How can I tell him? How can I give his mother praise?'

'I know I am right. Robert is your child, and now he is mine as well. And I will have no one say any different. You are a good man, Simon Clare.'

'Come here,' he commanded.

Phoebe leant into him and put her arms about him. His mouth swooped down on hers, hot, hungry, devouring her like a starving man. There was a dark intensity to the kiss that she had not experienced before. Her hands clutched at his shoulders as the overwhelming hunger swept through her, burning with the intensity of the hottest fire.

His hands slid down her back and cupped her buttocks, clasping her to him. Their hips crashed, the apex of her thighs meeting his hardness. Her back arched, seeking the planes of his chest. All the while, his mouth was on hers, and Phoebe forgot everything but this aching need growing inside her.

She wanted this man, wanted him beyond anything. She moaned in the back of her throat as his lips sank lower. She buried her hands in his crisp hair and held him against her chest.

'Do you want me to stop?' he whispered, his tongue just touching the skin under her neckline.

Mutely she shook her head. Everything but him had ceased to have any meaning.

'Good.'

They sank down to the carpet. With one swift motion, he loomed over her. Large, male and seductive. The light from the fire played over his features, making him seem more piratical than ever, ready to take and plunder. Her hands reached for his waist and pulled his shirt free. She ran her fingers up his back, felt his hot skin as he ground his hips into hers.

'Phoebe.'

She reached up and touched his scar, marvelling at his face and the intensity of his look.

Her breasts strained against her stays and her

hips lifted off the ground, needing to meet that hardness again, wanting him.

He moved her skirts and his fingers brushed her curls, softly at first, but then with a firm stroke. One finger slipped inside her, moving like cool water against her. Her whole body ached.

She opened her thighs and willed him to continue. He loosened his breeches and she saw the full extent of his arousal. Days ago it would have frightened her, but now she reached out and touched its silky hardness. He groaned as her fingers closed around him.

Impatient hands moved her thighs wider and he plunged forwards as her hips rose up to meet him. The great fire within consumed her, consumed them both and forged something new within her. Its white-hot intensity and an awareness that she had never known before, spiralling, lifting her up and up until she knew that she had been born for this. Their cries rose up together.

For a long time afterwards, they lay in each other's arms, saying nothing, just being there, limbs entwined. She held back the words saying that she loved him. It seemed in a way that no words were necessary. He placed a gentle kiss on her forehead. 'Thank you for bringing light back into my life.'

'My pleasure.' She forced her voice to sound normal, but felt it catch in her throat.

His arms went out from around her and he rolled away, leaving her.

Phoebe lay regarding the gilt ceiling as she heard the door click. He needed her physically, in the same way that she needed him. Their fierce joining showed that. Her fingers explored her lips. He needed her physically, but she was not sure if he needed her emotionally. Would it be enough when her heart ached for more?

Chapter Fifteen

Over the next few weeks, life continued. Phoebe knew she depended on Simon more and more, but the only sign of affection that he gave her was their fierce joining. At other times, he appeared remote and distant, more concerned with work than with her.

He did, however, spend time with Robert and their relationship blossomed. Phoebe hated how much she resented their evenings spent poring over plans for a travelling engine and other inventions. She knew she should be rejoicing, but she couldn't help wanting more of Simon for herself.

He never mentioned the proposed wedding trip and she was loathe to bring it up. Some day, when the time was right, maybe she would mention it.

With Jenny and Mrs Satterwaite's help, the ball gown took shape—a white silk underdress, with an over half-dress of Pomona green and cascades of white lace. She kept the dress carefully out of sight, never mentioning it. She wanted it to be a surprise for Simon. Its low-cut neckline showed her shoulders off to perfection.

As she took one last look in the mirror on the night of the ball, Phoebe wished that Edmund hadn't pawned her pearls—they would have looked lovely with the dress.

It bothered her that Edmund had not thought to reply to her letter. In a few short weeks it seemed that she had become completely unnecessary to their existence. Or rather, she supposed, straightening her skirt as she waited for Simon to appear, they had become unnecessary to hers.

'There was a problem at the colliery,' Simon said, coming in to the entrance hall. His eyes blazed appreciatively. 'I had not realised I was so late. Is it time to leave for the ball?'

'Past time.' Phoebe forced her lips to smile.

Simon ran a hand through his hair. 'It will take me but a few moments to wash and change.'

'Then hurry.'

He leant and kissed her bare shoulder. 'I had

worried that you were not going to have a dress, but I see I was mistaken.'

'Worried, why?' She put her hand to her throat.

'I had stopped into the modiste a few weeks ago and she proclaimed ignorance of you. Then you never mentioned going anywhere else.'

'Diana had a length of cloth. She gave it to me. I knew the exact style that I wanted. Diana even insisted on paying Mrs Satterwaite. It is her wedding gift to me.'

'Trust my sister.' He sighed. 'And what did you do with the money? Did you give it away? Is that why you had to make the dress yourself?'

'It remains under my handkerchiefs.' Phoebe met his gaze. She had delayed the moment of reckoning, but she had to explain now. 'I am hoping to persuade you to take me somewhere, so that I can purchase some more lengths. But please may I go to a different modiste?'

'Is there some problem with the modiste in Ladywell?'

'I have no wish to look like Lady Bolt or her daughter. I want to be able to choose where I go and which styles I wear. I am no doll to be dressed as you see fit, Simon. I am a grown woman with ideas of my own.'

His eyes travelled down the length of her gown. 'I suppose I must be grateful that my wife is such a determined woman. I was wrong not to trust your judgment on this. I only sought to help. Use the money for whatever clothes you desire.'

'Thank you; now run along and change.' A tiny bubble of happiness filled her. Tonight was going to be wonderful. She half-closed her eyes and practised a few steps to the quadrille. She was determined to show Simon that she could be an asset. She could be part of his life.

He changed far more quickly than she had believed possible. And her breath caught as he came down the stairs in his evening clothes. His black satin knee breeches fitted him exactly and his shoulders filled out the tailcoat to perfection. 'If you continue to look at me like that, Phoebe, we will not make it out of the door, let alone to the ball.'

She smiled shyly. 'I will be good.'

'You are always good, Phoebe.' He ran a finger about her neck, sending a shiver down her spine. 'But you are not wearing any jewels.'

Her tongue wet her lips. 'Is it a problem?'

'I think you will like these.' He withdrew a slender box from his coat pocket.

Phoebe's fingers trembled on the clasp. Inside she hoped that they were not Jayne's jewels. That would be wrong. 'The clasp on the box is stiff.'

'Allow me.'

His strong fingers took it from her unresisting ones. Phoebe was unable to stifle a gasp. Her pearls and the ear bobs that matched lay against the blue velvet. 'How…how did you get them? How did you know?'

'It is not my doing, but Coltonby's. He paid your stepbrother for them and then gave them to me.' He picked up the pearl necklace and Phoebe felt their coolness against her skin. His palm brushed the back of her neck. 'Brett acted on my behalf when he discovered the situation. I believe your brother approached him when he deposited your trunks with him. I was waiting to see if you would trust me.'

'About what?'

'Your brother sent a letter, and you did not trust me with the contents.'

'He sold my pearls without asking me. I could not have asked you for the money. I would not have even known where to start,' Phoebe whispered as her insides twisted. She should have trusted him. 'I was…ashamed of my stepbrother and his actions.'

'But you had done nothing wrong. I waited, Phoebe.'

'I feared your anger.'

'You have nothing to fear from me. Next time, let me help you. And do not tell me that there will not be a next time, Phoebe Clare. You love your stepbrothers. Together, we can find a way to help them. You are far from being alone.'

Together. Phoebe's stomach knotted and she concentrated on tying her wrap. She kept finding more reasons to love him, but he had not asked for that. She had to be content with the physical. And yet she knew that she wasn't. It was no longer enough and she wondered if it had ever been enough. She wanted to hear from his lips that she was important to him. Was she asking for more than he could give?

A loud knocking interrupted them. Simon raised an eyebrow as Jenkins opened the door.

Simon's heart sank as he saw the man standing there, twisting his cap and face creased with anxiety. 'Is there a problem, Dodds? I only left the colliery an hour ago.'

'Clay and water have been leaking into that old tunnel, the one we were using to bypass the fire damp.'

'You have been using timber to prop it up. We agreed on the strategy this afternoon.'

'That's just it, master. One of the timbers has given way. It weren't put in properly. There has been a slippage.'

Simon went cold. 'How many men are down there?'

'Three—Frank Armstrong, Tommy Jameson and Wor Al. The rest got out. It was the start of the shift, like.'

Wor Al. Albert Dodds. Dodds's eldest. He had only started work at the colliery a year ago, but had already proved himself an able worker. He had been one of the men to help put out the fire on the engine. He had prevented the young Satterwaite boy from being killed and then had worked tirelessly to save what he could of the engine. Simon had already earmarked him for advancement. The neckcloth pressed into his throat, choking him. 'Where did the clay slip happen?'

'Just before the junction with the third tunnel.'

'Then there is a chance they might be alive. Someone will need to go and check.' Simon stared at his foreman. 'Has no rescue party left yet?'

'I wanted to volunteer, but I also knew that you

would have to be told. Your orders still stand and it isn't worth my life to disobey.'

His orders. Was everyone that frightened of him? No, not everyone. Not Phoebe. Simon turned to where Phoebe stood in her absolute loveliness. It was hard to believe that he had ever thought of her as a harpy. She was far more like some fairy creature who had happened to land on earth and in his bed. He knew how much this ball meant to her and how much he wanted to show her off to the Tyne Valley society. But there was no question with the colliery in danger, with those men underground. Someone had to go, and he knew suddenly who it had to be and what he had to say. 'Phoebe.'

'I understand.' Her face was pale. 'You do what you have to do. There will be other balls.'

'Thank you for understanding.'

'Your colliery is more important.' She gave a sad smile, and he heard the unspoken hurt—more important than her. But he knew his duty. She had to trust him to return.

'They may have made it out already,' Simon tried to reassure her. He could not promise to stay above ground and he hoped that she would not ask him as he refused to lie to her. There were so many things he wanted to say. 'But I have to go.'

'Then I am coming with you. I will wait with you.' She gave a decisive nod.

'Coming with me?' Simon stared at her in astonishment. His heart leapt. She wanted to come with him. He had not wanted to ask, but she had read the unspoken message in his eyes.

'If the men have been rescued, then we can continue on to the ball. If not, I do not want to sit here and worry, twiddling my thumbs, feeling useless.' Her laughter sounded forced as she put her hand on his arm. 'It is no good drawing your brows together and looking stern, Simon Clare. I have made my mind up. I might be able to provide some comfort to the miners' wives.'

'Phoebe.' Simon fought to keep his voice steady. It seemed incredible that Phoebe would want to come with him. He knew she was an enthusiastic partner in bed, far more so than he had ever dared hope for, but he did not expect this. It might make it all the harder to do what he knew he had to do, but he needed her by his side.

'And if you tell me not to come, I will simply disobey you.'

'She will, too, master,' Jenkins said behind him. 'And I would help her. Orders or no.'

Simon stared at his butler in astonishment. Had

he lost all power in this household? Had everyone seen through him? The worst thing was that he wanted her there with him. He wanted to hold her hand and to feel her simple presence for those last few precious moments. 'I see that I have no choice in the matter. You may come with me, Phoebe, but you must promise that you will stay out of the way and not get involved with the rescue effort.'

'I promise, Simon.'

He turned to go and stopped. 'Remain here a moment, Dodds. I have to kiss *my son* goodbye.'

'Very good, sir.'

The tower rose in the falling dusk, silhouetted against the sky. Phoebe did not want to think about the three men trapped below the surface and what might be happening with them.

All the way, she and Simon had sat in silence. She had hoped that he would explain what was going on, and what he hoped to do. And she did not like the parcel that the valet had passed to him just before the carriage wheels had begun to turn. Why would he need a change of clothes?

'Nearly there.'

He reached over and took Phoebe's hand. 'I am grateful that you have come, truly I am. It helps knowing you are here.'

'Why did you kiss Robert goodbye?' she asked in a tight voice.

'It might be a while before I see him.'

'Are you going to go after the men? Why did you tell Dodds to wait?'

A muscle jumped in his cheek. 'I won't lie to you, Phoebe. If the men are not up, I will go down after them.'

'Is there a way to get to them?'

'Yes, but it is through a dangerous tunnel. There is a chance that the gas from the fire damp will have gone. I will go down with the lantern that Robert and I discussed the other night. I have made a modification or two that might work. It is my chance to try it.' He gave a crooked smile, but Phoebe knew it was a front. He was not going down there because he wanted to test his theories, but because he cared about those men. 'Don't look so worried. This experiment could make mining much safer.'

'Who am I to stand in the way of progress?' Phoebe wanted to ask him to stay with her and keep her safe. There was no need for him to even be here. Most colliery owners would not be. They would be safely dancing with their wives at the Grand Allies ball, leaving the comforting of the bereaved to others. But then they were not Simon.

He cared about his men and, looking around at the faces of those who were waiting, she knew that he had made the correct choice. Her heart bled for them and she wished she could do more. 'Every inch of the mine, isn't that what you said? Isn't that what you know?'

He leant over and kissed her lips, a bittersweet kiss. 'When I return, we will go to the Grand Allies ball and waltz. I can't promise the opening quadrille, but I can promise a waltz.'

She watched his back as he disappeared into the throng. 'I love you,' she whispered. 'You had better come back to me.'

Simon lifted the lantern high. The flickering light shone off the rock walls as he and Dodds trudged deep into the mine. The air was warmer here, far warmer than on the surface. Every sound was magnified a hundredfold. Here and there he could catch glimpses of the deep black rock, the black diamonds that they dug. Coal was easy to spot. Fire damp was invisible, deadly. It only gave the briefest of warnings—a flicker of the candle before the explosion.

'Won't be long now, sir, before we reach the fire damp.'

'I know that, Dodds. I know where we are.' Simon forced the words from his throat. He refused to think about failure.

'I think I can hear knocking, sir. Do you believe they are alive? Or is it just ghosts?'

Simon stilled and raised his lantern. The light flickered. His stomach clenched and sweat poured down the back of his neck. He glanced over at Dodds, whose face gleamed with sweat. They could go back now and perhaps save their skins. The memory of the way Phoebe's mouth tasted swamped him. He should have said something. He should have told her of his feelings. He knew that, whatever happened, her name would be on his dying breath.

The lantern flickered a second time, nearly went out, but then flared brightly.

'Sir?'

'I made a promise, Dodds. Those are my men. They work for me.'

'There is none that would hold you to it.'

'We go on. I have to know. If there is the slightest chance, I want them out alive.'

The dark mouth of the tunnel gaped black and wide in the fading light. Here and there clusters of men and women with shawls over their heads stood clustered about. Time dragged. Each breath appeared to last longer.

Phoebe kept her eyes trained on where she had last seen Simon. He had to come back. But the mouth remained blacker than the night.

'I did not expect to see you here, Phoebe.'

'Brett!' Phoebe glanced over her shoulder quickly before concentrating on the mine's black mouth again. 'Why are you here?'

'Diana and I heard. Tommy Jameson is one of our tenants. Nothing happens on the estate without one of us knowing. Has he come out? His wife and children are with Diana.'

Mutely Phoebe shook her head.

'Where's Clare? What is being done? No one seems to know.'

'He went down the shaft. He wanted to test his new lantern.'

Brett swore loud and long. 'Testing another foolish invention! He nearly lost his life the last time. Doesn't that man understand his responsibilities? Doesn't he understand his priorities?'

'He does. And that lantern is the only reason why the men might get rescued. He is going through a flare of fire damp.'

'What are his chances?'

Phoebe gave a small shrug. 'I don't know, but Simon has promised to waltz with me at the Grand Allies ball.' She held out a foot. 'See, dancing slippers. I suppose I should be practising right now.'

Brett squeezed her shoulder. 'I am sure he plans to. The fool.'

'He will return.' Phoebe blinked rapidly as the scene swam in front of her.

A great shout went up from the crowd. 'There's movement! I see a lantern! Someone is coming!'

'You see.' Phoebe hurriedly straightened her skirt as a great relief rolled off her shoulders. Simon had done it. All would be well. 'We might even make it in time for the opening quadrille.'

Without waiting for an answer, she pushed her way forwards. Every particle strained to see Simon, his broad shoulders—a lock of hair would be enough. One little glimpse would be enough. A great pit opened in her stomach as a single burly man stumbled out, holding Simon's lantern aloft. Dodds.

'Where…where is Simon? Where is the master?' Phoebe barely recognised her own hoarse cry.

Dodds gave a slight shake of his head. 'We tried, the both of us.' A great sob racked his body, prevented him from speaking.

'Where is Simon Clare, man?' Brett went up to him. 'Tell me now. Quickly.'

'He…sent me back…away. It were still there. That flare.' Another sob racked Dodds. 'He gave me the lantern. I have left the lift down, just in case…'

'Has anyone survived?' Phoebe asked, forcing her mouth to form the words.

Dodds sank to the ground and collapsed. A great groan went up from the crowd. Phoebe knew she should go and comfort the miners' families, but her feet refused to move. Brett's arm went around her shoulders, shielding her view.

'It is all over, Phoebe. He was a brave man.'

'Was? Is. He *is* a brave man.' Phoebe blinked back tears and moved away from Brett's shelter-ing arm. He had to come back. There were so many things she needed to say to him. Things she should have understood, but hadn't until that moment. She had accused him of not giving, but she was the one. She should have told him how much she wanted to be a part of his life. It was too soon. He could not die. She refused to abandon him. He was her other half.

'Phoebe, you must face facts. It was too danger-ous. I will get someone to take you to Diana. We will be here for you and Robert. You will always be part of our family.'

Part of his family. Phoebe knew that once her greatest longing had been to be part of a family. But standing there outside of the mine, she knew that she did not want that any more. Even within the circle of a family, she would be alone. Simon was her other half. He made her complete. She knew that she could not abandon him. And that she would wait here, until all hope was gone. He was alive. He had to be.

Phoebe pushed her cousin away. 'No, you are wrong. I know it. Simon will come out. He knows every inch of the mine. He could walk it blindfolded. Tommy Jameson told me so. I'd know if he were dead.'

'Phoebe!'

Phoebe elbowed her way past the crowd around Dodds. No pinprick of light relieved the all-consuming blackness of the mine. She took a step in, cupped her hands around her mouth. 'Simon Clare, you promised! You promised me a waltz!'

The only thing she heard was the ghostly echo of her voice—*waltz, waltz, waltz,* mocking her, becoming ever fainter, ever more phantom-like.

Behind her, she heard the murmur of voices.

Soon they would begin drifting away, going back home, back to pick up the pieces of their lives, but Phoebe knew she would stay there, until all hope was gone. She would wait. She had promised. And she would keep that promise. She would also make sure the families of the men who were in that mine were looked after. Somehow. It would give her a purpose in life.

'Waltz!'

She started. The word was stronger, deeper. Echoing back at her. Her heart leapt. Was he alive? Or was it her mind? No one else appeared to have heard anything. Brett still regarded her with sympathy in his eyes. She called again. Louder. Longer. Again the odd echo. Hope burnt within her.

'There's some movement! Can you see it?' a voice behind cried.

'Aye! I heard something. Are the wheels turning?'

A great roar went up from the crowd as people surged forwards.

Phoebe bit her lip, and prayed.

Two more dirty miners stumbled out, blinking in the final rays of the setting sun. Everyone began crowding around her, buffeting her, preventing her from seeing.

'Give Mrs Clare space!' Brett roared.

Suddenly she saw him. Moving slowly with a youth over his shoulder. Tired. Dirty faced, but alive.

'The lantern needs a few modifications, Phoebe,' he said after he set the youth down. 'Could not risk the men's lives.'

Phoebe blinked back tears. 'Yes, I know.'

'I found them huddled together just after Dodds went back. Albert has broken his leg. Then I couldn't risk candles. I nearly lost my way when I heard your sweet voice calling to me. Holding me to my promise. I followed it. It called me home.'

'No, your voice called me to my home.' Her eyes feasted on his form. She flung her arms around his neck and would have pressed her lips to his, but he held her off.

'I need to change. I am covered in coal dust. And I did promise you a waltz.'

Phoebe took his face between her hands and kissed him. 'I love you, Simon Clare, and I don't care where or when we waltz. Just let us be together.'

'But I care.' His fingers brushed her hair back from her forehead. 'You are my life, Phoebe. My love. My dearest wife.'

'Well done, Simon,' Brett said, coming up to them. 'I am proud to say that you are my brother-in-law. There is no finer man. You are a gentleman in the truest sense of the word. I would be honoured to do all in my power to ensure your dream of a travelling engine becomes a reality.'

'And I return the compliment, Coltonby. And sometimes dreams change. Right now, my dream is to be a good husband. Travelling engines and machines can wait.'

Phoebe squeezed his hand. More than anything, those words told her how much she was loved. She did not need words. Deeds were important as well.

'When you are ready, then,' Brett said.

'Will you look after things here while I take my wife to the Grand Allies ball? If I don't make an appearance, they will think I fell down a mine shaft or some such nonsense.'

'It would be my pleasure.'

Simon held out his arm. 'Shall we go, Phoebe? Shall we show them how the Clares can waltz?'

'I suppose we must. I would hate not to keep up appearances.'

Epilogue

July 1815

The sun beat down on Phoebe's straw bonnet. She resisted the temptation to pull it forwards. She breathed deeply. Northumberland on a still July day was stunningly beautiful, she had thought that today as the carriage passed the row of miners' cottages before they turned into the Ladywell colliery.

All the pumps were silent and a great viewing platform stood at one side of the yard. Many of the Grand Allies and their wives were already there waiting. She gave a nod to the Bolts and ignored Lady Bolt's sharp intake of breath as Phoebe carried baby Alexandra in her arms. Alexandra might only be six weeks old, but Phoebe refused to have her miss the day.

'We have finally arrived,' Diana said, coming to

stand beside her. 'Brett will be here in a moment. He is making sure that the horses are settled.'

'I see you were of the same mind.'

'I couldn't leave them at home. And Brett decided that they needed reins so they would not fall off the platform. Of course he has made them far too long. You would not believe the mischief two boys can get into.'

'Oh, I would believe it.'

'Where is Simon? He is not driving, is he?' Diana's brows knotted together.

'He and Robert are seeing to a last modification to the Elephant.'

'The Elephant?' Brett asked, capturing one of his twins around the middle just before he did a headfirst dive. 'I told you, Diana, the reins are too long. My wife never listens to me.'

Diana rolled her eyes, but Phoebe smiled. She was well used to their loving banter. They were both so happy with Paul and George.

'The elephant is because Robert swears Hannibal helped him to the design. And Hannibal had elephants. He would have brought the cat, but finally listened to Simon on the matter.'

'The boy will go far.'

'He has had several offers for engineering

training, but agrees that he should go to Cambridge like his father.' Phoebe gave a smile. 'My stepbrother Edmund tried to get him to think about Oxford, but he refuses.'

'As I said, Robert is an intelligent boy…' Diana said, laughing as Brett rescued the other twin from Lady Bolt. 'I hear that Miranda Gough is expecting. Hopefully a grandchild will help heal the breach.'

'I could not believe it when she ran away with that curate to Gretna Green,' Phoebe said. 'I had never seen her as curate's wife.'

'Once I told her to follow her heart, and I was so pleased that she did. She seems happy enough.'

A cheer went up from the growing throng of people.

'Here are the men of the moment.'

Phoebe watched Simon and Robert cross the yard. Robert had grown so much. It was hard to remember him as the pale boy from little over a year ago.

'Well, Clare, here we are,' Brett said as Simon mounted the stairs. 'Where is this elephant of yours? Will it actually go this time?'

'Albert Dodds has it under control, Uncle,' Robert said, taking a squirming Alexandra from Phoebe. 'I trust him.'

'Put your baby sister down, Robert,' Simon said.

'Let him, Simon,' Phoebe said, giving Simon's hand a squeeze. 'He is as excited as you are. And Alexandra loves her big brother.'

Simon's face relaxed slightly. 'Yes, she does. I just worry.'

'Perhaps we ought to have the demonstration of the infamous travelling engine, then,' Phoebe said, slipping her arm through his. He pulled her close and she could feel the tension in his body. At Simon's signal, a loud whistle filled the air, swiftly followed by a chugging noise. The crowd gasped as the engine moved forward, pulling four carts of coal. Slowly, steadily it went down the iron track towards the staiths. All around them, Phoebe heard the Grand Allies gasping and admiring.

'Clare, you have achieved your dream. You have created a travelling engine,' Brett said.

Simon's arm tightened about her waist. 'No, my life's dream is here in my arms and over there standing waving at the engine. My two children and my wife. A man cannot ask for more riches than that.'

'There I will agree with you,' Brett replied, putting his arms about Diana and their children. 'To our wives and our children.'

'To our families.'

Phoebe gave Diana a look and knew they were both thinking the same thing. Moments like this showed how sweet life could be.

* * * * *